Iron Rose Bleeding

Iron Rose Bleeding

Anne Azel

P.D. Publishing, Inc.
Clayton, North Carolina

Copyright © 2009 by Anne Azel

ISBN-13: 978-1-933720-63-0
ISBN-10: 1-933720-63-8

9 8 7 6 5 4 3 2 1

Cover art by B.L. Magill
Cover design by Barb Coles
Edited by: Day Petersen / Lara Zielinsky

Published by:

P.D. Publishing, Inc.
P.O. Box 70
Clayton, NC 27528

http://www.pdpublishing.com

Acknowledgements

After nine years and now fifteen book covers, I would like to thank Anne Azel for allowing a woman in another country the artistic opportunity of doing the covers of her many wonderful books.

In regards to the subject of this particular book and the artwork it inspired, I would like to acknowledge First Nation's artists, like Michael Robinson, for reminding us through art that our future lies in respectful stewardship of our planet Earth.

~ B. L. Magill

My thanks to Linda and Barb at PD Publishing and to my editors Day Petersen and Lara Zielinsky. Special thanks to B. L. Magill for sharing her remarkable talent.

~ A. Azel

Author's Note

The environmental information present in this story is accurate. Sadly, since the writing of this work, Earth's environmental crisis has worsened. Our isolated and special planet is very ill. If change does not come soon, by 2050, planet Earth will be dying.

Individuals can make a difference. Please consider recycling, reusing, saving energy, and lobbying your government representative to put the environment first before short term goals. Thank you for caring.

~ Anne Azel

To Planet Earth
Get Better Soon

In the beginning, turtle brought the rose coloured mud from the dark depths to create the Earth. The land was beautiful and turtle wished the plants and creatures of the land to live in harmony and peace.

~ Based on a First Nation's Legend

An Introduction

"As we acquire more knowledge, things do not become more comprehensible, but more mysterious."

~ Albert Schweitzer

A Background: Taken From Courtney Hunter's Logs

My eyes are grey, the colour of winter light. That's important. On that day so long ago, they were focused on the road ahead as I drove with the blindness of familiarity. My mind was elsewhere until any variation in the morning driving pattern snapped me back to awareness briefly, leaving a Morse code of impressions in my subconscious. I had taken the same route to work for over two years, but that day I experienced a heady feeling of not being connected to the humdrum world around me. It was disconcerting. I no longer felt a part — not by any action I'd taken but by the decision to take action. I remember my heart drummed with the rush of anticipated adventure and a trace of a smile formed on my lips. Indecision, perhaps wisdom, had held me back for many months, but that time had passed. That morning drive committed me to finding the truth.

I am Courtney Hunter and this is part of my story. It is also a part of the story of all of us.

That morning as always, I signalled and turned left off the main thoroughfare onto a straight, smooth, private road that bisected the fields on each side. On one side, the hay caught morning light and rippled with autumn gold. To the other side, the fields still lay under clouds, partially hidden by a bank of mist. A few minutes later, the road I travelled dipped out of sight of the fields into a valley copse of beech and then dead-ended in the parking lot beyond.

The lot was discreetly hidden behind a neat box hedge. For a second I sat, hands on the wheel, staring ahead of me at the greenery. It was the first wall of many, one inside the other like the set of painted wooden dolls I had been given as a child. It was the elaborate walls of defence that had first made me suspect something was terribly wrong at TAP International. The day I was finally looking into it, I remember setting my jaw in determination as I reached into the back seat to grab my briefcase and lift it over beside me before opening the door and getting out. I swung the car door shut and locked it, knowing that my personal mission had begun — my fate sealed with the thud and click of a locked car door.

Several metres past the hedge, a high electrical fence shut off one world from another. I headed over to the security gate and punched in my personal code. A small screen glowed green and I stood directly in front of the camera lens and swiped my ID card through for a facial recognition scan.

Electronic squeals and bleeps came softly from the speaker as the planes of my face were surveyed and a digital map was made of my features to verify against the record in the system's database. "Hunter...Courtney...you are scheduled for time off," stated a mechanical voice. "Indicate reason for access."

I tapped in number 24, the code for required overtime. More squeals and bleeps followed.

"Please stand on the white dot and look into the viewfinder." Dutifully, I shuffled over and took the correct position, having to raise my petite figure on tiptoes for an iris recognition scanner to photograph my eyes.

I had done my research. The iris is the only internal organ of the human body visible from the outside. This makes it an ideal tool for identification.

The scan would look for the random variations in the visible elements of my iris. The phenotypical features of each individual iris are totally unique for every person. Even identical twins have different patterning. The system, I knew, was almost impossible to fool. It could even pick up contact lenses stained with fake iris patterns. I knew it couldn't detect my emotions, yet it peered inside my being and so instinctively I tried to radiate calm confidence.

"Access granted."

The gate slid open. I stepped in and the gate closed behind me. I now stood in a three by three metre cage like a zoological specimen for the eyes of the security system.

Five steps brought me to the next security check. Without hesitating, I placed my left hand over the red circle that glowed on the screen beside the gate, waiting patiently while my fingerprints were recorded and compared. In an AFI system, a data file of significant loops, arches, and whorls unique to my prints were recorded and compared to those on file. An AFI system did not keep an image of my fingerprints nor could it reproduce them, but using its stored data, it could successfully identify me from millions of others. Another foolproof system of identification. Why?

I heard the power switch trip and the metal cover over the key slot slid back. I inserted my ID card key, waited, then removed it when the screen turned green. The security door slipped open and I entered, standing in the box formed by white lines painted on the cement until the door slid closed behind me. The mechanical voice came again.

"Access has been granted to...one...individual...Hunter... Courtney. It is now safe to step forward. Do not step back. Proceed forward."

I complied, knowing I was crossing through a laser net as I did so. The grid mechanism had received data from the other security systems to allow one break of the laser web. Anyone following would trigger the elaborate security system.

I squared my shoulders and strode down a fieldstone path bordered by high cedar hedges hiding the security fencing on each side. It was a prison walk disguised in country attire. A little further on, the walk split around a guard house and again I showed my I.D. card.

"Hi, Ian," I said into the speaker to the serious looking man dressed in the black jump suit on the other side of the glass. I liked Ian. We often worked together when I required some extra help in the archives. He almost summoned a smile as I handed my briefcase through to him for it to be scanned by the x-ray machine. I thought my voice that morning sounded strangely loud, and tight with tension, but Ian didn't seem to notice.

After a few seconds, Ian Philips waved me ahead to walk through the metal scanner. No bleeps. I was clean. He came out of the bulletproof booth to join me and handed me back my briefcase.

"Hi, Court. The system is showing you as having today off, but it has cleared you for entrance anyway. I bet you were called in because she is coming," he stated, managing a brief smile this time.

My heart skipped a beat, but outwardly I tried to give no indication that I had been unaware of this information. I gave the Mona Lisa smile, signifying everything and nothing, and took the green security tag Ian offered me. It would allow me to move freely about the green zone sections of the house and estate, and I clipped it to my waistband. "Have a good day," I stated with no further explanation, waiting for Ian to punch in the code to release the last gate that would open Taylor Punga's world to me.

I had asked Ian, when we were having lunch together one day, why such a redundant system of security checks was necessary. He had looked up from his soup with surprise.

"But, Courtney, a hand can be cut off or an eye plucked out. Redundancy is the only viable security."

I hadn't finished my lunch.

Once through and making my way along the path again, I was acutely aware of my aching shoulders and the sweat between my breasts. I forced myself not to loosen the tense muscles but to walk as I always walked each work day down this path.

Over the last two years, I'd gone through this elaborate security system many times. On good days it was fun, like being a spy. On days when the weather was unpleasant, it was a source of extreme annoyance. This was the first time it had made me nervous. Why did Punga need such a security system? It was redundant in the extreme. What did my employer have to hide?

Learning that Punga was coming to the estate made me consider changing my plans, but I decided I was committed to action and should proceed. I justified this decision by arguing to myself it might also give me the rare opportunity to see my boss, Taylor Alexandria Punga.

I had worked for her for over two years by then, had seen her only twice, and knew nothing about her. That is, almost nothing. My job was to archive the material that flowed in from Punga's busy schedule. In a way, I knew all and understood nothing. Finding out what motivated and financed Punga's life had become an obsession. Taylor Alexandria Punga was an enigma I meant to unravel.

When I was hired, I had been told Punga headed a think tank, but there was something going on in this complex far bigger than I had originally been led to believe. Stories didn't hold together. Places in the vast complex were out of bounds to me and the personnel very secretive. My enquiries had been stonewalled, and so I had made the decision that this was the day that I found out the truth.

From the moment I had met Punga, I had been curious about the tall, aloof woman. Suspicious might be a better word. Punga was far more than she seemed and whatever went on at this establishment was far bigger than I originally thought. I had to admit part of the source of my interest in my boss was the strength of Punga's personality. She simply radiated confidence and energy. That flame of deadly energy fascinated me until I fairly buzzed with curiosity. If energy was strength, Taylor Alexandria Punga was very powerful. I wanted to know how and why.

I grudgingly had to admit that Punga was striking, too, not in a pretty way but with the sort of beauty generated by a powerful charisma. Punga was mesmerizing, controlled, confident in her movements, and very mysterious.

Who was Taylor Alexandria Punga? She seemed to have incredible power, yet she had no title and held no official office. She was immensely rich, and yet had no visible source of income. She was present at every significant meeting in the world — or so it seemed — and yet never spoke or presented at them.

Discovering who Taylor Alexandria Punga was had become my personal project. That was why I had come in to work that day, even though it was my day off.

Access to the house was through a maze created by dry stone walls that edged high beds of flowering trees and plants. Here and there, water danced down garden rocks or goldfish flashed in a still, silent pool, moving from light to shadow. Every previous time I had walked through this beautiful area, I had promised myself if I ever had a house of my own, it would have a mysterious and magnificent entrance like this. That day, I barely noticed it.

As always, I came on the house suddenly from out of the gardens, reaching a stone wall and then having to turn to follow its curve to the brass front doors. Once again, I stood in a white box painted on the flagstone. The tag that Ian had given me automatically fed data into the security system, much like a garage door mechanism. The brass doors unlocked with an audible click.

I pushed through the one on the right and entered a quiet lobby, beautiful in its simplicity. A floor of black stone tile was divided by a long, rectangular pool of water. A rough cut slab of grey granite was the only means across. The walls on each side were polished teak and on the other side of the bridge, a glass wall allowed a view of a huge interior courtyard of thick vegetation. Here, even nature was walled in or out.

Turning left once I crossed the pool would take me into the green zone of the elaborate complex. These were the public areas — library, dining room, kitchen, meeting room, computer room, and staff rooms. Going right would take me into the red zone — the private chambers of Taylor Alexandria Punga and her personal staff.

For a second, I stood on the bridge focusing my thoughts, then I crossed and walked to the left, over the black stone floor, letting the security camera record me. As far as I had been able to ascertain, there was only the one camera in the main lobby. Clearly confident in their elaborate security system, this camera simply recorded who came and went through the door. It had blind spots. Its main blind spot was overconfidence.

I first took my briefcase down to the archival library where I worked and hid it out of sight. The fewer people who knew I was there the better. Not allowing myself time for second thoughts, I moved back up the hall to the lobby. Once under the entrance camera, I flattened myself against the glass wall, as I had planned, and edged along to the far right side of the lobby.

To be truthful, my heart seemed to be convulsing in my chest, which made me feel lightheaded and slightly ill. If someone had walked into the lobby just then, I would have been hard pressed to explain what the hell I was doing. Not for the first time that day, I felt crazy to be attempting this incursion. For a second, I stopped. I can still recall the sensation of the heat of the sun on the glass wall behind me. I see in my mind how my body divided the light from the window in two, casting my relief as an elongated shadow dividing the lobby in half. It was this shadowy image that betrayed me. The moment of hesitation passed and I steeled myself and moved on into a wide alcove on the far side of the room.

Punga's quarters were separated from the rest of the house by another set of brass doors. I bit my lip in concentration and wiped the sweat from my hands. I had no clear idea what I hoped to accomplish by doing this. If I did find evidence that Punga was up to no good, who was going to believe me? If I got caught, I suspected the consequences would be swift and serious. I had hesitated for months, my common sense and instinct for self-preservation overruling my compulsive need to know who Taylor Punga really was. Until that day.

It was too late for second thoughts. From my pocket I slipped the red tag that I had picked up and kept after it fell from one of Punga's coat pockets the winter before. I took off my green tag and clipped on the red. If the switch didn't work, the security system would automatically sound an alarm and pinpoint my location on monitors. I had witnessed practice drills many times. If the red tag didn't work, then the next intruder alarm would be for real, security personnel would come from literally everywhere and I would be carted off, goodness knew where.

I moved into the white box, the doors slid open, and I stepped into Taylor Alexandria Punga's very private world.

It was disappointing. I scanned the room, recording impressions. I'd entered a lounge area consisting of comfortable, distressed leather chairs and a sofa around a fireplace. The fireplace was natural stone, the walls silk, in soft, warm tan. The original art on the walls was an eclectic mix of well known twentieth century artists. Over the fireplace was a Jackson Pollack.

There were several oils by the Ash Can School, and a sketch I suspected might be a Picasso.

Everything was neat and tidy, and devoid of any personal items. Nothing was worn or scratched. The room looked as if it had been set up by an interior designer just for show. Everything was perfectly placed. Even the stainless steel briefcase bearing the initials TAP was placed with deliberate casualness on the granite block that acted as a coffee table.

TAP! The implications of the briefcase being there exploded into my mind that day and left me feeling faint with worry. I can act foolhardy but I am not a fool. I turned to beat a hasty retreat and found, to my horror, Punga standing right behind me.

Punga's body was lean and muscular. She was dressed in a black jumpsuit and her features were set in hard, classic lines. Startling aqua eyes snapped with anger.

"I can explain," I stammered.

"No, you can't," purred the deep, liquid voice.

We warned you.

She is the weak link.

This is a problem.

Startled, I looked around me. Had I heard voices? There was no one else in the room, only me and the towering Punga, who continued to look down at me with angry suspicion. Someone touched my hair and I nearly jumped from my skin. I whirled around. Still no one.

Surprising.

Perhaps you were right after all, Tap.

This development is alarming.

I looked around in growing annoyance, found no speakers, and then spun back to the tall, silent woman behind me. "Something touched me. What the hell is going on?" I demanded, fear giving me more courage than I felt.

Punga raised an eyebrow and looked at me condescendingly. "I believe that should be my question. You will come and sit in the chair over there," she ordered, pointing to one of the leather chairs near the fireplace.

"No, I won't. I'm leaving," I responded in growing fear as I tried to brush an invisible hand from around my arm.

Fear pumped adrenaline through my system. Things had gone badly wrong almost immediately. I had been a fool to think I could have gotten away with this invasion.

"That would be unwise and futile." Punga shrugged. "You will stay."

I felt my hackles rising. "I apologize for being in a restricted area. I shouldn't have been." I took off my red tag and pulled the green one from my pocket, trying to be assertive and get myself out of the hole I had dug. I tossed the red tag onto a side table and clipped the green one back on my waistband. "There is your tag back. I found the red one when it fell out of your coat pocket last winter. I guess I'm fired, but I certainly am not your prisoner." My speech stopped at the sensation of the cool, invisible fingers once again touching my arm. "What the hell is that?" I cried in frustration, pulling away in fear.

She hears.

And she feels.

She can not see.

Taylor nodded. "Yes. This surprising development supports my theory," she murmured.

I could feel myself starting to panic. Outwardly, I forced myself to remain calm. This wasn't the time to show fear. "What theory? And would you please let me go!" I demanded, violently pulling away from the invisible arm. Released suddenly and unexpectedly, I stumbled against the tall frame of Taylor Punga. Her body was unnaturally warm, like touching the hot sides of a teapot.

"Oh, shit," I whispered as strong hands took my shoulders and pale eyes burned into mine.

"I would prefer we not have a scene, Ms. Hunter. I repeat, please sit down."

That time I nodded, backing away in shock. I swallowed, pulled myself together, and slowly turned and surveyed the room. No one. Gathering my courage as best I could, I went over and sat down on one of the leather chairs with as much defiance in my walk as I could muster.

That would be a day that would change everything, and so it is a good place to make a start. It is nowhere near the beginning of the endeavour, of course. The project had been going on for some time and was near to reaching a climax. It is, however, when I became a significant element in the undertaking, and so a good place to make a beginning.

Chapter One

"Any beginning is a single seed that may someday be a multitude of life. We never know which beginnings will change the universe. Nature is random."

~ T'Tap

These are the events as we observed them.
We recorded them factually and objectively.
And now we report them to you.

Courtney sat still in the chair. Tap had not sat down; her remaining standing was a reflection of her method of control. That is, Tap did not control directly but passively. She stood silently observing Courtney Hunter. At last, she spoke. "Why?" It was a long speech reduced to its bare essence.

Courtney swallowed and squirmed in her seat. It appeared to us she did not wish to tell the truth but was afraid to be caught in a lie. "I don't know." This, also, was a short speech with a long meaning, mostly to do with guilt and avoidance. It was not a very satisfactory answer because it stemmed from a fear of expressing knowledge. And Tap was not satisfied.

Courtney, we sensed, would have liked to have stood again so as not to remain at a disadvantage, but Tap was too close, not so much looming but hovering near, and so Courtney was trapped by Tap's position. If she stood, it would mean she would be face to face with the annoyed woman. That would be a worse position than the one she was already in. It would invite confrontation. Wisely, she remained seated.

We knew Taylor Alexandria Punga was not satisfied with Hunter's lack of explanation. She stood close, hovering and waiting, and finally, in order not to be observed growing old, Courtney gave a longer speech that was more satisfying but shorter in its meaning.

"I have worked here for two years archiving material that you send me. The range and extent of your research is amazing, and yet you don't do anything with it. You live surrounded by security and wealth, and yet you have no occupation or income. You know everyone and no one knows you. I wanted to know."

Tap nodded, a smile not quite making it to her lips. "Am I not entitled to my privacy?"

It was a weighted question and it dropped heavily from a great height because Tap had the advantage of standing and Courtney Hunter did not. That was a great disadvantage.

Courtney stammered, "Of course you are. I realize I was wrong to come in here..."

"Nonsense," Tap stated, correcting her employee. "You would not have done it if you had not thought it the thing you wanted to do, and so your action was right for you. What was wrong for you was getting caught."

Courtney laughed, and then jumped up with a gasp when she felt an invisible touch to her mouth. The wall she hit was not a wall, but Tap. Courtney stumbled and stepped aside. She skittishly went to put her back against the wall. Tap remained where she was, allowing us time to observe Courtney Hunter. We noted that the woman's eyes were grey. A most unusual shade. This was important.

"What the hell is that?" Courtney demanded, using the back of her hand to wipe the touch from her lips.

"What?" asked Tap. We have noted that the word what used in this manner was not a question at all but a type of period that should end any enquiry.

"The thing in the room that keeps touching me."

This time Taylor Alexandria Punga did smile, but only briefly. It was cut short by a briefer explanation. "It is a type of security system."

"Doesn't it bother you?" Courtney asked. She sounded annoyed.

"No. I was meant to be here. You are not. You were about to tell me why you really came in here."

Courtney's eyes lifted and so made contact with the brilliant aqua ones that observed her. In the silence, we observed.

She is more aware than I would have expected.

Perhaps we should recheck our findings.

She is Tap's responsibility and so Tap must say.

Courtney drew herself up to her full height, which was not so tall, but she wore her body well because she was fit and so she looked taller and more confident than she was. "I came to learn about you because you fascinate me. I want to know what you are up to, and now, I want to know about the voices, too."

Tap nodded. "It would not be easy, and having started, you would not be able to stop."

"And having started, you would not be able to stop" was what Taylor Alexandria Punga had said, and yet Courtney Hunter had stopped only a short time later. She had been left in a room to which Tap had taken her, and she had been there for a good amount of time. The door was locked and there were no windows through which to frame an escape. We felt this was wise until Tap could reach a decision on what to do with Courtney Hunter.

She was to observe later that it was, as conventional rooms go, very unconventional to her. The walls were rag rolled in a misty swirl of blues, greys, and lavender. The floor was grey stone. Along the length of one wall ran a narrow channel of water, bouncing over smooth grey river stones. A recess in the wall formed a platform bed which was neatly stacked with pillows, duvet, and sheets in grey silk. A grey stone wall bracket formed a nightstand.

There were two alcoves. One was small and had a rod to hold clothes. It was empty. The other was bigger and held a toilet and a shower, but no basin or mirror. The toilet was not a toilet as Courtney knew it. It was a stainless steel basin recessed into the floor, which one squatted over. It was designed in an Eastern style and there was a stainless steel button on the wall to flush the basin clean. The shower, too, was strange to her. There was no curtain or door, just a stainless steel basin in which to stand. The water came through holes in a ceiling fixture. It, too, was stainless steel, as were the hot and cold water controls on the wall. In this room, the tiled walls were steel-grey, as were the towels that were stacked neatly on a recessed shelf. No doors, except the one that was locked, no windows, no furniture. It was a no room and Courtney felt the no. At the time we were not aware of Courtney Hunter's negative reaction to the room.

She would report that for a while, she was grudgingly content with the no. After all, she reasoned, she had trespassed. But after a while, the no became intolerable, and then simply rude. Eventually, it became a worry that bordered on fear. She was not prepared to be held as a prisoner.

As Courtney Hunter saw it and she felt she saw the situation very clearly, having had considerable time to see it — there were only two ways in and out: the first was the door which was locked, and the second was where the water exited. At the time we did not understand her reasoning and were shocked by her actions.

Taken From Courtney Hunter's Logs
The water channel seemed my only means of escape. I decided to go with the flow.

I removed the layer of stones and placed them carefully aside. The channel was about two feet wide and about eighteen inches deep once cleared. Looking under the lip where the channel disappeared near the wall, I saw that the water flowed through a metal screen and then dropped.

I considered various possibilities and concluded it was unlikely the house had different plumbing for the various water channels. More than likely, the one that I crossed in the lobby was part of this same system. I tried to visualize a likely pattern for the flow of water while I used the round end of my metal nail file to remove the screws that held the metal screen. I laid down in the channel to have a look, and shuddered. The water was cold. Dimly, I could make out a large holding tank. On the other side was another rectangle of light framed by green plants where the overflow escaped. I smiled. The room must back on to the inner courtyard of the house.

I went feet first, which — as my mother would have said — was my way, to step where angels feared to tread. It was a squeeze, but I have tried to stay in good shape so with a push I slipped through and splashed into the water tank below. The water was cold and dark, and smelt of plastic and mould.

I gritted my teeth. It might not be the most pleasant place to be, but I felt that I would have moulded too, had I remained prisoner in that room a minute longer. I had chosen to escape and I now found myself in a very cold and not very pleasant place. Out of the frying pan and into the fire, my mother would have said.

I wasted no time swimming to the other side and grabbing hold of the grate. It was going to be harder this time — and it had not been easy the last time — to remove the screws, as they were on the outside. I used my fingers to bend some of the thin wire far enough so that I could wiggle my fingers through. It was a tight fit and only accomplished after some deep scratches to my hand and a great number of muttered oaths. Slowly, shaking with cold, I worked the screws loose, bending the grate back as I made more room to manoeuvre.

Almost too cold to move, like a lizard seeking sun, I slid from my prison into the light. For a few minutes, I lay gasping on a rock in the warmth of the rays that beamed through the glass above into the inner courtyard. Then caution returned and I slid off the rock and back into the cold water.

I knew my situation was desperate and so I threw my exhaustion back like a blanket. The aluminium grate needed to be replaced so that they would think I had not gotten this far. I needed them to be delayed from searching the holding tank for me. I knew that I could not further my escape until the sun had set.

Once this job was accomplished, I moved with relief back onto the warm land to rest.

From Our Report

Tap looked at the rocks that had been removed from the stream of water and then looked at the grate that had been removed and set aside. Her eyes went back to the rocks. They had been very carefully arranged to spell, FUCK YOU. We observed that Tap fought to keep her features neutral.

She has bested us.

It is amazing.

Very resourceful.

Tap's decision was made without consideration, as action was needed immediately. We sensed that Tap was aware that she could be putting herself in danger, but Courtney Hunter's escape was a far greater danger. Tap took off her shoes, dropped to her belly, and wriggled through the hole. Head first was her way, although at this particular moment we felt she was not necessarily using her head. Tap hit the cold water with a gasp and we immediately felt her body heat bleeding, haemorrhaging out. We were afraid. Several strong strokes took her to the overflow gate at the far side. Her fingers, now blue, wrapped around the metal and shook the frame. It was screwed in place but the metal grid had been bent, as if someone had tried to push a hand through. Tap reasoned that Courtney Hunter could not have gotten through, and she had not returned to the room, so she must have drowned. We sensed that thought distressed her greatly.

Against our advice, Tap dived, and dived, and dived. At last she once again held onto the grate, her strength and body heat completely gone, but she had not found Courtney's body. Tap had stayed in the water too long and now we weren't sure if she could make it back across the tank and force her body back up and through the water into the room. Tap had become the prisoner and her situation was desperate. She shook the grate with all the strength she had left, hoping to dislodge the metal. The strands bent beneath her fingers as she slipped closer to unconsciousness. We summoned help.

Taken From Courtney Hunter's Logs

The rattle woke me from my exhausted stupor and fear gripped my heart. I looked through the branches and saw Tap's hand wrapped around the bent grill. Panic erupted inside me until I noted the hand was an ugly shade of grey-blue. I fought to calm myself and think rationally. A memory stirred in my mind.

"Are you all right?" I had asked last winter as Taylor Alexandria Punga had staggered into the library.

"Cold," the woman had revealed on this, our second meeting. "I got too cold."

I had helped my boss to a chair and brought her a hot cup of tea. Taylor Alexandria Punga had recovered slowly, thanked me, and left. It was then that I had found the red tag that had fallen from the woman's pocket. It was this tag that had planted the seed of the idea that had brought me, and now her, to the water grate. Now once again, Tap was in trouble.

Hard decisions are often made by instinctive reaction, then given elaborate explanation after the fact or dismissed with the words, "I don't know." Later, when I was questioned, I fell back on the latter to explain my actions. I didn't know. I still don't.

"Hold on," I ordered as I knelt in the water and started to remove the screen. It was easier this time. The screws were not fastened as tightly and I was working from the outside. I could not see Tap from where I worked and that worried me. All I could see was her hand. It was now white and claw-like. The last screw fell into the water and I reached around the screen to grab Taylor Alexandria Punga's wrist. It was ice cold. Dead weight.

I sat on my bum, placed my feet on either side of the grate, and pulled — fighting with all my strength not to lose her. An arm and shoulder appeared. Gasping with the effort, I risked letting go with one hand and made a grab for Tap's collar. Gradually, inch by inch I pulled the body from the water. It was a body, not a person. It was still and cold and unresponsive, like the cold body of death. I felt panic returning. Struggling, I pulled the long form clear of the tank and up onto the warm rock ledge, then flopped down myself, gasping.

I remembered the first time I had met Taylor Alexandria Punga, it had been hot. We met on a hotel terrace in Vancouver and had coffee. Tap had sniffed at hers, but drank very little. We had gone through my résumé. My life, reduced to two dimensional symbols on flat white. It was a good résumé but a boring life. I liked to think there was another side to me that wasn't on my résumé, but in my heart.

Tap was offering a fantastic salary for archival work. A few years in the job and I would be out of debt, or at least only in the debt that it is appropriate to be in.

"I do not want you. You are too qualified for the job."

It was an arrow through my dreams. Its point was ludicrous and so I protested.

"But I want the job. I can handle it easily and the money is good."

This was true. Looking back, however, after the incident in Geneva, which has not yet come into this report, I wondered if even then the attraction to the enigma that was Tap had not been there. Had I been suspicious of the woman even then?

"You will leave for a better position and I need someone to stay."

"I will stay."

Maybe then Punga saw some of my heart and less of my résumé, because we came to an arrangement then and there. It was a good arrangement and it had lasted two years, one month and eighteen days. Then it had changed.

Now, I remember pulling Tap from the holding tank as a scene in sharp contrasts — like an Escher drawing in black and white, perspectives distorted. The body was cold, the rock warm; the shadows dark, the sunlight brilliant. My emotions were fired by worry, and the dread of the guns that were soon trained on me, and there was an ice ball in my gut.

Punga was taken away. I protested, wanting to stay with Tap until I was sure she would recover. My protests went unheard. I was returned to the room.

The grate and stones had been replaced and the stone floor was dry. Had I escaped? The no of this room was even louder now. This time what Tap called her security system was present — like invisible bodies pushing against me. If I tried to go near the water channel, the force pushed me back. Exhausted and emotionally drained, I grudgingly accepted the no. I showered to get warm and found to my surprise when I returned to the main room, a red jumpsuit lying on the bed. I switched from towel to jumpsuit and slept amongst a jumble of sheets and pillows rather than bothering to make the bed, too emotionally and physically drained to care.

From Our Report

We must go back and review the rescue from another angle. Each angle is another viewpoint and so another event. When we sounded an alarm after Courtney's escape, security personnel charged about, knowing only that there was a security breach. We were not able to help them. They then realized that Tap was somehow trapped in the water system, and lastly, that an intruder had her in the courtyard. They had charged in, assault rifles at the ready, fanning out across the space like birdshot from a rifle. To their surprise, the intruder was Courtney Hunter, whom many of them knew, and she held Tap gently in her arms.

They were separated, the bond between the two still, silent women cut with surgical precision. Tap was carried away gently. Courtney was taken roughly. One silent and still, one loud and fighting her keepers.

We were both relieved and confused. How had this happened? Nothing like this had happened before. Courtney Hunter had outsmarted us and this should not have happened. Stranger still, Courtney Hunter had not made good her escape, but had pulled Taylor Alexandria Punga from the holding tank. This could not possibly have happened, and yet it had.

What are we to do with her?

It seems most regrettable.

Termination is for the best.

Chapter Two

"Complexity leads to a need for corporate conformity. With conformity, critical thought is lost, and at this point, social structure starts to rot from the inside out. This is why all empires fall."

~ Saianna

From Our Report

Termination is the state of coming to an end, not by choice or by nature, but by decision. A decision was made and that was — regrettably — to terminate Courtney Hunter. There was no anger or malice in this decision. The decision was simply an observation that termination was necessary and regrettable. Courtney slept through this decision-making process, as did Punga.

So when Courtney woke hours later, she was not yet aware of the possibility of her termination and would not be aware of that decision until the Geneva incident, which has not yet entered this report.

Taken From Courtney Hunter's Logs

I woke feeling frustrated and angry. Every step I had taken since deciding to use the red tag had gotten me deeper and deeper into trouble. I was happy for the anger; it was keeping my growing fear at bay. I was terribly hungry and had extremely sore muscles from my struggle to escape. The sore muscles I was willing to tolerate; they had been earned. The hunger I was not prepared to accept. Under the Geneva Convention, I had certain rights as a prisoner, one of them being food. I stretched, enjoying the sensation of my cramped bones straightening into place, and then rolled in one movement from the bed and onto my feet. "I need food," I announced loudly into the empty room, assuming that I was being monitored by the security system. "I'm hungry."

I thought it a reasonable request at the time, although at that point I didn't know I was about to be terminated. I wouldn't learn of this for some time. Still, one is entitled to a last meal. Does the food lie heavily on their stomachs, those that ate and were terminated? One wonders. I didn't wonder. I grew angry instead. I had come back and saved Taylor Alexandria Punga's life, and I felt I deserved better treatment. I'm an individual who tries to be proactive. Although I will admit that my actions, when motivated by anger, can at times come very close to spite.

I took a pillow, walked into the bathroom area, and stuffed it over the drainage hole of the shower. The security system did not react at first and when it did, it was too late; I had managed to get the water running. I was finally pushed from the alcove just as the water topped the rim of the stainless steel basin and started to run across the floor in a spreading fan of trouble. I took the time to smile.

Then I stopped struggling against the security system's force field and ran back into the main room, bouncing off the walls, back and forth like an India rubber ball out of control. The security system could not seem to keep up, and on my third bounce I was able to break through to the channel of water. I picked up a stone and hurled it, then another and another, heaving them in all directions with as much force as I could muster. I didn't think it would shut down the security system; I was just trying to cause as much of a disturbance as I could in order to get their attention.

The stones bounced and rolled and rattled about, and still I threw more, using up my angry energy. I had played for the local softball team for years and I could pitch. And I did, over and over again. I threw until I couldn't throw any more. When I finally stopped, much to my surprise, I couldn't feel the security system around me. The water spread. The stones, now left alone, remained in a helter skelter pattern on the floor of the room. I had simply reacted, and in doing so, I seemed to have made some progress.

There was silence, then the door opened. Ian entered. "Court, what are you doing?"

"Getting my point across."

He crossed the room and disappeared into the alcove to turn off the water. I ran to the door. It was locked. I knew I needed a red tag to get through the doorway. Ian wore a red tag. Once again, I didn't think, I just reacted, turning to face Ian. "The door is locked."

"Yes."

"But you can open it."

"Yes. What do you want, Court? Why are you doing this?"

"I want food, I want to see Punga, and I want my freedom."

"No."

I was a cornered animal and, as such, my flight or fight instinct was on full alert. Flight was being curtailed by Ian and so fight became necessary. I picked up a fist sized stone and hurled it at Ian with considerable force. It was a high, fast ball that caught

Ian between the eyes. Much to my surprise, he buckled and dropped.

I ran to Ian and knelt down beside him. He was breathing and seemed okay. Relief flooded through me. I hadn't meant to hurt him; I only wanted out of there. The red tag was fixed to the collar and wouldn't come off. I hesitated for only a second, then I undid Ian's jumpsuit and, with some difficulty, pulled it from his body. I slipped the black jumpsuit on over my red one and stood in the square. The door opened and I once again made my escape.

From Our Report

Courtney had proven herself to be both resourceful and unpredictable. She did not escape into a corridor, but into a domed courtyard. This one had a small circular pool in the centre of a room. The room was empty except for a magnificent bougainvillea that grew up the one wall and partly across the glass dome. The dome was dark; night had come on while Courtney had been held in the room. The area was lit by a single light in the centre of the dome. Courtney did not find it illuminating. The surveillance camera recorded that, for a minute, Courtney stood still, considering, as her eyes took in the strange room thoughtfully.

We anticipated that the logical thing for her to do would be to find a way out. But once again, we were surprised.

Taken From Courtney Hunter's Logs

I could have tried to escape again, but then what? No one was going to believe my wild story. I would be without a job or a good reference, and worse, I would still not know what was going on at TAP International. That would weigh on my mind for the rest of my life. This reasoning sounds brave. The truth is, I was very scared. I didn't think there was much chance of me escaping from the compound, and so my best defence was to do what they least expected. Besides, I had made my decision and it had not changed. I meant to find out who Tap was and what was going on there. Like Daniel, I'm inclined to walk into the lion's den.

A number of doors led off each side of the interior square. I started opening each one in turn and saw some very interesting things, which I'll talk about later in this report. Finally, I opened the door to the room where Taylor Alexandria Punga lay. The room was very hot, and a number of people in black jumpsuits stood around looking worried. They looked more worried when I walked in. Worried and bewildered. I took some satisfaction in that. They did not react. I suppose at first they did not realize that I had not been released but had escaped yet again.

"Has anyone called a doctor?" I asked, pushing through to where Punga lay on a mattress resting on a shelf protruding from the wall. Little else was in the room. Punga was covered in layers of sheets and blankets. No one answered my question. I rolled my eyes in frustration. For a bunch of people who supposedly belonged to a think tank, they surely didn't seem to know what to do. I knelt down beside the woman, reaching out to touch her arm. The arm was cold, but not as cold as it had been.

Out the corner of my eye, I saw Haichen look over at Lamount for a brief second, then her eyes shifted to Franz Scheidt, who was head of Security. He nodded his head once ever so slightly. Her nod in return was barely perceptible. "You can't be in here, Courtney," Haichen Lai said, stepping forward and placing a restraining hand on my shoulder.

"Look!" I snapped, standing up. "I have had it. I'm hungry, tired, and royally pissed. I've worked with most of you for over two years, and it seems I'm the only one not in on the big game. Well, that just changed. I want to know what the hell is up around here."

No one responded. Clearly, I was a situation without precedent. Finally from behind them, a quiet voice asked, "Is that Courtney Hunter? What is going on?"

It was Haichen Lai who answered. "Tap, it appears that Courtney has now escaped a second time and—"

"Enough," Punga cut in calmly. "You are all to leave, please. Courtney, you stay."

"I want food," I demanded.

"Bring food and drink. You know her. Bring whatever she likes." The group looked uneasy, but after a second's hesitation, Scheidt herded them from the room.

"Why?" Punga asked. It was a small question which demanded a complex answer.

I crossed my arms and looked down at Tap with eyes narrowed in determination. "I will not be held prisoner. I have not done anything to warrant imprisonment. And I came back because you were in trouble. I would not let you die."

I saw Tap gather her strength around her like a blanket. "You will wait outside the door for me. When the food arrives, please come in and eat with me. I need your word that you won't escape if I allow this."

"You allow nothing. But you have my word that I will not escape until I have eaten and talked with you."

"Agreed."

From Our Report

Tap's agreement, although only one word, was a very big speech, a policy statement really. It led to a rather disturbing picnic and a series of events quite startling in nature and resulted in the need for this enquiry.

Courtney left. She did indeed wait in the domed room by the pool. She was to write in her report later that, not being stupid, she had used the time to consider possible avenues of escape. She noted with some amusement that one was reasonably sound and two others would take daring and some remarkable luck. These two, she said she favoured.

Alone in the room, Tap blinked. When she blinked again, it indicated to us the degree of her surprise. We knew Tap felt she had never met anyone quite as spunky and resourceful as Courtney Hunter. Although she had sensed from the moment she had interviewed her that Hunter had much to offer the project, she had not anticipated that her quiet archivist to be a potential revolutionary. Once Courtney had left the room, Tap let the fatigue show again in her face. This worried us. Tap lay staring at the ceiling, as if she would find the answers written there. It is rare that Tap is taken by surprise, and rarer still when she is bested at her own game. The day's events had not only sapped her strength, but had made her revisit some of the decisions she had made.

We have recommended termination of Courtney Hunter.

It is regrettable.

But necessary.

"No," Tap snapped, snuggling below the blankets to get warmer. "At least, not yet."

But, Tap, she has broken into your chambers.

Escaped through the water channel.

Hurt Ian and escaped again.

"How was Ian hurt, and how badly?" Tap enquired calmly, lying still, her eyes closed. Yet we knew Tap found this disturbing news.

Rugia Malwala sent him in to talk to Courtney Hunter.

She was going mad.

She hit him with a river rock.

It knocked him unconscious.

She took his uniform and tag.

And thus she escaped again.

Tap sighed. We sensed she was beginning to understand the danger. Courtney Hunter was a law unto herself. That is to say, Courtney Hunter was unpredictable and creative in the decisions and actions she chose. "Had she been set on escaping, she would not have come in here. There will be no termination at this time."

Perhaps we would have debated this decision, but at that point the food arrived, followed closely by Courtney, who had said she was very hungry. It appeared she could smell a toasted cheese sandwich and a carton of chocolate milk from beneath its plate cover.

"You may go. I will be alone with Courtney Hunter while she has her meal," Tap commanded, and so we left.

Taken From Courtney Hunter's Logs

It was an unusual request on the part of Taylor Alexandria Punga to ask to be alone with me, but I did not realize the significance of her actions at the time, nor did I care. If Tap wanted to dismiss the person who had brought in the food, that was all right with me. At that moment all I cared about was calories, and the more the better.

"You will call me Tap in the future. What is that I smell?"

I looked down at the pale figure, lying on her back as if asleep. "Aren't you afraid I might bludgeon you to death with my milk carton?" I asked, one eyebrow raised in sarcastic query. However foolish, I find I can't resist pulling the tail of tigers. And Punga was undoubtedly a tiger.

Those strange, aqua eyes opened and looked directly into mine. "Should I be?"

I repressed a shudder. For a second, I was very close to panic. Nervousness well disguised as bravado loosened my tongue. "No. Why don't you sit up and join me, Tap? There's lots. I'd just like to go on record, in case we ever meet again after today, that I mostly like a toasted processed cheese sandwich and chocolate milk at lunch, because it fits so nicely into my tummy and into my budget."

I saw Tap blink rapidly. I had surprised her. That was good. I needed to keep them all off guard. It was my only defence. I forced the fear back and hoped Tap couldn't hear my heart pounding. I sat cross legged on the floor and took bites of my sandwich between slugs of milk. For a minute I wore a brown moustache, and then wiped it off with my napkin. I suspected I had surprised Tap on a number of levels. I didn't think she was used to being told to do something, even something as simple as joining me in lunch. I also didn't think she was used to ever having her name spoken in a tone of friendship. I had meant my request to have a degree of warmth to it.

Tap sat up and gingerly took half a sandwich from the plate I offered her. She sniffed it.

I laughed. "Do you always sniff your food? You sniffed your coffee the day you hired me, too."

Tap's face hardened and she bit down on the sandwich, chewed deliberately, and swallowed defiantly. By the look on her face, the concoction was acceptable — just. I had a feeling it was the first time that Tap had lowered herself to eating a toasted processed cheese sandwich.

For a little while, we ate quietly. Tap ate little; I ate a lot. It was only when I had eaten my fill and was just savouring the last few mouthfuls to fill up the more remote corners that I opened up the conversation. It was, in fact, not so much a conversation but very much more a negotiation.

"Tap, I do want to learn what is going on around here, but I will not be held a prisoner. What you did to me is illegal and that worries me. I won't be a party to any activity that is illegal. If that is the case, I'm out of here."

"Are you afraid of nothing?" Tap asked, once again lying down and covering herself with blankets. She had eaten only half a grilled cheese sandwich but judging by her colour, I wasn't at all sure even that much had been a good idea.

I looked at the pale woman wrapped like a cocoon. "I was afraid you would die," I admitted.

"It was close in the tank. I had considered the possibility that you might have drowned and I searched for your body." From the tone of her statement, I assumed Tap considered her actions well beyond the call of duty and I should be grateful for the risk she took.

I, on the other hand, found her remark condescending and insulting. "Gee, I really feel bad that was an annoying possibility. But I'm relieved to know that you weren't worried. Why do you go to all those environmental and world health conferences if you care so little about human life?"

The pale, cold eyes focused on me again. "I strive to be objective. It is not good research if it is tainted by emotion and personal bias. There must always be reason above passion."

I snorted. "You are one flawed human."

Tap was on her feet in a second and looming over me, bristling with anger barely in check. "I am not flawed!"

I sat back in shock, fear lancing through my heart, and looked way up — because Tap was very tall — into a face taut with anger. Frowning, I forced myself to look unafraid and stood slowly. Although I still had to look up, I felt I was at less of a disadvantage. "OK, you are not flawed. You know, Tap, humans have weaknesses. It's unrealistic to think otherwise." Tap jerked when I reached out and touched her arm, then she seemed to compose herself with effort. My eyebrow rose in disbelief. "If a person didn't know you weren't flawed, a person might assume that you have a fear of being touched."

"I have no fears."

Which, of course, was a lie, but one that I don't think Tap knew she was making, believing that she did not have fears but only uncertainties. Uncertainty is rooted in the fear of unpredictable consequences. This, however, is different from being afraid. To be afraid is to not face your fears. Perhaps at this time, Tap did not know the difference between fear and being afraid.

I couldn't help laughing. "Yeah? I have plenty."

"You do not seem to fear anything."

I put my hands on my hips and looked up at Tap in exasperation. "I didn't say I was afraid, I said I had fears. I'm not the least bit afraid of you; you are just a big bully."

Tap walked away and I wondered if I had pushed too far. She stood quietly for a minute and then turned to look at me. "Let us start again." I felt my insides relax. She meant she had realized that she had not handled the situation well. "If you are to train here, then you must stay here. Once classified information is given you, it would be a security breach to let you go."

I know this time the uncertainty and shock showed on my face. I was about to commit to an unknown, but I was very much afraid that not to do so would be far worse.

Chapter Three

"Clubs and other such organizations do not exist to bring people together, but to exclude others."

~ Tap Zad

From Our Report

We left, but we observed. It is our right. Tap knew this. She stood looking at Courtney with an expression that showed considerable frustration. It was the sort of frustration one feels when trying to find the missing end on a spool of thread — one should start at the beginning, but there is no beginning to be found. It was impossible to explain the truth to Courtney Hunter. Even if presented with it, Tap doubted very much Courtney could understand. Instead, she tried to explain away her organization's actions. Logic is both the key to solving and to obscuring the truth. It was the latter she meant to achieve.

"Consider a small event in the past. Do you remember some years ago now when the American surveillance plane was intercepted by a Chinese fighter?"

"Yes, of course. The fighter came too close and clipped the wing of an American aircraft. The jet fighter crashed into the sea and the American plane had to make an emergency landing in Chinese territory."

"Yes, then what happened?" Tap asked, crossing her arms and looking at Courtney with interest.

"The President took a very strong stand that the plane and personnel must be returned immediately, and they were."

"No."

"No?"

"The President had the Secretary of State feel out the Chinese Embassy in Washington, who communicated the strong line that was going to be taken by the Chinese government. They needed help. I was contacted and I made the arrangements. The President was allowed to take a strong and threatening stand. This was necessary to appease the American people and was acceptable to the Chinese government, who had no problem with the United States portraying themselves as world bullies and spies.

"The Chinese were given a formal apology for the death of their airman. This was necessary in order for the Chinese to save face. They would have preferred that it was the President that made that apology, but they could not push too hard because they need foreign currency and the support of the World Bank to pay for the Three Dam Project. American investment is an essential part of their development plan. The Americans were able to save their own face by having the Secretary of State make the apology."

"But—"

"I am not finished. There had to be a price paid for the release of the flight personnel. The Chinese would have liked to imprison the spies for life. The price was the surveillance system that the United States had planned to establish in Taiwan. The crew was returned. The President got to brag about taking a strong stand against the Communist threat, and a month later the US quietly dropped their surveillance system."

"But—"

"The President used me to broker a deal. He played the role he was told to play in order to get out of a very embarrassing political situation. The control was mine."

Courtney laughed. "You are arrogance personified."

"I speak only the truth."

At least of a sort, we knew.

"So, where were you when 9-11 happened or the war with Iraq started?"

Tap noted the sarcasm. It is a tool of attack when defences are starting to weaken. Her reply was concise, reducing major events to the bare essentials.

"My services were not required. Decisions had been made well before the event."

"I thought you said the President has no control."

Tap smiled. "You are a good debater, but you confuse diplomacy with might. Those two elements do not co-exist, although they are often made to seem so for propaganda purposes. The fate of Iraq was decided not by Bush, but by Bin Laden."

"What?"

We sensed Tap's impatience. She did not show it.

"Revenge for 9-11 was deemed necessary by the American people. They saw this as important so that the US would not seem weak to the world. They also felt that the people who died that day deserved justice. That prevailing attitude gave the Bush administration the window of opportunity for which they had been waiting."

"I don't understand."

This time Tap showed her frustration by holding up a hand for Courtney Hunter to be quiet while she explained.

"The Bush Administration was already looking for a reason to attack Iraq. Even under the Clinton administration, efforts had been made to paint Saddam Hussein in the worst possible light. There had been over 3,000 inspections for weapons of mass destruction, and at only three installations had the inspectors run into any difficulties. Yet the American on the team, after receiving a call from the US, went public about how it was impossible for them to do a proper inspection in Iraq. The rest of the inspection team was surprised and shocked by his statements.

"You see, Iraq had become a weak link in the US foreign policy in the Middle East. Saddam Hussein had been a thorn in the side of his Arab neighbours, attacking Iran in a violent and prolonged war. America saw Saddam Hussein as an Islamic moderate standing against Fundamentalism. But then he attacked Kuwait, which led to the war called Desert Storm. The US knew that attacking Iraq would not destabilize the region. The other Middle East countries would be content to watch as Saddam Hussein, the former US puppet, was removed from power for turning against the hand that had controlled him for so many years.

"9-11 allowed the US to do what it had always wanted and that was to move into oil rich areas like Afghanistan and Iraq, and make sure they controlled the oil. Emerging developing nations will soon be making greater and greater demands for oil. It was necessary to make sure that the US needs were met first. The weapons of mass destruction were simply a device for justifying the war. The American people had to feel the war was justified."

"That's wrong."

Tap shrugged. "It is the politics of this world. I have nothing to do with any misinformation nor do I broker arms. I work in the sphere of diplomacy, not military might."

"I'm glad to hear that," Courtney observed dryly. "So you are telling me that you run an international consulting service for world leaders. Do you do anything illegal?"

This was a very difficult question and Tap considered carefully before answering, responding with cautiously chosen words.

"I run nothing, but sometimes help if requested, then I provide my services for a price. Humanity has common moral and ethical values; however, laws vary greatly from country to country. I try never to violate a law of the country with which I am dealing. Sometimes, however, it is necessary for the greater good."

Courtney looked thoughtful, then frowned. "Tap, you need to lie down again and get covered up. You don't look well."

"You have caused me much trouble."

Tap did not mean this as a criticism, but as a statement of fact. She had much to do and had wasted an entire day on Courtney and on being ill.

Courtney reacted immediately. "Hey! Get real. You locked me up. I should have escaped, called the police, and lodged a complaint. Instead, I came to you and gave you a chance to explain."

We sensed the anger rising like lava through Tap's frame. She had saved this impossible woman's life, against our advice, by putting a hold on the order of termination, and at the moment, she was totally flummoxed as to why she had bothered. We observed Tap's fight for emotional control. She managed to respond neutrally.

"You are not in a position to threaten me. It is my good will that protects you. I remind you that you have broken into and entered my home."

Courtney blushed. We suspected she was now feeling very uncomfortable with her poorly formed decision to use the red tag to gain access to Tap's chambers, and although we knew she would never show it, we believed she was very fearful about the situation in which she found herself.

As we had come to expect, Courtney Hunter went on the defensive. "I didn't break anything, and you didn't give me any time to enter. I was barely across the threshold when you and your weird security system showed up."

Tap was growing impatient with this troublesome woman.

"I need your word that you will stay, learn, and be part of my organization. There will be no more escape attempts."

We sensed Tap was not well and needed to lie down and cover up, but to do so would be to show weakness. That was not an option. Tap needed this matter concluded.

"Can I go and come as I please?" Courtney bargained.

"Once you have completed your training. Until then, you may wear a red tag and have access to most areas," Tap stated.

We were surprised. We knew this decision was going to cause problems. We wondered why Tap felt it necessary. Tap, we knew, suspected Courtney Hunter had much to offer, although she was not yet sure just how much of a role Courtney would play in her plans. At this point, we did not realize either. We failed. Complacency makes us blind to the future. We did know that if Courtney did not agree, then she would be terminated. That would be regrettable.

"How long is the training?" Courtney asked, her chin up with determination.

"A month."

This was not so much a truth as it was a lie. It would take at least a month for Courtney to do some basic reading. After that she might be given an opportunity to be a participant in our undertaking. She could never, we thought, be told the truth, but she could be a willing subject. That had never been attempted before.

"I'll need some things from my apartment," Courtney held out stubbornly.

She seemed to feel she was doing very well at striking a bargain and things were turning in her favour. This was not true, either. She was, had she known it, only a hair's breadth away from death.

"Tomorrow. I have no time to deal with this issue today."

It was Tap's final concession. If Courtney argued, Tap would give the order for termination. We sensed Tap was very cold, shivering, and she knew she needed to lie down.

Courtney opened her mouth to argue, then closed it. She must have decided that she had made her point and achieved her aim to learn about Tap's organization.

"Tomorrow. OK."

Those two words saved her life.

The door opened and Haichen Lai entered silently.

"Haichen, you will see that Courtney is given a proper outfit, red tag distinction. You will escort her through the administrative areas and explain anything that she wishes to know about."

"Yes, Tap," Haichen Lai responded, keeping her face and voice neutral despite her obvious surprise.

A smile almost made it to Tap's face. "Go now, Courtney Hunter. And please find a room that you are prepared not to escape from."

Courtney did smile and reached out to touch Tap's arm, which shocked both Lai and Tap. "You rest. Your lips are turning blue again."

We did not understand Courtney's concern for Tap's well being. Perhaps she did not fully understand the gravity of the situation in which she now found herself. Tap watched them leave with thoughtful eyes. Even then, the seeds of the decisions she would make started to take hold.

This is not right.

Is this wise?

These are uncharted waters.

"Enough. I will rest."

Dismissed, Haichen hurried Courtney from the room.

We suspected Haichen was confused by the change in Courtney Hunter's status. She would not doubt, however, that Tap had a logical reason for this change. She would know that it would be best to make sure that Courtney saw Haichen in a positive light. Tap's relationship with Courtney would have seemed very informal.

"It is good to find you are now part of the organization, Court. I have always found you very obliging and efficient in your job."

"Yeah, well, I was a little surprised today to discover I wasn't seen as part of the organization. How is Ian?"

"He will recover, but has a large area of swelling and bruising on his frontal eminence."

Courtney stifled a laugh at the double meaning of this statement, knowing that Haichen would not understand. Instead, Courtney shook her head in disgust.

"I usually have better control. My pitch was high. I was under pressure."

Haichen smiled, although she had probably not meant to. Courtney Hunter showed great nerve. That was to be admired.

"This room is where our uniforms are kept. Tap prefers that we change twice a day. You come here and pick out your size and transfer your tag."

The room was empty except for hundreds of black jumpsuits that hung from the rods that lined the walls. "Where do we change?"

Haichen looked surprised. "Here. Oh, of course, you would not understand. We are very open here. We live and work together, so there is no embarrassment in changing in front of others."

When in an awkward situation, we have observed, Courtney Hunter will often be flippant.

"One big happy family, huh?"

Inside, we understood, Courtney felt uncomfortable by this revelation. She was a little afraid she might have entered some commune not to her liking. Despite her abnormal amount of curiosity about others, Courtney Hunter was a private person. Such contradictions are common among the human race.

Haichen felt the need to correct her charge. Haichen saw things in black and white, and could not bear misinformation. "Oh no, none of us are related. Except, of course, by the genetic similarities that we all share." She chuckled, enjoying her joke.

Courtney smiled, although she wasn't sure what was funny. Haichen went on. "The A suits will have to do for you. You are very short. A is the closest we would have. You will please change now and give me back Ian's tag. I will get you your own."

Courtney could be rash in her decisions, yet we noted she never made the same mistake twice.

"Tell you what — I'll change while you get my new tag. Then we'll swap."

"You do not trust me?"

"After the day I've had so far, I wouldn't trust my own sweet grandmother if she was decked out in one of those jumpsuits."

Such expressions are a way to express considerable negative meaning indirectly.

Haichen was concerned. It appeared that Courtney Hunter had much favour with Tap and so she did not want to displease her, yet she knew that Courtney had twice tried to escape. Tap would be displeased if Courtney were to succeed. "I understand your caution. You will change and then we will go together to get you your own tag."

"Agreed."

Courtney felt she was doing very well in asserting her rights, we sensed. It is easy to feel pleased with yourself when you have no idea of your possible termination. This she would not learn until Geneva. The events then would, of course, change everything.

After Courtney had changed, they went to a room to the right. Here a number of men and women whom Courtney had never seen before worked in near darkness. The only light came from the reds, blues, and greens of each computer screen, which made the room glow like some alien world.

"Courtney Hunter has been granted red status, Rugia," Haichen said to one woman who nodded after the briefest of hesitations and, without looking up, went through a series of security checks on Courtney. The last item to appear on the screen was a brief statement: *Courtney Hunter is to have red status.* In large, bold letters, it was signed simply "Tap".

The woman typed again and a few seconds later a machine spat out Courtney's red tag. Courtney clipped the tag to her pocket and they left. Rugia Malwala's intelligent, thoughtful eyes watched them go. Then, turning back to her screen, she entered an access code and typed: Subject: Courtney Hunter. Event: Assigned red clearance by TAP's order. Please advise.

Now that Courtney was properly clothed and tagged, Haichen took her on a tour of the red zone area. Off the domed courtyard there was the computer and uniform room, the room in which Courtney had been held, the room in which she had found Tap, and a communal dining hall, kitchen, and a state of the art library.

In this last room, Courtney had a good look around. All books and data were stored on a server. The people doing research sat in comfy chairs with small swivel tables on which they placed their data pilots. The data was presented on wall-mounted monitors. Haichen explained that novels and data could also be downloaded, should Courtney wish to read in the privacy of her quarters.

The last door off the domed room led down a corridor off which was a huge gymnasium and, at the end, a sauna, showers, and a large swimming pool. They turned right and the corridor opened up into the interior courtyard that was much larger than Courtney had realized. Haichen explained that the rooms that formed the north wall of the garden were the private quarters of the house staff.

"I do not know where you wish to establish your quarters. Our only guest room is the one where you were—"

Plans have changed.

You are to bring Courtney Hunter at once.

Tap wishes to speak with her.

Courtney wisely forced herself not to react or look around her. We sensed she was not about to let Haichen know that she did not fully understand.

"It looks as if our tour has been cut short," Courtney Hunter observed.

Knowledge was power. Lack of knowledge was weakness. Courtney planned to play her cards close to her chest until she knew what was going on around here. That is, she did not wish others to realize how little she knew or how little power she had.

Haichen showed shock at the realization that Courtney had heard the voices. She recovered quickly. "I will take you back to Tap's quarters."

"No need. I know the way. I'm sure you have things to be doing and I don't want to keep you from your work."

Courtney spoke with authority, testing her newfound power.

"Very well, as you wish," Haichen agreed immediately. "It has been a pleasure to show you around."

We sensed Courtney Hunter's surprise.

Courtney Hunter had anticipated a power struggle. Haichen must suspect that Courtney was closer to Tap than she actually was. Courtney smiled her thanks and walked as casually as she could back to the room where she had last seen Tap. She was well aware Haichen followed some distance behind and watched with interested eyes until Courtney crossed the domed room and disappeared into Tap's quarters.

The room where Tap had been was now empty. The cushions were back in place and the sheets, blankets, and pillows gone. Courtney crossed the room and knocked on the door at the back.

Enter.

Wait within.

She will come.

Courtney forced herself not to answer or react to what she heard. Instead, she opened the door and entered a room that was beautiful in its simplicity. Here the walls were rice paper in frames of polished camphor wood. A gentle, warm breeze from wall vents stirred the spicy fragrance of the wood into the air. The floor was white stone, and along one wall a channel of water bubbled over black river rocks. Had it not been for the gentle breeze, the room would have been unusually hot.

A door at the back opened and Tap entered.

Chapter Four

"Books give not wisdom where none was before. But where some is, there makes it more."

~ Sir John Harrington

From Our Report

After Courtney had left to be outfitted, Tap dressed in a fresh black jumpsuit, but her casual dress was not in keeping with her thoughts. She was preoccupied. Tap was about to make a significant decision with considerable repercussions. We did not fully comprehend Tap's thought processes, as we were focused on Courtney Hunter at the time.

Tap felt the key to solving our situation had been handed to her at last, and only in the nick of time, but to use that key would be to change fundamentally who we are forever. Would the others follow her? Was this a decision she and the others could live with? Tap had been wrestling with our problems for a long time, but the desperate course of action she now considered was based on a sudden insight. This illogical behaviour is referred to as "going with a gut instinct". Such behaviour, when successful, is highly respected. When it fails, it is then referred to as reckless or foolhardy.

Although time was short, Tap was not about to share her thoughts with anyone yet, least of all Courtney Hunter. Tap walked with casual confidence across the room and was surprised to see the apprehension, perhaps even fear, in Courtney's eyes at the sudden summons. Tap concluded Courtney had begun to wonder what role she would play and whether she truly wished to be a part of the organization.

The reality was Courtney Hunter was totally out of her depth. There was no familiarity or point of reference for her day's experience, and from now on there never would be. We had concerns. Courtney was not one of us. She did not belong. We did not as yet know what Tap planned. Nor did we understand what was unfolding.

"There has been a change of plans. I will be leaving in seventy-two hours. You will accompany me."

Tap could see Courtney forcing herself to look into Tap's eyes and not let her gaze waver. It was not easy for Courtney. We sensed this pleased Tap. Too often today, Tap had found herself at a disadvantage with this woman.

"Where and why?"

Tap allowed herself the pleasure of showing her frustration with Courtney's stubborn nature in the form of a snort. Then she turned away and walked to her desk, settling herself gratefully in the leather chair. She was, in truth, still very cold and weak from her experience in the holding tank. With a sigh, she closed her eyes. Tap needed rest but there simply was not enough time now. "We are going to Italy. Rome. There we will hear a series of lectures on the world economy. There is much you will need to learn before then."

The door opened and Tap did not bother opening her eyes. She knew it would be Samuel Singh bringing two data pilots. She heard him walk quietly across the room and gently place the equipment on the desk, as if not to disturb her sleep, though Singh was well aware that Tap was not asleep.

"I think she was hit by a bus, but I don't think she got its license," Tap heard Courtney joke. "How are you, Sam?"

"Fine, thank you, Court. Welcome." Sam smiled then left without another word.

"I was not hit by a bus, Courtney Hunter. I got too cold in the water tank and so I am tired. I have the heat rather high in this room. I hope that will not be a problem."

"It was a joke; I like to be called Court; and no, it will not be a problem."

"Sit and read then, Court. There is much that you will need to know."

For once Courtney followed Tap's instructions without query, sitting across from her in the visitor's chair. She must have wondered how many visitors had sat there without her knowledge. Two years, and Courtney was only just learning that a whole program functioned behind the façade of the organization for which she had worked. She had no idea what she had gotten into. Perhaps if she had, she would not have acted with such bravado.

Tap handed Courtney one of the units and she opened up one of the files on the data pilot and started to read a report by the US Navy on ice thickness in Antarctica. She squirmed a good deal over the next three hours, and finally ended up partially unzipping the front of her jumpsuit and rolling up her sleeves. It was more than warm in the room, it was hot, but although uncomfortable, Courtney did not complain.

Tap was perfectly comfortable and finally starting to feel recovered from her ordeal. She became preoccupied with her own reading for a time. Courtney read through two lengthy reports. Tap read considerably more. Tap saw Courtney tightening her jaw in determination as she forced herself to focus on a report on island elevations. A change of pace was perhaps in order.

"Did you notice anything in the rooms where the security system was functioning, Court?" Tap's quiet voice seemed to boom out in the still room.

Absorbed in her reading, Courtney started. "What?"

Tap's eyes focused on her with some intensity. She did not want to miss any body language that might tell her more than Courtney's words.

"I wanted to know whether you detected any physical evidence of the security system I have in place."

"I heard it, and I could feel it. It's creepy. How is it done? It must be some sort of energy force."

"I suppose you could call it that. I know you heard and felt it, I want to know what you saw."

Courtney considered this directive for a few seconds, perhaps letting her mind replay the events of the day. "I didn't see anything. Why?"

"I am curious as to how easily the system can be detected. Were you aware of the system before today?"

"No."

The answers were not so much answers as they were pieces of a puzzle that had just been tumbled from their box. We and Tap considered them, letting Courtney return to her reading. For some time there was silence again in the room, except for the gentle bubbling of water over rocks.

"Why do so many of the rooms in the red section have water running through them?" Courtney asked as she clicked another file closed.

Tap looked up with an annoyed frown and then thought better of the sharp response that was on her lips. Instead, she leaned her long form back in the chair and looked over at the stream. "Water is the life force of all living things. Human cells, you know, are ninety-eight percent salt water. Humans never really left the ocean, you see; the sea is simply inside their cells."

Courtney said nothing. She was letting Tap muse aloud, hoping to gain insight. We were in a very quiet cat and mouse game.

"Seventy percent of this planet is covered by ocean. The Pacific Ocean alone covers half the planet's surface." Suddenly, Tap swivelled her chair to look at Courtney. "Do you know how much freshwater this planet has, Court?"

"No, not really."

"Five percent. The world's population at the moment is over six billion people. By 2025, it will be nearly eight billion, all clustered around that one polluted, depleting water hole." Tap turned back to look at the stream of water flowing along the wall. "Water has a special meaning to me. Where I come from, there is one big river. My surname means water or source."

"Where are you from?"

Tap stood. The cat and mouse game was over for the time being. She had things to do.

"I will expect those articles read by tomorrow. Haichen will accompany you back to the library. I am sure that you have archival work to do. Good day, Court."

Such sudden changes in subject do not enlighten, but are used to close the paths of communication. Courtney understood this and we felt her frustration.

From Our Report

To observe only those in power is to miss the complexities of any given situation. We must, too, always watch the others. We watch and we record when we can.

Haichen joined Dr. Gene Lamount as soon as she had seen Courtney enter Tap's business areas. She quickly reported the strange events of the day. "I do not understand. I have never understood why Tap chose this place. How long will we be here working in the dark until Tap feels she can reveal her plan?"

Lamount's voice was neutral as he busied himself at his lab table. "It is best not to think too much about why Tap does what she does. We will know in good time. In the meantime, there might be safety in ignorance." This, of course, he said to ease his own conscience. Lamount was a man with many secrets of his own.

Haichen looked around nervously. Certainly there was danger. "Yes, that is true, but there is also danger in not knowing where we are being led. Do you think Tap infallible?" It was a simple question but filled with layers of emotion. Lamount did not fully realize this.

"No, I do not think she is infallible, but I do think her very intelligent and a natural leader. Whatever Tap has in mind, it will be revealed in due course."

Haichen sighed in angry frustration. For a second, she let some of the boiling emotion within show. "I joined Tap because I thought it would put me in a position to advance quickly. Tap's fame and power, I thought, would pull me along in my career. Instead, everything went wrong. I am doing random research with no clear goal, and babysitting Courtney Hunter. This is not what I envisioned."

The young and ambitious often are impatient for success. They confuse success with happiness. They have yet to learn personal happiness is an elusive bubble.

Lamount looked up with startled eyes. Haichen had never before expressed such thoughts. He reached out without thinking and touched her arm, felt Haichen pull back instinctively, and then was surprised as she melted into his arms. He held her close but gently.

"These feelings we have for each other are a complication also," Haichen murmured against his chest. Lamount kissed her head tenderly but said nothing.

"If Tap finds out..."

"She will not," Lamount reassured.

"I do not know what to believe anymore." Haichen pulled away and made an effort to regain control. The mask of emotional neutrality descended over her features.

Gene Lamount sighed. "I will admit when I committed to this endeavour, I realized that it would mean considerable readjustment. Yet, I was not prepared for what we have been asked to do. Still, I am committed to seeing it through. I have to believe now what I believed then — that Tap's work is important. This project is either going to be a milestone in our history, or the biggest blunder known to mankind."

Haichen smiled at Lamount's wit, allowing the tension to drain from the moment. "Then we must tread softly and advance carefully, so we have a milestone, rather than a footnote in Earth's history."

Gene Lamount looked worried. "I trust Tap. I have to. There are... One needs to be careful."

Haichen nodded. "Yes. I wish I knew more about Courtney Hunter's role. I wish I knew if she is part of the project or a danger within it."

"Be careful."

Haichen would have said more but she felt her pager. "I must go. She wants me."

Lamount watched her leave then moved over to the computer that he had been at just before Haichen had entered the room. He read the brief message, already knowing its content. He typed back one word. *Wait.* Then he sent another message to a location only he knew. *Haichen Lai has doubts. We might be able to recruit her services in time.*

Taken From Courtney Hunter's Logs

Haichen met me and took me for a late meal in the green zone lunchroom. She explained those who had worked today in the green zone would use the lunchroom on that side of the house, while those working in red zone used the dining hall off the domed room. This meant that the few people I saw there working late were people I had met before. After tea, I was left to my duties as the house archivist. My tea with Haichen had helped me gain two more pieces to the puzzle: all of the people I worked with were "Tap's people". I had been the only "outsider", hired to do a specific job in the green section and then go home each night. The twenty others lived on site. Now I was the twenty-first.

Sitting at my desk in the quiet house, I was tempted to walk out and see what would happen, then thought better of it. I was committed for the next month and I meant to keep my part of the bargain. Besides, I reasoned, I had always wanted to travel and now I was going to Rome.

Suddenly my heart dropped and I sat up straight. I didn't have a passport. Already I was going to upset Tap's plans. I called Haichen right away and explained that I needed to see Tap. I was informed, however, Tap would not be available again that evening. I fumed for a few seconds and then reluctantly explained my problem.

"Do not worry. You have a passport," came the response.

One would think that such a reassurance would have satisfied me. It did not. How had I gotten a passport without producing any documentation? Who had arranged it? Why? And was it legal? Once again I thought about trying to leave before I got in any deeper. Again I rejected the idea. When I had entered Tap's private world, I had committed myself to a course of action that I meant to see through to my own satisfaction. There was no backing out. It was just not the way I operated.

I sat back in my office chair and considered. I needed to establish my new position, whatever that was, and test to see how much power I actually had. If Tap was telling the truth about what she did, what was her interest in me? I had gone from an employee definitely out of the loop, to a prisoner, and now, to Tap's trainee, all in one day. But what was I being trained for? With a sigh, I called up another file on my data pilot and started reading about the growth of world deserts.

I slept that night on the rug in the library. I had no intention of going back to the room where I had been held prisoner, which was, it seemed, the only quarters available. To use it would be a sign of acceptance of Tap's authority over my life. That wasn't going to happen. Already an idea was forming in my mind as to where I could live. It would suit me fine and it would certainly upset Tap's people and the merry little voice system that followed them around. That thought formed a smile on my face and I drifted off to sleep.

Despite the stressful day and late night I had the night before, I was up early and already putting my plans in motion. First, I made a phone call.

"Haichen, please ask Tap if it is convenient for us to visit my apartment around eleven. Tell her it would be best if we took my car and I will see to lunch in exchange for her help."

I was taking the offensive. Wars are not won on the battlefield, but by the subtle movement and shifting of troops and plans. I had read that in a history book once.

There was shocked silence on the other end of the line, then Haichen's voice came hesitantly, "I will get back to you."

I filled in my time working at my job in the library. There wasn't much to do now that Tap was there and no material flowed in from various conferences and resource bases. The call I had been waiting for came back within the hour.

"Tap will meet you at eleven-thirty in the central room that is domed."

"The central room, fine. Thank you, Haichen. Goodbye." I put the receiver down and smiled with satisfaction, feeling the familiar tingle of excitement running down my spine that I always got when I had a tiger by the tail. I got up and headed off to the red zone kitchens. I needed to know what Tap enjoyed eating because I had observed it certainly wasn't coffee or grilled cheese sandwiches.

A visit to the kitchen revealed a rather strange fact: Tap lived mostly on rare vegetables, which she ate with a hot, spicy mix of boiled grains. Occasionally she ate fruit and dairy products, but rarely ate meat or fish. It was a healthy if very boring diet. Having gotten the information I needed and organized things to my satisfaction, I returned to the library.

From Our Report

We had observed Courtney Hunter and knew her plans. They both shocked and amused us. Courtney Hunter was an unpredictable person.

Tap was punctual, partly because Tap always was punctual and partly because she was quite curious as to what Courtney Hunter was up to. This study was proving to be most interesting. Courtney Hunter was very difficult to predict. She didn't appear to be a spy. It didn't seem as if she had planned to steal anything. No, Courtney Hunter had entered the red zone simply out of curiosity. Tap was used to people and governments being very interested in her, but only for a reason. Courtney Hunter did not appear to have an agenda.

Tap was also used to individuals, both male and female, wanting to know her for more personal reasons, too, but Courtney Hunter didn't seem to fit that profile either. Nor had Courtney reacted as Tap expected. Tap had planned to scare the small woman by holding her in the guest room until the end of the day and then to release Courtney after she had fired her. She had been greatly surprised at Courtney Hunter's ability to escape, not once, but twice. She had been more impressed that Courtney had given up her escape attempt to come back and save her. Tap needed more data because, as stated earlier, a daring plan was forming in her mind.

We must confess we did not fully understand. Tap had not shared all her thoughts with us. But we, too, were starting to realize the importance of Courtney Hunter. She would need to be tested. If our suspicions were correct, as unlikely as they seemed, Courtney Hunter would have to be trained by us.

Tap found Court waiting by the well with a large knapsack beside her. "There wasn't a picnic basket to be had, so I had to improvise."

"We are going on a picnic, Court? I thought I was escorting you while you picked up any belongings that you will need for your stay."

"That too. Are you ready?"

Tap hesitated. "I have a number of vehicles and excellent drivers. Would it not be best to use one of these?"

Courtney snorted. "Not in my neighbourhood. It would be in the chop shop before you even found a parking spot. Trust me on this."

Tap looked at her with pale, serious eyes. "Why should I trust you?"

It was a good question, for in the last twenty-four hours Courtney Hunter had been very troublesome. She had entered an area off limits to her and then escaped twice and, in doing so, hurt one of Tap's employees.

Courtney blushed. "Good point. I'm right about this though."

Can you trust her?

You are taking a great risk.

Should you do this?

The questions annoyed Courtney. "Will you please turn off that stupid system and just think for yourself. Make up your mind. Are you coming with me or not?"

Tap was shocked and angry, then she appeared to calm herself with effort. "You do not understand. I forgive you. Yes, I am coming with you. I would not trust you out of my sight for a minute."

Courtney rolled her eyes. She appeared unwilling to acknowledge the truth of Tap's words.

Courtney Hunter exited through the formal living room and out into the lobby. They left by the front door and made their way through the garden maze.

Ian was in the security booth. He sported a large goose egg in various stages of nasty bruising on his forehead. Courtney Hunter went to him immediately.

"Hi, Ian. Look, I'm really sorry. It was a wild pitch. I never meant to hit you in the head. Are you all right?"

Ian straightened at the sight of Tap standing quietly behind the smaller woman. "Yes, I am fine. Thank you, Court. Tap, is there anything I can do for you?"

"Courtney Hunter and I are going out. We will follow the usual security procedures."

"Yes, Tap."

Courtney smiled. "See you later."

Ian Philips watched them go with a face reflecting nothing of the surprise he felt within.

We knew this was a new turn of events and very disturbing to others. Courtney Hunter seemed to have developed great power, but no one knew how or why.

They moved off down the cedar walk, through the security gates and on to the car park. A large pool of oil was eating its way through the asphalt under Courtney's dilapidated car.

"Court, is this vehicle of yours road worthy?"

"It will be. Get in. Oh, just move the garbage off your seat. I got breakfast at a fast food place on my way to work yesterday morning."

Tap opened the passenger door and sniffed. The inside smelt of dust, stale grease, and oil. At least one of these offensive odors she could eliminate. With a look of utter disgust, she gingerly picked up the bag of fast food remains and placed it on the sidewalk. "The groundskeepers will see to this."

Courtney Hunter was not listening. She was observed through the security cameras removing several litres of oil from a box in the back seat and lifting the hood to check the dipstick before pouring the oil in with a sigh.

Security watched her movements closely, keeping her every action centred in the crosshairs of their scope.

Chapter Five

"It is not the roots we are born with but those that we grow over a lifetime of experience that keep us grounded."

~ Edith Hunter

From Our Report

We knew Courtney Hunter had been raised in a series of foster homes after her parents were killed in a car accident. Her parents, Edith and Ted, had been free spirits — artists who travelled a lot and lived comfortably, if from one day to the next. A free spirit lives life for the moment and with zest. It is a good life for the individual, but a harsh one for those who must rely on them. Foster homes are like cocoons. They provide protection during growth, but in return can be restrictive of both body and soul.

Orphaned at twelve, there were no relatives or savings to support Courtney. Once she had worked through the pain and anger of the loss of her parents, she had made up her mind that she was going to find all the security she could in a steady career and remain unattached and independent. Never again was she going to be left alone and unprotected. This was how she explained her life later, after the Geneva incident. Now she simply explained to Tap that she was trying to pay off her student loan as quickly as she could and she had very little money.

She lived in a small apartment over a Middle Eastern restaurant. Four cardboard boxes packed neatly but tightly held the belongings she collected. Tap approved of her minimalist life style. She was not surprised by the living conditions of her employee. Social stratification was something Tap had read a good deal about and understood instinctively. If she felt anything at the struggle Courtney had experienced to get where she was, it was respect that the young archivist had met her goals.

They left. Others arrived shortly after and carried out Tap's orders. The landlord was paid off, the apartment emptied of all traces of Courtney's occupation, and her meagre and basic furniture taken and incinerated. Then the rooms were scrubbed from top to bottom with bleach and sprayed with a human blood agent. It would now be virtually impossible for any official agency to isolate and identify Courtney Hunter's DNA or fingerprints.

At the same time, her bank accounts were transferred many times and then disappeared completely. Her name was deleted from government files, school and university records, and even her driver's licence, social security number, and tax returns ceased to exist. No detail of Courtney Hunter's life was overlooked, right down to her membership with Amnesty International, her doctor and drug store records, and her library card. By the time Courtney Hunter was spreading out their lunch at the park, she had ceased to exist outside of her physical form.

This she did not know, just as she did not know she had been identified for termination, or she was now a key element in a daring plan Tap was considering. None of this would she know until much later. This would prove to be a problem.

We observed Tap and Courtney Hunter as they had their picnic.

Courtney smiled. "I asked in the kitchen what you prefer to eat so there will be no sniffing and turning up your nose."

Tap lay in the sun, soaking up its warmth with enjoyment. Nearby, Mallard ducks and swans swam on a lake. It was a pretty spot. The human race lived in small box warrens and yet built parks where they could be free. Their contradictory need for confinement and wish for freedom at the same time is a complex phenomenon.

Tap forced herself not to sniff her food. She would enjoy her food much better if she could smell it first. She was not sure why this offended Courtney. It was one of the things she wished to understand. At least today the food was closer to her liking. She spooned some of the spicy grain porridge on to her plate and then dipped one of the raw vegetables in the mix and bit off a bite. To her surprise, Courtney followed suit.

"You do not have to eat as I do."

"I didn't think I would like it, but I do. A bit crunchy and rather hot, but flavourful, and certainly good for you. Do you always eat like this?"

"At my home, yes. Tell me what you learned from your reading."

Courtney frowned. "There seem to be disturbing patterns and trends. There is clear documentation that the polar caps are thinning and glaciers, even in places like Greenland, are melting back at an alarming rate. In recent years, a large section of the ice shelf of Antarctica has broken off, and a year later the same thing happened in the Arctic. To date, about thirty percent of the ice cap has melted. The impact of this could be catastrophic in the years to come. First, it could very well result in the loss of many species that are cold desert or ocean dwellers. Second, the oceans rising only a few inches could flood many low elevation islands, coastal lowlands, and countries such as Bangladesh. Even island cities like New York, Montreal, and Venice would be in great danger of flooding. Already, there has been a significant enough rise in ocean levels to threaten a number of low lying islands in the Pacific and Indian Oceans. The Shechel Islands, for example, will soon be in danger."

Tap said nothing. She was content to lie in the sun and listen to how much Courtney had absorbed and what bias she would put on the information.

"There is some geologic evidence to support the hypothesis that the Earth never really came out of the last glaciation. In fact, while the coastal regions of the polar caps seem to be melting, the ice covering Antarctica has actually thickened. If this is just an inter-glacial period, what we should observe is a rise in ocean levels as the polar caps melt. This would result in greater evaporation rates and cloud cover. The clouds would hold in the solar heat, raising temperatures and causing the caps to melt more quickly. It would start to snow more at the poles, thickening the ice that would form new glaciers over time. These would inch forward over the land, lowering sea levels and temperature once again."

Tap shrugged. "This is nothing new, and it is a slow process that planet Earth has gone through at least three times before."

Courtney stood and carried some apple slices down to feed to the ducks. "Air pollution and the damage to the ozone layer are speeding up the process. Some scientists believe that by the year 2025 we will be beyond the point of no return. Even if we stop all emissions today, the material already in the air will continue to rise and eat away at the ozone layer for well over another hundred years. Some scientists believe that planet Earth is dying."

A smile almost made it to Tap's lips. She was pleased that Courtney has absorbed the basic information quickly and repeated it in a fair and objective manner.

Then Courtney surprised her. "It is pretty depressing reading. What do you mean to do?"

"Do?"

"Yes. You're gathering all this data; what do you mean to do with it? How can you help?"

Tap closed her eyes again and let the heat of the sun radiate through her. "I can not help. I simply observe and record."

"For whom? Your work seems pointless if you don't plan to use your data to help with long term planning."

"Do you understand chaos theory? In dealing with an infinite number of possibilities, it is impossible to predict a pattern. Even the smallest element in combination with others can change the course of events."

Courtney did understand chaos theory. It had grown out of early attempts to use satellites to track and predict weather. In the early sixties, scientists would brag that they would soon be able to accurately forecast the weather for weeks to come. What they learned was that they could only make educated guesses. Mother Nature was infinitely complex, and therefore unpredictable.

"If you have the information, you need to be making people aware of it so that they can work to change things for the better."

Tap sat up and looked at Courtney with serious eyes. "Societies, too, are huge systems that generate their own events chaotically. All the information I have on file is available to anyone with the education and knowledge to access it. Global warming is a concept known to most people, but they are powerless to change all the things that would be necessary to change in order to make any impact. And then what impact would they make? Events that form the fate of the universe are so complex as to appear random."

"That is a thoroughly pessimistic view. I'm sure that there are people who are working with dedication to deal with these issues. The human race is resourceful."

Tap watched as Courtney threw bits of fruit to the flock of ducks crowded near the shore.

"Oh yes, there is much going on. A new world order is just around the corner. I wish to record these events. There is much merit in keeping good records."

Tap stood and hesitantly took some vegetables and fed them to the ducks gathered around Courtney. A large swan with two young cygnets following her waddled up on shore, its graceful beauty now reduced by earthbound gravity. It was a huge bird. Tap threw it some scraps. It dropped its long neck and scooped up the offerings and waddled closer.

"Why did you enter the red zone without authority?"

Courtney turned to look at Tap. "I told you. Your organization fascinates me. You fascinate me. I want to know who I'm working for and what you are up to."

"I see." Tap absently dropped scraps to the birds around her. Courtney Hunter was a surprising development. Tap was rarely unaware of what was going on around her. Things were changing just as unpredictably as chaos theory would indicate.

We, too, observed, but as is our role, we did nothing.

We sensed Courtney did not wish for Tap to question her reasons for her actions. Perhaps she was not sure she understood them herself.

"If the data is available to all, then why gather it?"

A question can be a tool for avoidance. Courtney was avoiding a topic she did not feel comfortable in pursuing.

It was at this point that Tap got between the swan and its cygnets. With a loud honk, the massive bird spread its wings and came at the startled woman. "Tap, watch out!" Courtney warned, and pushed the taller woman out of harm's way. Courtney slipped and, as she fell, was aware of white wings and a pecking beak.

Taken From Courtney Hunter's Logs

The next instant, I had only the warm sensation of floating in a tranquil sea of energy. No, I wasn't floating; I had no form. I wasn't suspended in, but part of, the current around me. It was a strange world of sensations and yet one that seemed distantly familiar. I was aware that I wasn't alone, and yet I could not sense any form near me. What I could sense was a joining, being a part of something separate and yet also part of me.

Then, a second later, I felt myself suddenly confined and weighed down. I gasped for breath and found myself lying on the grass with Tap kneeling beside me. My confinement was my own body, and the weight, the air that I breathed.

"You are all right, Courtney Hunter?"

I was anything but all right. I felt disorientated, queasy, and short of breath. The latter sensation had a lot to do with my disorientation.

"I think so. What happened?"

"The swan attacked and you leapt in front of me. Perhaps you were knocked out."

There are so many ways to avoid truth. A suggestion can lead others away from enlightenment or towards it. Truth is rarely a tangible element but rather a slowly changing perspective. I was immediately suspicious.

I shifted slowly, forcing my reluctant body to respond again to commands. I felt lightheaded and queasy, as if I had motion sickness. I looked around. The ducks and swan were swimming a good distance off, as they had been when we first arrived. How long had I been unconscious?

"I'm okay now. I'm sorry I worried you."

"I was not worried. I knew you were not in danger," Tap responded. "Once again, you have come to my aid. I was not aware that swans could be so violent. You are not hurt?"

"No, I'm fine. I don't suppose the swan would have done much damage, but swans and geese are very territorial and are strong enough to break bones if they're angry," I explained.

I got to my feet gingerly and looked around. Some leftover vegetables sat in a plastic container on the grass. We hadn't thrown all the scraps to the birds. My eyes wandered back to the ducks and swan swimming some distance away. Something just didn't feel right.

I turned to look at Tap, who now stood watching me closely with interested eyes.

"What really happened?"

Tap shook her head. "We must be getting back. I have much to do. I thank you for this picnic. It was most interesting."

From Our Report

We watched with interest. For a minute, Courtney stood her ground, looking at Tap with hard, cold eyes, then she turned without a word and started to pack up the picnic remains. Tap did not help but stood quietly watching. She noted later she had been deeply shaken by the events but had tried her best not to show any reaction. What had happened was totally out of her realm of knowledge and experience. It should not have happened. Tap knew what was important for the moment was keeping these events secret. We, too, could not understand Courtney's experience. We, too, knew that this knowledge must be kept secret until we knew more.

They walked together to the car in silence. It was only when Courtney had slung the knapsack into the back seat and gotten into the car that Tap spoke again. "I would appreciate it if you did not make any mention of the swan incident or your being unconscious. I do not want Security to overreact, as they have a tendency to do."

"All right," Courtney agreed, as the old car started with difficulty. Then she turned and looked Tap square in eye. "But I will expect to hear the truth about what happened here today as soon as possible."

They drove back to Tap's estate without any further talk, and Tap quickly excused herself and disappeared into her quarters.

How could this happen?
We sense your distress.
Are you well?

"I am fine. Courtney Hunter is totally unpredictable. This will prove to be a very interesting opportunity, but one that will be stressful. Leave me."

Thinking herself alone, Tap finally allowed the events of the day to impact on her completely. It was clear they shook her to the core of her being. She would have to be careful with the knowledge she had gained today. She knew all too well that there was an informer in her organization.

We must know why this happened.

We must proceed with great caution.

There is an enemy in our midst.

Security Report 7248
Reporting Officer: Ian Phillips
To Commanding Officer Franz Scheidt

Rationale: The evidence removal team noted Courtney Hunter's neighbour had questioned where and why Courtney Hunter had moved. It was thought advisable to do a suspect profile of this individual.

Individual: Percy Dingwall, male

Address: Apt. 2, 289 Woodmeadow Avenue.

Occupation: Mail Carrier

Age: 39

Description of Apartment: Dingwall lives across the hall from the apartment rented by Courtney Hunter. The two story building is cinder block on three sides with a yellow brick façade. On the first floor is a restaurant. The second floor has two apartments. The one to the west side has been occupied by Dingwall for twelve years.

The apartment is identical in size and shape to the one occupied by Courtney Hunter on the east side of the hall. There is a small kitchen, living room/dining room, bathroom, and bedroom. The fixtures are in keeping with a middle class building built in the 1970s. Although the building has been maintained, there is no indication of any major remodelling since that time.

Description of Search: Dingwall has no photographs indicating family or friends. His apartment is without wall pictures and tables; shelves, etcetera contain no ornaments or art. The apartment is functional in the extreme and very clean and orderly.

Clothes in the closet are neatly ironed and organized by season and colour. Dingwall favours navy and dark brown.

A wicker chest used as a coffee table contains twenty-seven journals. They are lined and filled with observations of people to whom Percy Dingwall delivers mail. The entries are all written in the same black ink, using an inexpensive ballpoint pen. The writing is small, cramped, and angular.

Each journal is leather bound in black, and is dated by year rather than individual. The exception is the journal he keeps on Courtney Hunter. This journal contains photos as well as written entries.

Individuals who have moved out of his postal delivery area have black ribbons marking their last entry. Percy Dingwall has managed to collect considerable information on individuals by looking at their mail. He also records observations of family members and events at houses where he delivers the mail. He has observed Courtney Hunter since she moved into her apartment twenty-eight months ago.

Significant Points:

1. Dingwall knows Courtney is an archivist working for Tap Enterprises.

2. He knows the address of Tap Enterprises.

3. He has tried to access information on the company.

4. He is suspicious of Courtney Hunter's sudden move.

5. The details he has collected on individuals indicate he might have opened and read the mail before delivering it.

Conclusions:

1. Percy Dingwall does not appear to have any family or friends. He appears to live in a fantasy world based on his observations of his clientèle.

2. He seems obsessed by Courtney Hunter.

3. He does not seem to be a stable individual.

Recommendations:

1. Percy Dingwall should be kept under observation. Further intervention might be required.

From Our Report

We, too, were aware of Percy Dingwall. We noted he did not know Courtney Hunter socially but had wanted to. She had one of the apartments over the restaurant and he had the other. He knew quite a bit about her, even though he had never said more than hello in passing. He checked her mail. We were surprised to learn this was not difficult, as he was her mail deliverer. Such persons are hardly ever noticed and yet have access to incredible amounts of confidential information.

For example, he had observed that Courtney Hunter got pay stubs from TAP International and subscribed to Librarian Monthly. She got alumni letters from the same local university he attended at night, and she was often overdue paying her bills. He had delivered a number of second notices. No family or friends wrote letters or sent cards to her, and she supported the ASPCA and Amnesty International. Her dentist lived across town and when she needed medical attention, she went to the local walk-in clinic. We concluded, to our surprise, the human race guards their privacy closely and then has their secrets delivered to their doorstep.

It appeared to us Percy Dingwall liked knowing about people. He had many friends, few of whom he had ever met. This man enjoyed being a mail deliverer. We suspected even after he completed a degree, if he ever did, he would not change his occupation; he would miss his mail family. Knowing them while they knew nothing of him made him feel both powerful and safe. He kept black notebooks containing data on the houses, stores, and apartments he visited, and recorded any information garnered in small, tight handwriting. He always used erasable black pen so it was possible to correct a mistake. We sensed Percy's horror of making a mistake. When someone left his mailing area, he marked their page in his notebook with a black ribbon. He kept these notebooks in a wicker trunk used as his coffee table. Only Courtney Hunter had a notebook all to herself. We feared Percy Dingwall was obsessed by her and this worried us greatly. He had no books or TV or radio. His world consisted of the people on his route.

We sensed Percy Dingwall felt his life was full and satisfying, until Courtney Hunter disappeared. He concluded Courtney Hunter should not have disappeared. We hoped that Percy Dingwall would take no notice, being used to what he saw as irresponsible people not filling out postal change of address cards. This had happened all too often to him. Surprisingly, the problem was that Tap's people made sure there was a change of address card. Percy Dingwall noted immediately it was not Courtney Hunter who had filled it out. We had not considered the mail deliverer would know Courtney's writing and realize she had not been the one who signed her name. This discrepancy worried Percy Dingwall.

We sensed the people who came and moved Courtney's belongings bothered him, too. He had watched them through the peephole in his door. They had worn black jumpsuits with no company patches. Percy Dingwall had noted it had not taken long to remove Courtney's property, but it had taken a very long time to clean the place. Afterwards, the apartment had smelt of chemicals.

We observed: Fate is not easily controlled.

Chapter Six

"Home is not where you live but where they understand you."
~ Christian Morgenstern

From Our Report

We had watched, not understanding at first. Later, Haichen Lai blinked in amazement at what she saw. Security had contacted her with a bizarre tale she couldn't quite envision. Because the story involved Courtney Hunter, she had immediately stopped what she was working on and had gone to see for herself. Their quiet and hard working archivist had proven to be a resourceful, stubborn, and totally unpredictable element. She was also a personal project of Tap's, and therefore had to be handled with extreme caution and care.

Just how she was to deal with the latest development, however, she had no idea. There in the centre of the courtyard gardens, on an island formed by a splitting of the water channels, was a small orange tent. Courtney Hunter had reached the island — consisting of three trees and some hibiscus bushes — by removing rocks from a nearby garden wall to make stepping stones across the channel of water.

Carefully, Haichen stepped across to the island. "Court? Are you here?"

The orange flap flipped back and Courtney Hunter crawled out and stood to look at Haichen with a smile of pure devilment.

"Hi, Haichen. I thought they would probably send you or Ian. What do you think of my new quarters?"

"It is a pup tent, Courtney Hunter. Camping is for the wilderness. Why have you set up a tent in Tap's courtyard?"

"I needed a place to stay while I'm in training. I won't stay in a room where I have been held prisoner, and there is no other suitable place. Besides, I like it out here. How big is this courtyard?"

"It is about a quarter of a hectare. You have no washroom or power source," Haichen reasoned.

"I will use it only to sleep and store my stuff in. I can use the library, dining hall, and gym facilities, so this is really all I need. It suits me fine."

"But, Court..."

"Tap did say I should find a place from which I would not want to escape."

Courtney smiled when she said this, we noted. Haichen later reported it was not so much a smile as it was a dare, but Haichen did not dare argue. Courtney Hunter was Tap's project.

"If this is suitable to you, then it is an appropriate choice. Do you need anything?"

"Nothing I can't find myself. Thanks for stopping by, Haichen."

The worried woman nodded. Realizing she had been dismissed, she took her leave. She would report the developments to Tap and let Tap handle the troublesome archivist.

We were amused but not worried by Courtney's actions.

We knew Tap was deep in her research and recording, and was bothered by another issue, as well. Security had reported on Courtney Hunter's former neighbour, Percy Dingwall, who lived across the hall from Courtney Hunter's old apartment. He was a skinny, short man with bad acne scars and thinning hair. As noted in our report, he earned his living as a mail carrier. Franz Scheidt, head of Security, had gone to Tap personally to discuss him after he had read the report prepared by his junior officer, Ian Phillips.

Franz Scheidt was an older man. He'd served in the last war and wore the scars of his bravery. Tap, too, had fought in the war. Scheidt was fiercely loyal to her, Tap knew. War forges a bond deeper than blood.

"Percy Dingwall could be a problem. He is a very unusual man. He does not appear to socialize with others. His co-workers find him quiet and strange."

"He is unstable?"

"It would seem that way. He appears to live in a fantasy world where the people to whom he delivers mail become his friends. He worries about those who are in debt or are having problems, keeps notes on how their children are growing up, and puts a black ribbon on the last entry page when someone moves out of his area or dies."

"Courtney Hunter was in his books?"

"He has a separate book for her. He seems obsessed by her. He has even taken pictures of her and has them glued into the book. Since we moved Hunter out, he transferred his route. He now delivers post here. He has been asking a lot of questions about where she went."

"What cover story did you use?"

"That she was part of a training program and has been reassigned to work in Africa."

"Monitor the situation. Chances are he will redirect his obsession after a while."

"There is one more thing Tap."

"Yes."

"He believes in UFOs. He thinks that aliens are living on the planet observing the humans."

Tap laughed, something she rarely did, and only in front of one as loyal as Scheidt.

Scheidt smiled, quietly honoured that Tap would be so relaxed in his company. He was of the old school. His family had served Tap's for three generations. How proud his grandfather would have been to know what honours he had received in battle, and now, to work so closely with Tap. Still, he was glad his grandfather, an Honoured One, had not lived to see the troubles they now faced. It would have broken his heart.

"I do not think we need worry too much about him. I doubt very much if he has much credibility. Still, keep an eye on him, Scheidt."

Scheidt took his leave.

This is a troubling development.

We must move with caution.

Yet time is short.

"Yes, time is short."

So it was late in the afternoon, we noted, before Tap clicked on the report that Haichen had sent her. The report was brief and to the point.

Time: 14:23

Subject: Courtney Hunter

Location at time of report: green zone library.

Note: Courtney Hunter has set up an orange nylon pup tent on the small island in the courtyard. She plans to use this as her quarters. I have talked to her. She seems firm in this decision, noting that you requested that she find quarters from which she would not wish to escape. HL

We knew this message had also been read by Rugia Malwala, who sent it on to her contact. Tap did not know this.

Tap blinked and read the memo through again. We sensed her bafflement. Then she shook her head in disbelief. Tap thought perhaps it would be safer to terminate Courtney Hunter, after all. She never did what you expected. If she was terminated, then potential future problems of a very serious nature could be avoided. Tap had killed, but had never given the order to terminate anyone. She did not doubt she could, but she felt it would have to be for a very good reason. This is how she justified her decision at the time to not terminate Courtney Hunter. Later, she would be able to admit her decision was not made with complete objectivity. Even then, she had been thinking along daring lines. Time was short. We now agreed with her reasoning. We, too, were becoming aware of the possible importance of Courtney Hunter.

"Send Courtney Hunter to the red zone library immediately."

Tap clicked the message off and then had second thoughts about her decision, we sensed. She thought it might be best, considering the strange and disturbing events that morning at the park, to avoid Court until the new trainee had found out what was going on. She had, however, made Courtney Hunter her subject, and that commitment could not be ignored. Already she had gained from her decision by the morning's experience.

She waited for confirmation and then walked down to the library. Court was, of course, already there. It would not do for Tap to be seen waiting.

"I have ordered some more reading for you on educational movements. You will please read these and be prepared to report to me later this evening."

"OK."

Tap nodded and turned to leave, then stopped and looked back. "Was the tent necessary?"

"Yes."

Tap nodded, pleased she had not sensed or felt anything unusual, even though she had stood close to Court. What happened that morning at the park was an unexplained anomaly. She turned and left.

"What do you know about the Club of Rome?" They were sitting in the dining hall over coffee. Later that night, Tap had gone to look at the little orange tent in amazement, as had many others during the course of the day. She then sought out Courtney Hunter and invited her for a coffee. Tap was not fond of coffee. She drank it because she knew it was a ritual in the day to day social bonding process people needed.

"Not much. I know it is a great honour to be asked to give a lecture for them. I believe one of their mandates is to gather data, so I guess you have something in common."

This statement was made with an undertone of sarcasm, we noted. Tap chose to ignore it. Sarcasm is a tool of criticism used to convey a meaning far deeper than what is being said.

Tap nodded. "In a way, yes. The Club of Rome functions outside of any political boundaries and is a non-profit organization. They are essentially a think tank, providing a forum for discussion and debate on various topics. They invite significant scientists, economists, business people, civil servants, and heads of state to speak. This information is then made public for people to consider and use."

"Use. I like the sound of that word. Is this where we're going? I take it there are to be a series of lectures on the environment, since that's what I have spent the majority of my time studying."

"Yes, it is where we will be going, but the lectures will be by leading economists talking about the economic restructuring."

Courtney grimaced. "That sounds deathly dull."

"It is not. It will be your job to understand the essence of what is said and be able to relate its significance to your studies this week. The recent world recession is a warning. I wish that you understand better what that warning is and what the future might hold for the world economics."

"OK. Why?"

"It is part of your retraining."

Courtney frowned but said nothing. We knew she wasn't sure she wanted to be retrained. We felt her decision to be careful and not start questioning what she felt to be true.

"You will now tell me what you learned this afternoon."

"Some rather disturbing things. Some years ago, a report circulated that was based on a study of technological knowledge in the United States. It was noted that the cutting edge of technology came out of the military and filtered down to researchers, who tooled the ideas for industry that then passed them on to consumers. Lastly, these technological breakthroughs end up being taught in schools. This filtering down of information takes about fifteen years."

"Good, go on."

"The US at the time was concerned about the inroads that the Pacific Rim nations had made in industrial markets and so adopted a policy to reduce this knowledge transmission delay through a number of means."

Tap smiled. Courtney had a good mind and was able to extract the essential information quickly and see the underlying patterns. "Go on."

"Their first step was to tender contracts to new companies to write innovative curricula. The biggest contract was given to a company that was a partnership between Disney, the Pentagon, and Microsoft."

Tap was well aware of such companies but wished to put Courtney at ease. The woman seemed tense around her. "Strange bedfellows," Tap observed with a smile.

Small talk which seems at first to be meaningless fulfils a role in establishing alliances and identifying common world views.

"Yes, very strange." We sensed that Courtney was tempted to go on and express her concerns about manipulation of thought, but checked herself. What Tap did was record objectively; Courtney stuck to the facts. "The next step was to increase educational standards. This was done by discrediting public education. The public then was willing to support charter schools and reduce funding to remedial programs that no longer appeared to be getting results. Governments could then funnel money to those that they felt were 'worth' educating, while disenfranchising weaker students. The trend is to improve all standards but to direct monies to the bright and wealthy. Progress is evaluated through standardized testing."

"You are now talking about governments. Explain."

"The US is certainly not alone in its policies. Canada and many European countries have followed suit. Education is geared to producing science and math graduates to be the bullets in the economic wars that policy setters see as the future trend."

"A bias is showing," stated Tap, raising an eyebrow. It is often difficult for people to divorce emotion from reason.

Yes, a bias.

Yet she has learned a lot.

But has much more yet to learn.

Courtney folded her arms and looked at Tap with a good deal of scepticism. "It is a strange sort of security system that offers opinions."

"Yes, it is."

Courtney waited. Tap offered no more. "Are we finished?"

"Almost. Explain to me, Courtney, why we are going to hear these lectures at the Club of Rome."

"Because they're the missing piece of the puzzle."

Tap nodded and stood. "They are one of the missing pieces. There is yet more to the pattern. Good night, Court."

"Good night, Tap."

We noted Courtney returned to her new quarters feeling disgruntled and out of sorts. We sensed she was pleased Tap seemed satisfied with her training. She appeared to be working to her full potential to impress Tap. This was wise of her. We also sensed Courtney Hunter felt a growing emotional bond with Tap. This did not surprise us. Many have.

What she was learning, we knew, was upsetting to her. That of course is the irony of an age of knowledge. Information overload has resulted in a public which would rather watch sitcoms. Knowledge is held in trust by a few who may not necessarily be trustworthy. Courtney Hunter went to bed early and read more reports until she fell asleep with her data pilot still in her hand. Such dedication is admirable.

It was her dream that made us aware. The dream was more sensation than images. There she was again, part of an endless warm sea. One of many — many in one. Courtney felt whole and at peace. She had only to reach out and she would know...

Then her eyes opened to darkness, the smell of nylon and mould. She could hear the water bubbling along its channels. She lay on her back where her dream had left her and stared into the darkness, wondering what it all meant: her park dream; her unconscious dream; her awakening.

We noted this with astonishment and awe. Courtney Hunter had grey eyes, as the prophecy had foretold. She also had awareness. She would need to be trained by us.

We sensed, too, that Tap woke with a start, her heart pounding and sweat coating her body. With effort she regulated her breathing, then she slid from under her sheets and walked to the shower. The hot water helped revive her, but it did not fade the memory of the dream. It was most unusual. She could not recall having had a dream before and now she was fully awake, she found she could not recall the images. For a long time she lay in the darkness of her room thinking. Her people did not yet understand the enormity of their situation. She did. The plan she was now forming was going to drop a large rock into a still, deep pool. That is, she was going to upset the traditional thoughts and practices. She was not yet sure of the consequences. She did know that keeping her plans from her brother was key to any chance of success. We agreed. Yet we knew secrecy would not be easy.

Chapter Seven

"Travelling is the ruin of all happiness! There's no looking at a building here after seeing Italy."

~ Mme D'Arblay

From Our Report

We observed Courtney had no time to think in the next few days. She had hours of reports to read and sessions with Tap being questioned on what she had learned. She was fitted for several suits — a beige, raw cotton suit jacket with several straight cut skirts, and another with two sets of slacks. Her shirts were linen or silk and cut with a conservative collar and short sleeves. On the day they were to leave, she found her suitcase packed and ready for her, along with a passport and tickets. A helicopter would take them to New York where they would connect with a regular commercial flight to Paris and, lastly, a commuter flight on to Rome.

Courtney wore the underwear and suit delivered to her tent that morning and carried the black briefcase she had been given for any notes that she wished to take with her. The briefcase was labeled in gold: C. Punga — TAP.

A Lincoln pulled up to the main gate and Courtney recognized two of the security officers sitting in the front seat. It wasn't until this time that Tap arrived. She wore a soft, tan suede pantsuit with a black silk shirt. As always, she was all business.

"You are ready, Court?"

"Yes. My passport says my name is Courtney Punga and that I have diplomatic immunity. Why has my name been changed? By whose authority?"

"Mine. Until you complete your training, it is necessary for you to travel incognito. Shall we go?"

For most of the trip, Tap read. Courtney did her best to follow her boss's example but, we felt, she was excited and nervous. She watched everything with the excitement of a child, while below the thrill of new adventures, a growing fear smouldered. We knew she must have questions about why had her name been changed and whether her passport was legal. For now, we felt, her questions needed to remain unanswered.

"Do you ever sit still?" Tap's voice showed her irritation. Irritability is often a sign of deep stress and the cause of the irritability is rarely what it seems.

Courtney froze. Tap had been grumpy for the past few days but now she looked really angry. "I'm sorry. I'm excited. I've never travelled before, and today I have been in both a helicopter and a plane. Pretty good first time, huh?"

Tap looked at her with a mixture of surprise and wonder in her eyes. "I forget sometimes that there are more people on this planet that have never used a telephone than have seen a computer."

"I can use a computer." Courtney did not like to be seen by Tap as inexperienced. She would be surprised to learn that it was some of Courtney's experience that Tap found most upsetting and was the main source of her boss's irritation.

Tap simply nodded, however, and went back to her reading. Tap was upset for a number of reasons. First, the incident at the park and the dream she'd had were of great concern. It was a very delicate matter and she would have to be very careful. Naturally, she hoped the incidents were isolated and simply some strange reaction to the strain she was under. She knew, without us advising her, that it was very important her brother not find out about these two occurrences until she had resolved these problems.

Second, there was the report in her briefcase on Courtney Hunter. She had read it over and over. Courtney's past would be an added complication. Court had lived an unconventional life with her birth parents, and a lonely and restricted life in foster care. She had shown remarkable strength and determination in getting her education and bringing order to her life. There had been lovers. A long and steady relationship with a boy at university ended when Courtney turned down his proposal then a short, casual relationship with a woman. It was the detailed data on Court's private life that upset Tap. It was important there be no doubts or questions in regards to Courtney Hunter's past. She would have liked to question Courtney Hunter about her private life, but knew this would not yet be appropriate.

They worked in stony silence, each reading reports with a studied intensity neither really felt. Tap's mood deteriorated further when her vegetarian meal was served. She sniffed at it suspiciously and sighed. Courtney looked down at her own filet mignon with delight, then she shyly reached into her bag and brought out a container of grain porridge and cut vegetables that she had had prepared in the kitchen before they left and slipped it onto Tap's tray. "Thought you might like this."

Tap looked at her in surprise and then smiled. It was a real smile of delight, not the stiff, strictly controlled smile Courtney had seen in the past. We sensed Tap's smile made the effort worthwhile. Courtney thought she had pleased her boss.

"Thank you, Court."

"You're welcome."

The rest of the trip was uneventful. Boss and trainee worked side by side in happier frames of mind, reading and preparing for the lectures. It was hard going for Courtney, who was too excited and disturbed about her day to stay focused for long on the reports. She also found economics boring and usually totally out of step with social needs. When she expressed this view, Tap patiently reminded her that business dealt with fulfilling societies' wants at a profit and not with meeting social needs at cost.

It was late in the afternoon, Rome time, when they were finally through Customs and had registered in their hotel. To her surprise, Courtney found she was sharing a suite with Tap, and her security personnel shared the room next to them. They were staying in the small but luxurious five-star Bernini Bristol, built in 1870 and renovated in recent years.

Courtney looked in wonder at the elaborate and rich design features, the eighteenth century tapestries, and the antique furnishings. This was another world Courtney Hunter knew nothing about. Once their room had been checked by Rugia and Franz, the two security officers with them, and their bags had been brought in and the porter tipped, Tap disappeared into her bedroom. A few minutes later, Courtney could hear the shower running.

Courtney unpacked and hung up her clothes. She felt trapped and frustrated. Here she was in Rome and it looked like her first experience travelling was going to be reading in a hotel room and listening to lectures at the Club of Rome, the understanding of which were way over her head.

She showered, dressed in blue jeans and a t-shirt she had managed to smuggle along in her carry on, and tried to read yet another report. Her restlessness led her from one seat to another until she finally ended up on the salon couch, gazing wistfully from the window. It was a business trip, she knew, but she couldn't be asked to work twenty-four hours of the day. Her jaw set in a familiar strong line and she slipped off her seat to walk over to Tap's bedroom and knock on the door.

"Enter."

"Tap, if you have nothing planned for me, I think I'll go out for a bit and see what I can of Rome."

"That is not possible. You may not leave until your month's training is up." This was muttered from behind a report that Tap read as she lay on her bed wrapped up in one of the hotel's thick terrycloth bathrobes. The silence that followed made Tap look up with concern.

When their eyes met, Courtney tried once more. "But, I might never see Rome again."

Tap put down her papers and looked at Courtney with interested eyes. "The Bernini Bristol is located at the beginning of the Via Veneto. We are within walking distance of the Spanish Steppes and the Trevi Fountain. These places I could take you to now. Would this suffice?"

"That would be wonderful, Tap, if you don't mind. I don't want to take you away from your work."

Tap would have liked to answer honestly that Courtney Hunter had already done so, but she had learned such demurrals as Courtney had made required not truth, but a show of willingness to be put out. Tap was not willing, but felt she might learn from the experience and so agreed. Still, she did not respond, but got up to dress for the outing.

Courtney beat a hasty retreat as Tap stood and slipped from her robe. Such comfort with nudity was not part of her upbringing, she later explained to us. Tap, for her part, was amused by Courtney Hunter's uncomfortable withdrawal.

They walked side by side down the Via Veneto. It was a lovely evening, the sort when the gold of the setting sun mellows old stone and brick into enchantment. Flowers and colourful banners hung from street lamps and balconies. The area was scented by spicy sauce and garlic as evening meals were prepared. They talked little and simply enjoyed the sights and sounds of Rome.

Tap watched Courtney with pleasure as the smaller woman stood in delight in front of the elaborate backdrop of the Fontana di Trevi.

"It was built in 1735 by the architect Salvi under Clement XII. The statues and bas-relief around it were designed in the Bernini School. That is, the underlying pattern is very geometric and the arrangement mathematically balanced for shape and form. It was designed really as part of the façade of the Palazzo Poli."

Courtney was only half listening. She fished into her pocket and came out with a coin to throw into the clear, cold water.

Legend had it that whoever drank from the fountain or threw a coin into its waters was sure to return to Rome.

"Are you superstitious, Court?"

"No. Just a romantic. Here, Tap, you throw a coin, too." Courtney gave Tap a coin and this is how Tap came to participate in her first superstitious act.

"But I have been to Rome many times and will come again."

"Please."

Tap nodded her assent and, after looking around to make sure no one was likely to notice, she threw the coin over her shoulder into the fountain as she had seen Courtney do. We found this amusing.

They walked in a big circle as they strolled down the picturesque streets until they reached the Piazza di Spagna. Tap explained in her serious way that the famous Spanish Steppes, all 1,772 of them, had been designed to harmoniously follow the slope of the hill, and that the pool and fountain at its base, known as the Little Boat, had been designed by Bernini.

Courtney listened politely to her tour guide/boss and then, with sheer devilment in her eyes, she ran down the stairs to the water's edge. Tap was right behind her. With a playful laugh, Court halted her forward motion on the very last step. They stood for a minute, close together — Tap a dark form behind a delighted Courtney. Courtney did not turn. To do so would have been to show fear. She looked out across the pond instead. "I wasn't running away."

At that, Tap felt some of the tension drain from her body.

"It is a beautiful place," Tap observed, stepping back.

This was not so much an observation but a quick change in mood. Tap found herself very close to liking Courtney Hunter. That realization was less shocking than she would have thought. She wondered if she would ever trust this woman enough to consider Court as a colleague, perhaps even a friend. What would be the harm? Naturally, she rejected this train of thought almost as quickly as it had come, as she had the dream. Her position and her name would be compromised if she lost her objectivity. Courtney Hunter must remain an outsider, even if her plan was to go forward.

They stood for a while admiring the beauty that was Rome, then they walked quietly back to their hotel in the gathering dark.

They ate in the luxurious dining room, Courtney immensely enjoying the wonderful food and wine. Tap ate her vegetarian plate with disinterest and drank a good deal more wine than the archivist. Upstairs again, they retired to their separate rooms to work until sleep came.

We noted Tap had her second dream. She found herself on the Spanish Steppes again. Music played softly in the background. It was a haunting, spiritual melody, more the whisper of wind through ancient hills than structured notes. The fountain's water was a cool touch on her hot skin and Courtney Hunter was nearby. They had been talking, as they had earlier that evening, enjoying the evening as individuals sharing a mutual experience. They felt close. It was most strange.

Tap woke from her dream with a start. She lay staring into the darkness for a long time, trying to come to terms with the enormity of the situation. Courtney Hunter's decision to enter Tap's private world had set into motion a chain of events proving to be both surprising and unnerving. Caution was needed, we advised.

From Courtney Hunter's Logs

I was unable to sleep. I'd been having an honest talk with myself about just what I was doing. The truth of the matter was that I felt I was in way over my head, and if I had any sense at all I would be swimming for shore with all my might. I was overwhelmed and felt it advisable for me to get out of my present situation as soon as possible. That said, the second truth that I had to face was my natural curiosity about Tap and her organization was changing. I felt almost protective of Tap. I didn't think Tap was as confident as she seemed. There was a vulnerability about the powerful woman that brought out my maternal instincts. This wasn't good.

I also realized I was changing. I was becoming more aware of issues and wanted to know more. Tap challenged me in ways no one had ever done before. I respected Tap and enjoyed our sessions together. That worried me, too. I needed to remember Tap could very well be a very dangerous person.

How did Tap see me? At times I had thought we could come to trust each other but this evening, when I had dared to be playful, Tap had reacted instantly and darkly. I sighed in frustration at this thought. Every ounce of my common sense told me that I was getting into a bad situation and keeping a distance from my boss would be wise. My gut reaction, however, was curiosity. Curiosity, the old saying warns, killed the cat.

Who was Tap and what was she up to? I wondered. I thought there was something not quite right about her organization and her activities, and yet there was nothing I could really put a finger on. It was very late in the night before I finally drifted off to sleep.

From Our Report

A firm knock at her door brought Courtney awake the next morning in a drowsy stupor. "Court, we must leave in ninety-three minutes," Tap stated through the door. Tap had already been up with us for some time. In our talks, we suggested for the first time that Courtney Hunter might fit the prophecy, as unlikely as that seemed. We sensed Tap was not surprised and the acknowledgement pleased her. At this time, we did not know the full extent of Tap's plan. Tap does not share all her thoughts. We were concerned Courtney's train of thought could lead her to answers it would be unwise for her to know at this time.

Courtney rolled from the bed, we were sure, more in fear of Tap's disapproval than from any great desire to face the day. She showered and dressed quickly, and was ready with her briefcase when Tap walked from her own room. Rugia and Franz waited downstairs with a limousine, and once the women were safely inside, they proceeded to the meeting. Other than saying hello to Court, Tap ignored her, reading through material on her data pilot instead. Annoyed, Court soaked up the sounds and sights of Rome through the tinted window.

At the lectures, Court was impressed by how many people knew Tap and treated her with the greatest respect, even at the Club of Rome, where people were used to mixing with the famous and powerful. Again we followed her thoughts. Courtney wanted to know who Tap was and what hold she had on so many. Court felt intimidated.

She followed one step behind Tap in the lobby and once in the lecture hall, she sat quietly, listening intently to the lectures. We sensed it was a very stressful day for her. This was not a world to which Courtney was accustomed, and she was nervous about how little understanding she had of the complex economic structures and trends presented in the series of lectures throughout the day.

When they left in the evening, we sensed Court had a splitting headache, dazed by the facts and figures bombarding her all day. We noted she might not be capable of completing the program that Tap had planned for her.

"You are uncharacteristically quiet, Court," Tap observed, as their limousine pulled silently away from the curb.

"I think my mind has blown a gasket," Court groaned, rubbing her temples wearily.

"You are ill?" Tap asked with some concern.

Court looked up into eyes both worried and curious. "No, just a headache. I meant that I feel tired from the stress of trying to understand what I heard today. I'm sorry, Tap. Most of it went over my head."

Tap shrugged. "I anticipated that it would." She was relieved, as we were, there was not anything seriously wrong with her trainee, and she turned back to the papers on her lap.

"What does that mean?" Court demanded, turning to look at her boss.

Tap looked up and frowned in puzzlement. We and Tap had noted that Courtney Hunter's mood swings were quite unpredictable.

"It meant that I was aware that you do not have either the knowledge or intellect to understand some of the concepts discussed today," Tap clarified.

"Thanks a lot," snapped Courtney, her grey eyes blazing.

Tap's frown deepened. After a second or two of consideration, she said neutrally, "You are welcome," then went back to her reading, not knowing how else to deal with Court's unusual reaction.

We were to learn later that at this same time, miles away, the informant was meeting with Tap's brother in secret. No easy feat over such long distances. The information gathered was reported clearly and concisely.

The leader's anger grew and radiated outward. "My sister is planning."

"Planning might not be the most accurate choice of words. She is researching with some intensity and, as of yet, I have not discerned a focus."

Sharp, angry eyes looked up and the other was quick to revise any conclusion to agree with the leader's. "She is up to something. Her research is not random; I just have not yet determined her focus."

He considered. "Continue to monitor events closely. My sister is a dangerous woman, and cunning. Do not underestimate her."

Chapter Eight

"There is no passion in the mind of man so weak, but it mates and masters the fear of death."

~ Francis Bacon

From Our Report

They ate late that night in an almost empty dining room. The click, click of cutlery against bone china seemed to echo about the room. To our surprise, Tap was annoyed that the silence seemed far more deafening than Courtney's continual banter. "You will tell me, please, what you learned," Tap requested politely, when she could no longer stand the silence.

"I thought my lack of advanced education and dull intellect made my understanding of the issues of little importance," came the quiet but acidic response.

Tap blinked, then blinked again as she considered the implication of what Courtney had said. We, too, did not immediately understand. "You feel that by giving you an honest assessment, I have insulted you? Would it have been less insulting if I had patronized you?"

Courtney put her utensils down with some force and looked at Tap with annoyance. "No, it would not. But I've been working my tail off to absorb all the information that you have required of me, and I feel I have done a pretty good job of it. So I resent being dismissed as lacking knowledge and intellect."

"Did you fully understand the economic issues discussed today?" Tap asked.

"Of course not," Courtney barked in annoyance, folding her napkin and dropping it on the table.

"You do not want dessert?" Tap asked in surprise.

"No."

"You always have dessert," her boss stated, lifting her hand slightly to get the attention of the waiter. In rapid Italian, she explained to him what she wanted and, with a nod, he left.

"I have been pleased with your efforts, Courtney Hunter. There is no shame in reaching limits. If you will please indulge me, I have asked the chef to prepare something special for us. There is a small library that is quite comfortable. I thought we could talk about what you heard today while we have a dessert." Tap stated this formally but with studied warmth, as she leaned back in her seat and met her trainee's eyes. This behaviour of Tap's was new to us. We did not understand fully the plans Tap was forming at this point. If we had, we would have strongly advised against them.

"You never have dessert," Courtney stated, meeting what she considered "those strange aqua eyes" without blinking.

Tap sighed softly. "Court, I am trying to meet you half way. You will please indulge me and not be so difficult."

"Is that your way of apologizing?" Courtney asked.

"Apologizing? I never apologize. I do as I wish. That is my right." We felt Tap's controlled anger beneath the surface of calm.

It was fortunate Courtney chose to bite her tongue so a sharp retort would not escape. She realized she was in Rome at Tap's expense, and as arrogant as Tap's conversation might seem to her, it would not do to criticize — at least not at that point. We felt Courtney was experiencing a growing feeling of anxiety Tap might be far more powerful and dangerous an individual than she had realized. Some very significant and famous people had shown great respect towards her boss that came unsettlingly close in its appearance to fear. Courtney, we realized, had noted this.

A heavy silence fell again. Tap frowned and looked at Court, her eyes reflecting her frustration and annoyance. Court sat stone faced and angry, her eyes fixed on a spot over Tap's left shoulder.

"We will go to the library now and have the dessert I have ordered, and you will tell me what you have learned." Tap stood.

Court followed her out of the dining room, pulling faces at Tap's back. Such acts, although considered immature, are often committed to relieve emotional tension.

The library, however, did seem to have a mellowing effect on the ragged emotions of both women. It was small and intimate, and a fire crackled in the hearth. Dessert, too, pleased both of them. It was a dish of bite sized balls of Italian ice cream served on a silver pedestal tray filled with dried ice that billowed trails of mist onto the table. Each ball of ice cream was dusted with a different kind of ground nut. Inside was fresh fruit ice cream, and in the centre, a piece of the fruit itself, each marinated in a different liqueur.

The tension between them relaxed and Court hesitantly gave a summary of what she had learned. "I'm afraid that the maths left me well behind but, as I understand it, the general gist of the meeting was that the world is facing an economic crisis. Certainly, in our lifetime, significant raw materials such as oil, gas, and copper will run out. Britain and the US have already peaked in the use of their oil reserves. Canada is now finding the refining of the

Alberta tar sands economically feasible, due to the high price of oil."

"Meaning?" Tap asked as she helped herself to another ice cream ball.

"We have essentially tapped most of the oil that there is and we're now in the process of using it up at an alarming rate. Even new finds in the Gulf of Mexico and off Newfoundland will not meet the world's needs. In fact, old coal driven generators, once closed in Europe and North America as an air pollution hazard, are being reopened to provide a reliable, cheaper, domestic power source. New nuclear reactors are being built as well.

"The recent world recession was triggered by bank loans with not enough economic strength in natural resources or manufacturing behind nations to cover those debts. This is the tip of the iceberg in terms of the economic meltdown that lies ahead of us. As climate change and shrinking resources impact on the world more and more, nations' inability to meet their debts will lead to a near collapse of the current economic system."

Courtney frowned and looked moodily at the fire. Tap said nothing, waiting for her trainee to continue.

"There were other elements that worried me more. It is very distressing that only twenty percent of the world's population, primarily the Western world, controls eighty percent of the world's wealth. Recent growth in terrorism seems to have a direct link to the hopelessness and poverty of some nations. As resources and opportunity run out, 'have not' countries are becoming increasingly scornful of the 'have' countries, while the 'have' countries are becoming more and more concerned about the developing nations' demands for a piece of the economic pie."

Tap nodded, pleased that Courtney was beginning to put her various studies together. "Earth is a beautiful paradise floating in a vast, cold universe. Yet it is bleeding itself to death," Tap observed. "It is like a blood red rose: so very beautiful, and yet it fades so quickly when picked. Perhaps that is part of its romance — that its beauty can last for only a brief time."

Courtney looked up into Tap's eyes with interest. She had not heard Tap talk with such passion before. She had assumed that Tap was all about logic and reason, not passion. "The First Nations have a myth that it was turtle who first brought the rose coloured soil from the deep depths to make the land. Do not give up on our world, Tap. We might be seriously wounded, but we're an *iron* rose bleeding. Humans are very resourceful, and our will to survive is iron strong."

Tap looked with curious eyes at the woman whom she had brought into her system. Certainly, Courtney Hunter had displayed that sort of iron will. It was one of the things that had attracted Tap to her. "Tell me then, Courtney, what makes this planet bleed?"

"So many things," Courtney sighed. "An increase in terrorism, famine, and war are all around the corner as the world fights over its dwindling resources. The gap continues to widen between those countries in the microchip age and those in the medieval age. United Nations' studies indicate that poverty and ignorance breed violence, oppression, and disease. Terrorism, the rise of fanatical leadership that gives false hope to the disenfranchised, and the rapid spread of new diseases like AIDS, hepatitis C, and new TB strains, are all examples of this."

Tap, who had been listening with one ear as she watched the fire, looked up in surprise when she heard the catch in Courtney's throat. "Is there something wrong?"

"Tap!" Courtney snapped, getting to her feet and pacing about in the small room. "Everything is wrong. Don't you see how serious a situation we're facing?"

"Yes. I strive, and so must you, to remain objective," Tap observed. We felt Tap's annoyance at Courtney's rudeness in pacing about in front of her. It lacked respect. We marvelled at Tap's control. "Please sit down and continue."

With eyes blazing, Courtney sat.

Tap smiled. Courtney had chosen not to sit in the wing chair opposite Tap, but to curl up on the rug near the fire. The firelight highlighted the gold of her hair and bathed her form in its soft glow. Tap found the image strangely appealing. This disturbed her.

Seeing Tap waited for her to continue, Courtney gritted her teeth and tried to appear objective. "In terms of education and focus, economically competitive nations are certainly preparing a new generation to win the economic wars ahead, but that might not be enough. The looming population crisis the world is facing, the threat of global warming and the destruction of the ozone layer, rising sea levels and the displacement of millions of people as a result, are all adding to the potential for a major world crisis twenty or so years down the road."

Tap nodded. "Any other factors?"

"Yes, many. The proliferation of nuclear weapons. The destruction of farmland, the overuse and misuse of fresh water supplies, the pollution and over fishing of the oceans, the reduced genetic pool in hybrid plants...there are problems rising on so many fronts." Courtney sighed, feeling a real depression starting to envelop her.

"Your conclusions?"

"We will survive, and come out of this turbulent time better and stronger," Courtney said with feeling. We sensed the confidence of her statement renewing her hope.

"You are a born optimist, Courtney Hunter."

"And you, Tap, what are your conclusions?"

"I, too, believe in the iron rose," Tap murmured. "I have bet my existence on it."

Neither one of them spoke for a very long time. To do so would have been to give up the moment of hope, and neither one of them wanted to do that. It was finally Courtney who shifted to look up into what she thought of as "Tap's remarkable eyes". "I don't think we're being objective." She smiled.

Tap blinked, then seemed to focus herself. "Passion is not necessarily irrational, but can be directed to achieving greatness. There is no doubt that this planet faces dangerous years ahead, far more dangers than perhaps you realize. Yet, I think it might not be logic that saves this world, but passion."

This statement was the first time that Tap had expressed a changing focus, both of her goals and her viewpoint. Had others in her organization heard her, they would have been shocked. We were shocked. It was a first conscious step on a path that Tap had been walking for some time. It was, for her, the first pattern of order in the chaos into which her life had been thrown.

Courtney nodded and went back to staring at the fire, her thoughts far away. Tap watched her subject with renewed interest.

Caution reduces society to safe, secure patterns that interbreed, weakening society from within over time. Bold action breathes in life and advances a society greatly, that is, if it does not kill. Tap wondered which fate awaited her people.

Chapter Nine

"Authority doesn't work without prestige, or prestige without distance."

~ Charles De Gaulle

From Our Report

Courtney Hunter lay in bed staring at the light patterns on the ceiling. We monitored her thoughts. For two years she had archived data for Tap. She had been aware of the subject matter, but not of the pattern and significance behind it. Now she was beginning to understand the focus of Tap's research. She realized Tap was cataloguing the events of a planet in crisis. But there had to be more to Tap's work than this, she decided. Courtney Hunter drew the following conclusions. First, Tap was far too powerful and assured to be simply a historian or diarist. Second, Tap must have some vested interest in all of this. We were concerned. Courtney Hunter was drawing too close to the truth.

Courtney Hunter was again wondering what the hell was going on and what she'd gotten herself into. By this, she did not literally mean she had gotten into some form of deity punishment for a wrongdoing, but simply that Tap's organization might involve her in trouble.

She was forced to admit it was her own strong streak of curiosity about Taylor Alexandria Punga and her organization that had drawn her into the situation where she now found herself. Now, having spent time with Tap, she realized Tap was well beyond her league. The thought of working and training under Tap was both irresistibly fascinating and absolutely terrifying. This sort of opposing reactions is typical of people. It is what makes them both foolhardy and great.

Courtney Hunter still had no idea who or what Tap was, but she did realize she was immensely rich, brilliant, and powerful. She had the money, resources, and connections to make even the most powerful figures in the world fear her. Courtney Hunter pondered why Tap was interested in training her. She had no special skills or talents. It just didn't make sense to her. We must admit at this point in time it did not make complete sense to us either. Although we did suspect Courtney Hunter might fit the prophecies in some ways, the absurdity of Courtney Hunter being The One seemed to far outweigh the possibility.

Courtney Hunter felt warning bells were going off loud and clear. We knew she had admitted to herself she was good and scared — not now so much for herself, but for the world and what might be happening behind the scenes. We watched as with a shaky hand, she touched her fingertips to her lips and blew a kiss out the window. *I believe in you, my iron rose.*

Tap, too, laid awake for a very long time. We knew she felt that training Courtney was a new and alarming experience. In a way, a devastating experience. Tap felt shaken to the core of her being. This concerned us. A leader must be decisive and remain detached from others. Never had Tap imagined the key to her future might be found in the little librarian who had worked so quietly and efficiently for her for over two years. Her mind had barely begun to grasp the importance of the role that Courtney might play in the events ahead when her whole world tilted. Tap felt her mind respond as if it had suddenly woken into a new dimension of understanding, which, in fact, it had. She now found herself looking at life not as a burden of responsibility, but with passion and excitement, the raw emotion of an animal. It was both shocking and wonderful, all at once. The depth of these thoughts she kept from us at this time, but we sensed the change.

Her decision to train Courtney was an immense risk that could threaten everything, perhaps even bring about Tap's ultimate downfall. She was well aware that informants would have already passed the disturbing news on to her brother, but she felt the risk justified. Courtney, Tap felt, was the key to the problems she faced. Her plan was as daring as it was radical, and the fallout, even in the best case, would be considerable.

What plan?

We must know.

We are here to guide.

"Do not trouble yourselves. My thoughts are mine for the time being."

The next day, Courtney had to struggle hard to keep focused and absorb any of the information she heard. The presence of Tap beside her was almost physically draining. That morning, Courtney had been awakened again by a knock on her door. At breakfast, which they had in their suite and not at the conference as they had the day before, Tap had read the morning papers, sharing them politely with Court but saying little.

Courtney would have liked further discussion of their conversation of the night before. She felt she was starting to understand the parameters of Tap's research, but she still had no idea of her goals. Humans are not comfortable without clear goals. When none naturally arise, they must create them artificially. Tap's body language clearly indicated this was not the time for continuing the discussion. So Courtney waited. They rode in silence to the meeting, keeping to their own sides of the bench seat in the limousine, and once there, the day followed the same structure as the day before.

It was the afternoon lecture by the United Nations' representative of the Council on World Poverty that at last made Courtney focus. The figures were shocking. Courtney had already read a few papers referring to the coming world population crisis, but here was the actual data, presented in a very scary manner. Countries such as Pakistan, India, Colombia, Brazil, and Bangladesh were already experiencing crisis situations in some areas. Canada's population density was only 2.5 people per square mile, while India's was 233.1 people per square mile. It had taken the world twelve thousand years to increase its population to one billion humans, but the current rate of growth had taken the world's population from five billion to six billion people in only eight years. Bangladesh and Vietnam would double their populations in less than thirty years, Ghana in less than twenty years. Already the strain on the world food supply had reached critical proportions. Twenty years ago, the world maintained a five year surplus of food. At present, that margin of safety had been reduced to mere months. The impact this growing crisis was going to have on the global economy was staggering.

It was a very sober Courtney who slid into the seat beside Tap that evening. "You are tired?" Tap asked.

"No, overwhelmed by the staggering extent of the problems facing the world in the next few years," sighed Courtney.

"Do you wish to change your assessment of your bleeding iron rose?" Tap asked, watching Courtney intently. Body language and expression are a far greater indication of feeling than words.

"No, no," Courtney answered slowly, deep in thought. "But I'm beginning to realize that the solutions are going to mean very hard decisions, and not everyone in this world will survive this crisis. Fifty years down the road, the world will be completely different than it is today."

Tap's brief smile expressed a far deeper understanding of what lay ahead, but she chose not to share that knowledge. Courtney would not see Tap again that day. Tap informed her briefly she had business to attend to that night and a meal would be sent to Courtney's room. "Please do not try to escape," Tap stated bluntly, but the implied threat was somehow not as strong because Tap raised an eyebrow and smiled.

Still, as Courtney ate her solitary meal in their suite, she was very aware she was, indeed, a prisoner. She suspected she would not get far if she were to try to leave the hotel. Just to assert some independence, she spent her meal thinking of possible ways to escape. Then, with a sigh, she settled down to read. She felt if she did much more reading, her eyeballs were going to fall out. People often express negative feelings in colloquial expressions.

Courtney woke to find the sunlight playing across her bed. The smell of coffee and fresh bread drifted through the door. Groggy, Courtney looked at the clock and was shocked to see it was almost nine o'clock. Then she saw the note:

Today, instead of flying back, we will go sightseeing. TAP

Perhaps not the most congenial of notes, but it pleased Courtney. She knew Tap had changed her plans in order to allow Courtney to see something of Rome. She smiled happily, folded the note, and carefully put it away inside her briefcase. Then she slipped from the bed and went into the bathroom.

It was a beautiful day and Tap did her best to be a good guide. Her sense of presence and tall, straight bearing seemed to part the crowds of tourists wherever they went. The shorter Courtney followed gratefully in her boss's wake. They went first to the Vitale Vaticano. Tap explained that Vatican City had many outstanding art galleries and museums of art and artifacts collected or donated to the church over the centuries.

"It would be impossible, unfortunately, for us to see and do justice to all the fine works that are on display here. There are Egyptian, Gregorian, and Etruscan treasures. There is the antiquarium that houses the Roman antiques, and then there is the vase collection, the tapestries, the maps, and Raphael's works, and—"

"Please, Tap." Courtney laughed, cutting into the list that threatened to go on for some time. "Can we go to the Sistine Chapel? I've always wanted to see it."

Tap smiled. "A good choice for such a brief visit. Although it is a magnificent work and one could spend days looking at it, sadly, the crowds make it less than the spiritual experience it should be."

"Do you like art, Tap? I noticed in the room...aah...where you found me, that you had some significant work from the turn of the century."

Tap's eyebrow rose in amusement. "You are referring to the room I found you in the day you broke into my quarters? Maybe I should count to see if the pictures are all there."

Courtney blushed. "Very funny." She might have taken offence at Tap's teasing, but just then Tap took Courtney's arm and they made their way through the press of tourists to the ticket booth. The simple touch felt awkward, and too intimate. They moved apart again as soon as they could, both a little embarrassed.

"Two, please," Tap managed to get out through a throat tight with sudden stress.

"Twenty-six lira." Tap handed over the money and took the tickets.

"I could pay," Courtney stated, as Tap checked the time of their tour.

Eyes the colour of the green Caribbean Sea trained on her. "Courtney Hunter, this is a tour I have decided to take you on and so I must pay. Besides, I am wealthy and you have no money."

Courtney put her hands on her hips and looked up at Tap in mock annoyance. "Perhaps, but it was my wish to see Rome and therefore I should pay some of the expenses," she challenged.

The look of surprise on Tap's face almost made Courtney laugh out loud, but she felt a point needed to be made right there at the beginning. Courtney Hunter felt touring with one's boss was a difficult situation in which to be. "And I do have some savings. It probably wouldn't seem like much to you, but I can afford a ticket or two."

Tap shifted from one foot to the other, feeling just a little uncomfortable. As we knew, the truth was that Courtney's money had disappeared along with her identity, by Tap's order. "Your financial independence is not in question here. I know Rome and therefore I am better suited to take the lead," Tap stated, astonished Courtney would question her natural authority.

"I accept, and I'm grateful for the experience that you bring to our day touring, but that doesn't mean that you need to cover all the costs," Courtney explained, determination written on her face, holding her ground as a stream of tourists broke around them.

Frustrated, Tap tried to explain her position without revealing anything to her trainee. "I am your boss."

"Granted. And until my training period is up, I have agreed to accept your authority over me, even to the ridiculous extent of virtually being kept a prisoner. But today falls outside of the usual boss/trainee relationship and so I must insist on a more equal footing, otherwise I wouldn't be interested."

"You broke into my quarters because you were interested," Tap pointed out to her, with growing annoyance.

Court snorted in disgust and rolled her eyes to the heavens. "You are so arrogant. As much as I have admitted a desire to learn about your organization and have agreed to this training period, I don't feel that I am totally without a certain independence."

Tap was blinking in shock. No one had ever dared to call her arrogant. Worse still, she knew that the plan she was formulating revolved around Courtney Hunter's cooperation. She needed Courtney Hunter, it would seem, far more than Courtney needed her. Tap did not enjoy this realization. "You owe me thirteen lira," she stated rather stupidly.

Courtney smiled. "That's okay, you can pay this time. I'll get the next entrance fee."

Tap blinked again, trying to make sense of the rapid change in Courtney's stance. "You do not wish to pay for your ticket now?"

"Not this time." Courtney smiled, rather enjoying watching the supremely confident woman floundering in confusion. We were surprised at the power of Courtney Hunter's personality. Not many got the better of Tap.

"Can we go now to join the tour, Courtney Hunter?" Tap asked, still trying to understand the status of their present situation.

"Yes, I would like that very much, Tap. Thank you for buying my ticket." Tap smiled weakly, still looking confused, and Courtney, smiling, led the taller woman over to where the line was forming.

They stood at one end of the Sistine Chapel looking up and around in awe. Tap had manoeuvred them to the front of the group and stood close up behind Courtney in the crush.

"The Sistine Chapel is where the election of popes occurs, and most of the pontifical ceremonies take place here. It is a barrel-vaulted ceiling, as you can see, and is divided by a marble screen. That was common in early churches, to separate those lesser individuals from the powerful who worshipped closer to the altar." Tap's explanation whispered softly in Courtney's ear and the feel of the warm, lean form up against her were unnerving Courtney. Thoughts, that one should not be having in such a holy and tranquil place, seeped into her mind.

"The ceiling is, of course, by Michelangelo. He painted it at the order of Pope Julius II between 1508 and 1512. It was only gradually that Michelangelo became committed to the project. He had wanted to spend his time working on marble sculptures. We still have some of his marble work left unfinished."

"It is breathtaking, Tap. How did he ever do it?" Courtney asked, unconsciously backing against the taller woman in the crush of people as she looked up at the magnificent ceiling. "The ceiling is so high up."

Tap gritted her teeth. She was not used to being touched by her employees. "He stood on a wooden scaffolding and painted onto wet plaster. It is called fresco. Julius II wanted the ceiling to show the lives of the Apostles. Michelangelo convinced him to allow the painting of a much bigger image of the religious history of Christians as they wait for the Messiah. Note the heavily muscled peasant women. At that time it was illegal to study anatomy and to have female models, so Michelangelo's women are not very feminine by today's standards."

"Yes, I can see that, but still the overall effect is so powerful," Courtney murmured as she strained to see the fading colours and brushstrokes high above her head.

"Julius and Michelangelo had a very stormy relationship. Julius was a little short of money because of the wars that were going on, and Michelangelo felt he should be paid more regularly. It was not until twenty years later that Michelangelo returned here at the request of Paul II. Between 1536 and 1541, he painted the wall behind the high altar, his famous *Last Judgement*. Legend has it that the figure over there in the fresco is Michelangelo himself."

"Really? Neat. Who did the walls?" Courtney asked, becoming aware for the first time of the rich illustrations down each side of the chapel.

"The wall frescoes were painted earlier, between 1481 and 1483 by Botticelli, Rosselli, and Chirlandaio. The panels represent the lives of Moses and Christ."

"How do you know all this stuff?" Courtney asked, as they were jostled out to let in a new group of tourists.

Tap smiled down at Courtney with a twinkle in her eye. "It's all in the data files in my library."

Courtney groaned. "More reading. I should have known."

They found a quiet café and had morning coffee while they watched the hustle and bustle of everyday life in Rome. They shared a basket of croissants, Courtney topping hers with grape jam and washing it down with a latte while Tap sniffed at her own bread suspiciously and ate it plain, with a black coffee.

Courtney sat back in her seat and watched Tap with interested eyes. We found her musings strange. Courtney Hunter concluded it wasn't just that Tap was extraordinarily good looking, although she was, but that there was an aura about her of strength and danger. She likened it to a panther which arrogantly sauntered into town and sent everyone fleeing. Tap's hands, Courtney Hunter noticed, were long and graceful, and yet gave the impression of being strong and capable.

Courtney looked up to catch Tap looking at her. "Does my appearance pass muster?" Tap asked, not with conceit but with real interest.

Court blushed at being caught staring but answered honestly. "Yes. I'm sure you know you are attractive, but more than that — there is something...exotic about you."

Tap looked at her trainee with curious eyes. "Physical appearances and attitude must command respect. Beauty is not important. You are attractive, but what is important is that I find you unpredictable and resourceful. These are traits, if harnessed and mastered, that could be of use to my organization."

Courtney nodded but we sensed a chill of fear. Tap's words plucked the chord of her uneasiness. She did not wish to have any part of her personality harnessed or mastered.

Chapter Ten

"Space isn't remote at all. It's only an hour's drive away if your car could go straight upwards."

~ Sir Fred Hoyle

From Our Report

Tap reluctantly let Courtney pay for their morning coffee; with great embarrassment, we noticed. Then they slipped into the limousine that pulled up to the curb as soon as the women got up from the table, and drove over to the Piazza della Rotonda where the Pantheon stood.

To Courtney Hunter's surprise, Tap, who seemed usually to be very pragmatic, became almost excited as she described the structure of this building.

We observed Tap explaining as she stood in the centre of the black and white marble floor, arms spread in illustration.

"The original building that stood here was destroyed by fire in 80 AD. This one was built during the reign of Emperor Hadrian. The man is known for his military brilliance, but he was also a lover of the arts and had a great interest in architecture. This building is simply amazing. Look at the dome, Courtney. The central opening at the top allows the entry of air and light, yet the massive stone blocks that make up the dome are just as sound today as they were two thousand years ago. You see, it is as if a big balloon was blown up inside and the walls and dome expanded to accommodate it.

"The interior measures 43.40 metres and it is the same in height. The whole building is a perfect sphere. That is amazing. This place was built by hand, each block chipped into shape and lifted into place." Tap turned around, looking up at the structure with genuine admiration in her eyes and a sense of pride.

A woman passing by Courtney, leaned over and whispered, "I wish we had your guide. She certainly is enthusiastic."

Courtney chuckled and Tap went crimson with embarrassment. "I am not your guide," she stated with some indignation. We felt that Tap had chosen to be a guide on many levels, whether she was aware of her role or not.

Courtney Hunter laughed even harder. "Of course, you aren't," she pacified her boss.

Their next stop was the Coliseum. Tap paid the extra eight lira each so that they could go up to the second level. Looking down on the ruins of the floor and sub basements, Courtney began to understand Tap's excitement with the wonder of this early architecture.

"This place is contemporary with the Pantheon and was built at the order of the Emperor Vespasian. It was designed to be flooded so that the Naumachie, mock naval battles, could be staged here. They also held Munera or gladiator fights, and Venationes, actual wild animal hunts. The building held 97,000 spectators and the doors were labelled with the row numbers to allow for easy crowd flow," Tap explained seriously.

"It is unbelievable. Look at the size of it!" Courtney exclaimed, leaning forward to get a closer look at the passageways and cells in the substructure below.

"It eventually fell into disuse and became the city garbage dump for many years," Tap stated.

Courtney looked at Tap with interest. There was a sadness in the taller woman's eyes, an awareness of things cruel and violent. "You don't like this place, do you?"

We felt Tap's pain, but she merely shrugged. "War is an art, but one that is so dark that it leaves only sorrow, even for those who win. I do not see the entertainment in battle. Are you ready to go?" Courtney nodded and they left in a quiet, reflective mood.

They spent the remainder of the day walking through a nearby shopping area. Tap, who we knew dreaded even the thought of shopping, seemed to find enjoyment because Courtney was having such a good time. She found this reaction most unusual, as did we. Tap appeared to be treating Courtney Hunter as a friend. That was most strange.

Once again, they flew first class across the Atlantic. Courtney tried to read, but the article on the massive destruction of the rain forest by lumbering, and the impact that had in reducing rainfall to the interior areas, made her quite depressed. When she got to the part where the author talked about how 1965 was the last time the planet was able to produce more oxygen than was needed, and that every breath taken since had gone through four sets of lungs first, she gave up. *Maybe the average person has it right: watch sitcoms and don't think about the crisis that lurks just around the corner.* We did not understand Courtney Hunter's sadness or train of thought. Things are as they are.

We watched as she took her pillow and punched it into shape. "I'm going to have a nap, OK?"

Tap looked up, nodded then went back to her work. Courtney curled in her seat and placed her head on the pillow. Yet we knew she was aware of the silent, focussed woman who sat beside her. Tap was her boss, her instructor, and her jailer, and sometimes, perhaps, a friend. Just as she drifted off to sleep, Courtney remembered an old Latin quotation from her school days: respect your enemies and do not put too much faith in friends. We thought this good advice for Tap as well.

Security Report 8431
Commanding Officer: Franz Scheidt

After Courtney Hunter's move, Percy Dingwall requested a route change so he could deliver mail to TAP International. Percy Dingwall does not like secrets. He did like Courtney Hunter. He was fascinated by her. That fascination became an obsession the first day he delivered mail to TAP International and found Courtney Hunter's car parked in the lot.

"I want to report a possible kidnapping," he told the police. It is a vastly inaccurate word. Courtney Hunter was not a kid, nor was she napping. But there is no other word in the English language for the forcible taking and holding of an adult individual against their will, with the possible exception of "conscription". That word did not apply here, either, although TAP was to use it.

"Courtney Hunter was conscripted into one of our training programs. She is currently doing field research in South Africa," Tap told the police. "She asked if she could leave her car in our parking lot for safety reasons."

"Why did she give up her apartment and who moved her things?" they asked.

"Court is in a three year training program that will take her to our offices all over the world. She simply did not need to maintain a place to live. When she is in town, she will stay in the guest quarters that we provide for our personnel. Our company handles the moving of all our people if the move is job related."

The police were satisfied. Three is a comforting number, and "training programs" sound successful, not threatening. Percy Dingwall was not satisfied. Percy Dingwall was obsessed.

He delivered the mail to TAP International via a back entrance. The facility is surrounded by a high electrified fence and tall rows of cedar trees. He would drop the mail into a metal box built into the fencing gate. There was never anyone around, but we could tell by his body language he knew he was watched. He had noted the surveillance cameras mounted on poles like electronic sentries stationed on the high ground.

After several trips, he found a high piece of land further down the road where he could pull onto the side of the road and observe the fence through binoculars. From where he stood on top of his delivery van, he could see extensive gardens. We hoped at first he would conclude that TAP International might be some sort of agriculture research centre. However, our investigations revealed Percy Dingwall's research at the library had uncovered vague references in the press to TAP International being some sort of think tank. He wrote this information in his black book and recorded two questions: What did TAP International think about? Did Courtney ever think of him?

From Our Report

After detailing his observations, Frank Scheidt reported to Haichen. "Haichen, he is there again."

"Did we ascertain how much he can see from his vantage point?"

"Not much. He has observed our personnel picking up the mail and can see most of the kitchen gardens. I will continue to monitor him and keep to the normal routines, but we must be ready to act if necessary."

Haichen nodded. "I will keep Tap advised."

We agreed. Sometimes the best defence against a possible threat is to carry on normally and to not indicate you are aware of being observed. Boredom leads to disinterest. Only if necessary would Franz Scheidt hit hard and without mercy.

We noted with concern the information about Percy Dingwall was passed on to other sources.

The next few days were very busy for Courtney Hunter and she did not see Tap after they arrived back at the estate. Courtney was archiving the data they had brought back and keeping up on the reading that arrived daily on her computer. On the third night, she was awakened by the sound of Tap calling her name. She crawled out of her tent and stood under her boss's steady gaze. "You have kept up on your reading?"

"Yes. I've also archived most of the material you gathered at the conference. I'm surprised that I haven't been questioned about it."

"I have been away. It is not always possible for me to communicate freely. Sometimes situations are tense," Tap responded cautiously.

Courtney looked at her boss with curiosity.

"Are you in danger, Tap?"

Tap smiled warily and looked off across the garden. "My position creates danger for me but I am careful. You are not to concern yourself with such things."

"But I *am* concerned. My position here is not very clearly defined. I fear you might be both my jailer and protector," Courtney stated, watching Tap closely for a reaction. We felt Courtney Hunter's assumptions were correct.

For a second there was silence. "You are safe enough, Courtney Hunter, if you keep your end of the bargain. Come and sit down here on the rocks; I need to talk to you."

Courtney Hunter sat where she was asked. We sensed the tension and caution she suddenly felt.

"Is there a problem?"

"Yes and no. Your neighbour, Percy Dingwall, has been asking questions about you."

"Percy Dingwall? I don't know him."

"He lived across the hall from you and delivered your mail."

"Oh, okay. I never knew his name. He seemed sort of weird."

"He is. He thinks you have been kidnapped. He has told the police so. They have been here asking questions."

"I've been kidnapped? What did you tell them?"

We felt Tap controlling her anger and frustration at Courtney Hunter's statement. "I showed them your employment file and explained that you were in a training program for a month, that at the moment you are doing field work for us in South Africa."

"What! You told them I was in an overseas program, that I'd left the country? You can't do that."

Tap remained calm. "I did. And if they choose to follow the paper trail we have created, they will discover that one Courtney Hunter did go through Customs in South Africa."

"That wasn't necessary. I'm not a prisoner."

"You made the decision to enter my world. In doing so, you left your own. Whether you return to it has yet to be decided. For now, people will think you are working in Africa."

We felt both Tap's cold determination and Courtney Hunter's shock and anger.

"I tell you of Percy Dingwall as a courtesy to you. He is not a stable man. He has taken pictures of you and keeps a file on you, along with many others on his mail route. I have informed the police of this."

"Is it true or another fabrication you have created?"

"It is true."

We sensed Courtney Hunter's uncertainty. She did not know whether to accept Tap's word as truth. Tap had told the truth but she did not do so always. Truth is elusive.

"About tomorrow," Tap continued. "Each month, I have a meeting with my chief personnel and report to them on my findings. Tomorrow you will speak instead."

Courtney looked up into clear aqua eyes in surprise. We, too, are shocked. "Tap, do you think that wise? I sense some awkwardness, even resentment, about me having red security clearance."

"It is a decision I have weighed very seriously and I feel this is the course of action that needs to be taken. There are many things of which you are as yet unaware that I have considered in making this decision. Such presentations are part of your training. Can you be ready to present a summary of our data by nine hundred hours tomorrow?"

Courtney shredded a leaf in thought. We felt her insecurity but also her determination. "Yes. I think so," she said, with more confidence than she felt. She needed to prove she had a right to be a part of the organization.

Tap leaned back with a tired sigh and looked at the dome above. It was late and the courtyard lights had been turned off. Through the dome, a thousand stars shone brightly in the night sky. For a long while they sat in silence, looking at the stars overhead and listening to the soothing sound of water as it flowed over the rocks in the channel.

A satellite caught the light of the sun and slowly drifted in an arc across the sky. Tap pointed it out to her. "It is a French communication satellite," Tap explained. "An old one from the early nineties. I do not take the time to look at the stars enough."

"Do you believe in UFOs?" Courtney asked dreamily.

"What?" came the surprised response. Tap had been taken unaware and needed time to think where this conversation was going. "What?" is not always used as a question but as a means of forcing clarification to allow time for thought.

"You know — UFOs, little green men sightings." Courtney laughed.

Tap cringed. "Do you?"

"Well, not little green men or even flying saucers. The distance to the nearest planet that might be able to support life just seems way too far away to allow conventional space travel. It would take light years just to get here, even at the speed of light. But I do like to think that there is intelligent life out there. Don't you?"

"Yes, I believe the same. The idea does not scare you?"

"Of course not... Well, as long as they remain a theory. I mean if an alien was to beam down here, I'd probably have a heart attack." She laughed.

Tap smiled at Courtney Hunter's joke and then went on seriously, "I have made arrangements for you to share my accommodations, Courtney Hunter." This decision we knew of and did not approve.

Courtney's eyes got round. "What?"

"Accommodations are in short supply here, but my quarters have several rooms that are under...utilized. One of these will now be your quarters."

For a long time, Courtney looked into the eyes she found so remarkable. "You are a very strange person, Tap. You say and do things in such a...different way. I never know just where I stand. Is this a prison within a prison?"

Tap stood, using the time to formulate the correct answer. "You said yourself that you have noticed resentment. The closer you are to me, the safer you will be until you have finished your training."

Courtney stood and looked thoughtfully at her boss. "And the closer I am to you, the more danger I'm in, as well?"

"That, too. But that was a position you put yourself in when you chose to break into my world."

Courtney got what she needed for the night and together they made their way across the channel to the path in the courtyard along the front of the staff quarters.

Dark eyes watched them go, we noted. What was going on? What importance did Courtney Hunter have in Tap's plans?

Spies. We see but we do not interfere.

Tap and Courtney Hunter entered the office where she had first studied under Tap's guidance and crossed through it to enter a smaller room filled with electronic equipment. "Security," Tap explained, and keyed in some codes that allowed Courtney to follow her into Tap's private rooms undetected.

To Courtney's eyes, the room was different. Once again, there was little furniture. A desk and chair were against the back wall. The opposite wall was a sheet of water that flowed over metal and ran out a channel in the floor. There, two chairs and a couch formed a conversation area. The other walls were a soft, silver grey. Each of the three remaining walls had an abstract painting on it in gentle, muted colours and flowing lines. Courtney walked over to one and looked at it intently. It almost seemed to move. "Who is the artist?" she asked. "They're all by the same person, I can tell." Her back to Tap, she did not see the look of astonishment.

"They are by Tay Appala Punra," Tap answered honesty. When truth is not understood, it is as good as a lie.

"I don't know the name, but this work — it seems very familiar. They're beautiful."

Tap watched Courtney with deep, thoughtful eyes. Courtney Hunter understood more than she realized.

"Do you collect art?" Courtney asked.

"Not really. I have an interest in it. Art is the cutting edge of social change and thought. Understand a people's art and you understand who they were and who they will be," Tap stated, intrigued by Courtney's innocent remarks about the paintings.

Courtney Hunter was proving to be an unexpectedly unnerving subject of study. Yet each revelation strengthened the argument that Tap might have been right in not terminating Courtney Hunter too soon. As Tap had observed, there was much to be learned. We were amazed Courtney Hunter found the painting familiar to her. That strengthened Tap's argument.

"This will be your room." Tap moved towards a doorway to the right and Courtney followed. The room, as always, was sparely furnished, with a bed and small writing table. It did have the advantage of having a window overlooking the courtyard. Off to the side were a closet and a small bathroom, much like the room in which she had been held captive. This room, however, was smaller and lacked a channel of water.

"Thank you. This will do fine."

"I will leave you to settle in before you return to your studies."

Courtney nodded. We sensed a growing anxiety within her — fear, really — about her situation. Tap was polite and concerned, but there was always that underlying threat that she was more the prisoner than the trainee. Once again she considered escaping and rejected the idea. Still, we knew Courtney Hunter was very uneasy and would have some tentative plans in place for escape if she thought it necessary. It is a human quality to rationalize natural instincts away. This is the source of both their success and their greatest failures.

Courtney unpacked the few things she had brought. We observed and were aware of her thoughts. She felt she would need to take down her tent and move all her cargo over, but caution made her hesitate. She wasn't sure what sort of message Tap was sending by moving her to her quarters. Nor was Courtney Hunter sure she wanted that message sent. By moving into Tap's quarters, she was sending one of two messages: either that she was much closer to Tap than she actually was, or that Tap didn't trust her and was putting her under tighter control. Courtney wasn't comfortable with either of those insinuations.

We noted she decided to wait a few days before committing herself to any course of action. We knew this would not please Tap. We felt cautious. We did not know why Tap had made the decision to move Courtney Hunter into her private chambers.

One thing we and Courtney Hunter were sure of was Tap knew why she had moved her into the room. There was a motive behind the action. Tap was always a step ahead of everyone else. She was also holding back many of her thoughts from us. That was not right.

Rugia Malwala met Gene Lamount in the gymnasium later that night. It was a good place to meet because it was open to anyone, regardless of their position in the organization. This late at night, few people used the facility.

Rugia worked hard on the treadmill, conditioning her cardiovascular system. This was important and so she took it seriously, working out every day. Lamount was more inclined to work with the free weights.

Lamount placed the forty pound dumbbell back on the carriage and used the towel around his neck to wipe the sweat from his brow as he walked over to where Rugia worked out.

"Anything?"

Rugia shook her head. "No one knows, not even Haichen from what I can tell. There was no correspondence, that is certain. Tap finished what she was doing in the library and then walked down to the courtyard and talked to Courtney on the island. Next thing, Courtney is packing up her night things and following Tap to her quarters."

Lamount looked startled, almost disgusted. "You don't think..."

"No. Maria said that she had been asked to set up a bedroom in a room that Tap never uses. It was supposed to be her personal gymnasium but she has always used this one."

"Strange. I have no idea what is going on either. I will report this incident immediately, but he will not be happy that we do not know more."

"Tap is a shrewd opponent. Her brother is wise to fear her."

"He fears no one," Lamount responded sharply.

Rugia paled. "Forgive me. You are right. My frustration and fatigue have made my thought processes cloudy. I should go and get some rest."

Lamount nodded. "Do that." He watched Rugia hurry off with interested eyes. Was Rugia's remark carelessness, or was she disenchanted? Or had she been asked to test Lamount's loyalty? He needed to see Haichen Lai as early as possible tomorrow. She might know more than she was prepared to share with Rugia Malwala.

These issues that we record here are the beginnings of a cascading event horizon and should be noted with some interest.

Ignoring us, Tap lay in bed, thinking. She didn't doubt her decision was correct, but alone at night, with all activity stopped, the enormity of what she was about to do was overwhelming. She had meditated, seeking not answers but peace. We would have preferred dialogue so that answers could have been reached.

We note the following. The study of faith is an interesting subject. In all faiths there are layers of spiritual understanding. The unbelievers are those who have rationalized spiritual enlightenment away. Enlightenment is based on an act of faith, trust. Such trust in abstract concepts is not possible for the unbelievers. Perhaps they do not recall their dreams. Their beliefs are limited to those concepts that can be proven with scientific experiment.

The second level up from the unbelievers is the other extreme. They are those of fundamental belief. They confuse the comfort of spiritual ritualism with enlightenment. Ecstasy is not enlightenment. This is a dangerous group, who know the letter of the laws and the words of the text by heart, but know nothing of the philosophy or history behind it. They are judgemental, fanatical, and narrow-minded.

The third level of awareness includes those who understand the doctrine, philosophy, and history of the faith, and yet the shallowness of their meditations prevents them from finding true enlightenment. They are trapped by their own need to understand the path to enlightenment.

On the fourth level of awareness, the believer realizes doctrine is meaningless except as a tool to achieve enlightenment. These individuals have taken the first step into a greater understanding.

On the fifth plane, the physical world is revealed to be only one level of reality. The believer begins to see the great interconnectivity of the forces of the spiritual universe.

On the sixth level, the believer no longer sees the interconnectivity of the spiritual universe, but rather its simple, pure oneness.

By the seventh level of enlightenment, the believer sees for the first time the reality that is all around and of which they are physically a part but spiritually beyond. They can find joy in life and yet be separate from it. The enlightened are now awake to, and part of, the spiritual oneness of the universe. Few reach this level of awareness and peace. Fewer still move on.

Tap chose not to follow this path to enlightenment, not by conscious choice but by action. Her faith she has vested in is the future of this lonely blue planet drifting in a sea of blackness. Her decision to use Courtney Hunter in her plans will risk everything.

What shall we do?

This is not right.

It could bring an end.

Chapter Eleven

"Power tends to corrupt, and absolute power corrupts absolutely. Great men are almost always bad men."

~ Lord Acton

From Courtney Hunter's Logs

When I woke the next morning, I found myself alone in Tap's quarters. I felt rather awkward being in the area set aside for Tap only. I did not know what rights I enjoyed, if any, and what restrictions my movements in these private rooms might incur. Rather than risk more conflict at this time, I chose to restrict myself to my room and the room adjoining it.

I knew Tap was a busy person and had probably been up for hours. Tap seemed to function on very little sleep. Embarrassed someone might find me there, I showered and dressed quickly, and headed out. I wasn't sure just how I was to explain my new accommodations. I grabbed a coffee and a bran muffin for breakfast in the green section cafeteria and headed into the library to prepare for my meeting.

At 8:30 Haichen walked in. "Tap has sent me to escort you to the meeting room," she said. "You are ready, Court?"

I smiled and slipped my notes into a file folder. "Sure I'm ready." I tried not to give any indication to Haichen I was nervous. I wondered if Haichen knew where I had slept last night and how she might interpret that information. This whole situation was getting way too complicated.

"It is a great honour — that you have been asked by Tap to sit in on the meeting," Haichen explained.

"Is it? I thought I was part of the team now, even if I'm only in the learning stages."

Haichen stopped and looked at me with eyes that revealed nothing of her emotions. "There will be some who will not approve. It would be wise to be careful." I nodded but said nothing, not sure whether Haichen was giving me a friendly warning or threatening me.

They sat around a large, highly polished wood table in the red zone library. No one reacted to Haichen escorting me in. Either they had known ahead of time that I would be joining them, or they were being very cautious. No one made eye contact with me. They sat quietly waiting, each apparently lost in their own thoughts. It made me feel uncomfortable. Then Tap walked in and we all stood. Only after she had taken her seat at the head of the table did everyone sit down and appear to relax a bit.

Tap looked around, her eyes finally settling on me where I sat near the end of the table. "A change of procedure today — Courtney Hunter will present the data and field any questions."

No one's expression changed, and yet I could sense their shock and intensified interest in me. I felt like an exotic fish in a bowl. Squaring my shoulders, I looked around the table confidently and started delivering my report. An hour later, I was just winding down.

"The general consensus of the talks was that economic stress could have any number of possible flashpoints. Several areas in South America, the Middle East, and the Pacific Rim nations would certainly be areas of immediate concern. The growing fundamentalist views in many religions are also a factor which helps to narrow the probability spectrum. To pick, however, a specific country or countries from an extensive list of potential areas of concern would be risky. Such decisions are easy to see in hindsight, but the reality is there are many areas of the world capable of spearheading a major international crisis. We're a small global village and any group making waves affects us all greatly. For example, the 9-11 attack on the US and the War on Terrorism that followed demonstrated how vulnerable the world can be. Does that—"

The door slammed open and a man strode in confidently. He was tall and underweight and yet appeared to have a wiry strength. His eyes were dark and his hair more unruly, but in all other respects his features were very similar to Tap's. Everyone stood immediately, including Tap.

He halted and looked around the table, his eyes finally settling on me. His lip curled for a fraction of a second, then he looked at Tap. "Tay, I have been informed of what you have been up to." He spoke with a soft voice that had wonderful resonance to it despite the fact it was edged with steel. "I could hardly believe that you would dare to disgrace your family by—"

"I will dare anything to achieve our goal," interrupted Tap, and slowly sat down. She sat relaxed, looking at the stranger with a calm, defiant manner. I was completely confused, having no idea at all what was happening. I could see fear and indecision on the faces of the others around the table and did not understand why.

I wasn't sure what was going on, but I did know whose side I needed to be on. I sat. A second later, Franz Scheidt lowered his big, burly frame into his chair. I looked across at Haichen and met her eye in a steady, confident challenge. Haichen hesitated and then sank weak-kneed into her seat. Slowly, one after the other, they all followed suit. Rugia Malwala was the last to sit. I could sense everyone at the table was horrified. I feared whatever was going on the consequences might be terrifying. I tried not to show it but I was petrified.

The man gritted his teeth and clearly controlled his temper with difficulty. Spinning on his heel, he left. There was a moment of silence. I could feel the fear and dread from the others hitting me in waves. Only Tap seemed calm, her face devoid of any expression. Tap's eyes focussed on me.

"That was my brother. Thank you, Court, for a detailed yet concise summary of the lectures we heard in Rome. I must ask you to leave now, as I have matters to discuss with my senior personnel."

I blinked, trying to make sense of the sudden change in events. I was being dismissed. Anger boiled up inside me but I kept myself under control. I gathered up my file and stood. "Thank you for this opportunity," I said formally, and left. With forced calm, I walked back to my small office in the green zone and threw my papers on the desk. "Arrogant assholes," I muttered, and sat down to think things through.

I didn't so much think as I seethed. I thought I had worked hard to meet Tap's expectations and I had been the first to show my support of Tap at the meeting, so I was having trouble understanding why I had been essentially thrown out. I wasn't prepared to be used and treated so poorly by anyone. I, of course, had no idea what had just happened. Ignorance is not always bliss.

From Our Report

Tap looked around the table at the stunned faces. More had happened in the last twenty-four hours than in all the time that they had been working on this project. "First, you may speak freely at this meeting. Second, I am going to say what you already suspect and have discussed behind my back: I think Courtney Hunter is the key to our success here. She is my choice for a significant change of direction in our goals. Perhaps there are others, even some more suitable, but Court, by her actions, has become the central figure in my plans.

"I have to admit that bringing in an outsider has been as much a shock to me as I am sure it is to you. I am still learning to deal with the concept. One of the rules we established in undertaking this project was that we would maintain complete objectivity. I have to admit that I have broken that rule when I decided to work with Courtney Hunter. It was...a gut reaction, an emotional decision." Tap felt as well as saw the shock effect of her words on her staff. We did also.

"I have committed us to a course of action and the justification I give you now is based after the fact. I think we might be a lot closer to our objective than we realized. That is the good news. The bad is the consequences that we might be facing by changing our focus. My brother, I think, made his position quite clear. If any of you wish to leave my service, do so today. I warn you, though, not to expect my brother to trust you within his ranks. He will think I have sent you to spy. Today, the battle bell has been sounded. We are on the verge of a social revolution and perhaps even war. If you are not prepared to die at my side, leave now."

Tap looked around the room. Most at the table had seen battle. That, they would not fear. Now they were being asked to change their loyalty, to pick one over the other. They were being asked to go against everything they had ever believed. We realized now, we, too, were afraid.

No one moved. Tap continued. The implications of her words were like bombardments on our hearts.

"As much as I can, I have told you honestly how and why I have made these decisions. I am going to ask you each in turn to tell me if you feel you have compromised your objectivity by feelings or actions that involve you directly or indirectly with those outside of this project."

Some hours later, Tap sat alone in her private office. She was deep in thought. Her meeting with her personnel had been both interesting and shocking in nature. It would take her time to digest all the information that had been reluctantly and awkwardly presented to her. Time was something of which she suspected she had little. She would need to act quickly and boldly. The time for objective observation was at an end.

Tap, with respect.

We must speak.

There is great danger.

"I am aware of that. I have been in danger since the day I was born."

But you are the figurehead.

You must consider carefully.

Is this the right course?

"I feel it is. To be truthful, I can think of no other and time has run out."

Then it must be,
No matter what the consequences;
It is our path.

The door slipped open and Haichen quietly entered the room. We watched silently. Tap looked at her with interest, wondering if she was one of the informants in her midst. "We are going ahead with the project," Tap stated.

Haichen's only reaction was to steady herself by placing a hand on the back of the chair by Tap's console. "Will it be Courtney Hunter?"

"Yes."

Haichen said nothing. Today had been one nasty shock after another for her, we realized. She felt as if the world had tilted beneath her feet. Worse, she found she had divided loyalties. She had lied to Tap and she was not very comfortable with having done so. Like most, it was not the lie that lay heavy on her conscious but the fear that the truth might come out. No lie is a certainty and so lies are dangerous things. A lie is eventually always exposed.

Her meeting with Tap was brief and to the point, then she was dismissed. Tap watched her go with interested eyes. Haichen Lai, she had thought she could trust, but she knew Haichen had lied to her today. Why?

We knew that Haichen Lai sought out Gene Lamount as soon as she could. He only had to look at her face to know Tap had told her of her decision.

"You must not talk of it," he stated before she could say anything. "Not even to me."

"But...it...it is...not right. It is obscene. Surely, there are others...I can not believe this. Things are going from bad to worse."

Lamount placed his clipboard on the table. "No, not worse, but very...different. We have been changed by this place, you realize, by what we are doing. Was that not our mission? Can we fail now because we fear to be bold?"

"Bold? Or mad?"

Lamount smiled, pulling Haichen into his arms. "Is what we are feeling madness?"

"I do not know. I am not sure of anything anymore," came the reply from against his chest. "You saw how she treated her brother at the meeting."

"Yes."

"I was scared. I did not know if we should tell her about us. She asked about compromises with outsiders. I did not think... I know our feelings for each other do compromise our objectivity, but she was referring to those outside. I thought—"

"It's okay. Don't fret."

"But, Gene—"

"She has committed us to a course of action that is extreme, I will admit. To carry out her plan, she needs me...and I need you. That gives us some security, but only a little. We will share in her triumph or her death."

"This is not what I thought I would ever be involved in."

"You should have. Tap has always lived on the edge. It is what has made her great."

Courtney chose to read in a corner of the red zone library. This was not so much a change in routine as it was her way when upset. She did not want to be where she would be easily found.

Her reading did little to ease her mind. The detailed report was the results of a survey that had studied literally every acre of Britain for the last forty years. The results were staggering. Their statistics showed a decline in the bird and butterfly populations of from fifty-four to up to seventy-one percent. If this pattern reflected a worldwide trend, and it appeared it might, the Earth was in the midst of another great period of extinction. It was not a comet that would be the cause this time, but the effects of the human population explosion.

A tear rolled down her face. She observed later she was not so much crying as she was feeling the sudden weight of the enormous responsibility for the protection of her planet. Earth was a blue spaceship, alone in an endless sea of darkness. And those aboard were in deep trouble. They all knew this. As Tap had stated, the information was readily available to all, but still everyone waited. Everyone shrugged and said they could do nothing.

Was Tap right that the beauty of Earth was that it was like a rose that could not last and so must be cherished while still it existed? She knew she couldn't accept that and yet like all the others, she could think of nothing she could do to stop the wilting of her world.

Courtney was drawn from her depressing thoughts by the unexpected arrival of Tap. Like the others working in the library, she stood when Tap walked in; unlike the others, her eyes flared with annoyance. She had become increasingly aware of Tap's power. She was clearly far more than the "objective" observer she insisted she was. We noted Courtney knew she was walking a narrow path, but she felt she had a point to make about the way she was prepared to be treated while she was here. "When you have a minute, we need to talk," she stated firmly.

Tap raised an eyebrow, as if she had only just become aware of Courtney's ability to articulate, then smiled softly. "Very well. You will come with me, please."

A little taken aback at Tap's willingness to comply so readily, Courtney followed. She was led to an area of the house of which she had previously been unaware. It appeared to her to be a medical centre.

Courtney had only a quick glance around before she felt suddenly faint and the world spiralled in. Her last sensation was the kettle-warmth of Tap's arms around her.

Security Report 8504
Commanding Officer: Franz Scheidt

On monitors, I watched Rugia Malwala standing at the window of her room, looking out on the private acreage that rolled down from behind Tap's complex to a double row of mature cedar hedges in the distance that concealed the security fencing. The land was planted with crops all native to the area. The produce would end up on our plates during much of the year. They were another element of Tap's varied and eclectic research. Singh handled the records for the farm and through him, Rugia had gained information both intriguing and confusing. She could not yet see the pattern to Tap's research.

Fortunately for us, trying to follow the many threads of Tap's research was proving to be a daunting and frustrating experience for Rugia Malwala. The primary research going on in the greenhouse and barns along the west side of the property was twofold: first, the creation of hybrids using the local plants and some of those from Tap's native lands, and second, experimentations in small animal reproduction techniques, particularly those of pigs.

Tap was particularly interested in pigs. Rugia's enquiries of the garden staff indicated she wanted to know why. She was well aware that meat of any sort was rarely eaten by the staff. I knew her suspicions and questions would be passed on to Gene Lamount. I also knew she would not dare to ask Lamount whether he knew more. Lamount, she was well aware, had the ear of one far more powerful than Tap.

The blue van was still parked on the hill crest. Rugia Malwala knew from security reports the occupant was Percy Dingwall. He had quit his job and taken to spying on our activities from a hilltop a half mile away. Security had advised Tap of the problem. She had ordered a detailed background check on Percy Dingwall; that was all.

Rugia Malwala looked angry and frustrated as she sat down at her personal computer console to make her daily entries. I will continue to monitor her movements.

From Our Report

We, too, knew of Rugia Malwala's interest in Percy Dingwall. We did not act. It is not our role to do so. Nor did we anticipate what would follow. Tap did not see Percy Dingwall as a threat, nor did we. We were preoccupied. This was unwise.

A short time later, we waited near Tap. The course of history was to be changed. Tap stood looking down at the naked body of Courtney Hunter with some pride of ownership. Courtney Hunter had a beautiful, well-toned body. This was good, and Lamount had assured her Courtney Hunter was in excellent health.

"This procedure, it will not cause her discomfort or any bodily harm?"

"When she regains consciousness, she should be unaware the procedure has taken place," Gene Lamount murmured, as he checked that the necessary materials had been laid out.

Tap nodded. "Proceed," she stated and walked out. We stayed.

We notified Tap as soon as we sensed Courtney Hunter was awake. She woke and blinked in surprise. She was now lying back in her bed in Tap's quarters. She turned her head and looked around. In the corner was all her cargo, including her small tent, now rolled up neatly. What had happened? Fear washed over reason as she threw back the sheet and checked for any physical marks. She had all her fingers and toes; they hadn't taken blood; she was completely dressed; so what had happened and why was she here?

As if in answer to her thoughts a knock came at her door. "Yes?"

"It is Tap."

"Please, come in."

Tap walked in quietly and stood beside Courtney's bed. "You are well? You became unconscious when we entered the lab. I have been concerned. The doctor feels that you are all right, but I am glad to see you awake." Truth is little more than a lie when information is withheld.

"I passed out?" Tap did not answer but Courtney was not expecting her to. "That's unusual. I've never done anything like that before. Why is my tent here?"

"I ordered it removed. Just in case you are not well, you should not be sleeping so roughly. Also, I admit that I want you to stay here. It is a more convenient arrangement." This too was truth, but the reasons behind the statement remained obscured. Tap hoped Courtney would comply without making things difficult for her.

Courtney lay back, trying to make sense of the missing time. Nothing seemed too clear in her mind at the moment; perhaps she was sick. Frustrated, her annoyance at being kicked out of the meeting returned. "We never talked. Can we now?"

"Yes," Tap responded, trying not to show her unease.

"I was embarrassed that I got thrown out of the meeting. I was one of the first to show support for you and I've followed your leadership without question because of our agreement, but I'm not a fool. It's clear that there's a lot more going on here than I know about, and I'm angry at being left in the dark, and increasingly concerned that there are things going on of which I might not want to be a part."

Tap considered her words carefully. She was walking a very narrow line now and she could not afford even the smallest mistake. "I did not mean to make you uncomfortable, Court. But you must understand that there have been projects underway here for a long time and that, because of the nature of our work, we are privy to a lot of top secret information. We must be careful. My instinct tells me I can trust you, but my head has to remember to follow security procedures to the letter. There will be a time in the future when more will be revealed to you. For now, you need to trust that when I tell you I mean you no harm and I am not involved in the violation of any international laws, I am telling you the truth."

Courtney nodded slowly but her eyes remained sad and worried.

It was nearly a week later when Courtney realized she was in very big trouble. Tap had told her they would be leaving for Geneva to observe a conference of the World Health Organization in a few days time, and Courtney wanted to leave everything in order when they left. She thought she would also see what the local library had on the World Health Organization and was surprised when her card number was not accepted by the computer. She then tried to access her bank accounts — nothing. She tried her apartment phone number. A voice told her the number was no longer in service. She phoned the landlord and asked about herself, pretending to be a long lost friend. "She moved out the end of the month. Her friends that came to clean her apartment out said she got a job overseas in one of them developing nations." We felt fear clutch at Courtney's heart as she lowered the receiver to the cradle. She was a prisoner.

Chapter Twelve

"Not every truth is the better for showing its face undisguised."

~ Pindar

From Our Report

We followed Courtney Hunter's reasoning with interest as she paced around her small office, trying to work out what she should do. She considered escaping and felt she could, but decided they would undoubtedly track her down. They had infinite resources and contacts and she had next to none. She could call 911 and have the police rescue her. She had a funny feeling that by the time they arrived, there would be no trace of Courtney Hunter and the police would be made satisfied with whatever story was given to them.

No, she would have to bide her time and pretend she suspected nothing as she quietly gathered information. Once she knew what was going on there, the better her chances would be of working out how to get out of the situation. But what about Tap? Could she go on sharing quarters with someone who was deliberately deceiving her and holding her prisoner? For a few days, she could avoid Tap by saying she was not well, but then what? Courtney bit her lip and tried not to cry. Courtney Hunter's reasoning was flawless until she allowed emotion to interfere. We do not understand emotion.

Around noon, a message from Tap flashed on Courtney Hunter's computer screen. "You will please join me for lunch in the red zone library so we can discuss issues."

To our surprise, Courtney typed back, "Can we leave it and talk later? I'm not feeling well today." Tears of fear escaped her eyes and she wiped them away. Giving in to panic, we knew she had realized, was not going to get her out of this situation. The problem was far more involved than just discovering she was a prisoner. She had wanted to trust Tap. She had chosen to trust her and to care for her, and now felt betrayed. This information we found both shocking and fascinating. Courtney Hunter took a minute or two to compose herself, then went back to her work.

Naturally, it was only a few minutes later when Haichen walked into her office. "You are not well, Court?"

Courtney looked up in surprise into a very worried face. Unlike us, she hadn't expected them to react with concern. At that time, she did not realize why she was important to Tap. She reasoned she had passed out the other day so it would be understandable for Tap to be worried. She gave a weak laugh, trying to sound natural. "It's okay, Haichen, I...I...I'm just having a bad period." A second later, she felt her world swirl and she passed out.

Tap paced about, looking extremely upset. Haichen stood off in a corner, trying not to be noticed. She did not want that anger directed at her. The inner door opened and Gene Lamount stepped out.

"Well?" Tap demanded, turning to face him with eyes as cold as a glacier.

Gene shrugged. "She is not having a period and appears to be in excellent health." To be truthful, he was greatly relieved Courtney was not ill. He, too, respected Tap's temper. He tried not to show that fear in front of Haichen, who stood pale and worried in the corner.

"She lied?"

"It would appear so," Lamount responded, not liking where the interrogation was going.

"Why?" Tap demanded, now looking just as confused as she was annoyed.

Lamount glanced at Haichen as he shifted nervously from foot to foot. Haichen gave the slightest shake of her head. "I do not know. I can only report that, happily, Courtney Hunter is in excellent health." He could feel the sweat trickling down his back.

Tap paced the room and came to a stop in front of Lamount. "You will run the tests again to be sure. You are to keep Court well, is that understood?"

Lamount swallowed convulsively. "Yes, Tap."

"Go," Tap muttered, releasing him from her penetrating stare and resuming her pacing. Lamount again looked across the room at Haichen, then he executed a quick retreat.

Tap waited until he had gone and then turned to face Haichen. "She lied so she could avoid me, did she not?" Tap asked bluntly.

"Perhaps," Haichen answered cautiously.

"Go," she growled, which Haichen was very glad to do.

Tap, we advise caution.
Things are going badly.
Courtney Hunter is too unpredictable.

Once again Courtney regained consciousness in Tap's quarters. This time we waited with Haichen, who was there when she awoke. "Hi, Court. Are you feeling better?"

"I passed out again?" Courtney asked, feeling the cold ice of dread seeping into her gut. She wondered what were they doing to her.

"Yes. It might be the strain," Haichen suggested. "You have been working very hard, really doing two jobs rather than one."

"That might be the case," Courtney agreed, although she did not actually believe it for a minute.

Haichen looked relieved that Courtney seemed to accept the suggested explanation so readily. "Tap wanted me to express her concerns and to let you know she will meet with you tomorrow night, if you feel up to it." Deception is sometimes used to protect as well as deceive.

"Yes, of course," Courtney agreed quickly. She knew she would have to play along. She would have a much better chance of escaping somewhere safe once she was away from this house. Tap would not have so many people at her disposal. It was a relief to know Tap would not be around for the rest of the day, but how she was going to handle the situation in Geneva, she was not sure.

As soon as Haichen left, Courtney got up and once again checked herself all over for any indications she had been used in any sort of lab experiment. There was no evidence, yet she felt uneasy. She was almost sure, now, she was not passing out, but rather somehow she was being knocked out. The questions remained, how and why?

We observed Courtney spent the remainder of the day scouring the computer system for any lead to explain what was going on and why she was being held by these people. There were literally thousands of documents, but nothing indicated a mandate or program involving her. It was late that night, as she lay alone in her quarters wide awake, that she realized the answer was probably not in the main database to which she had access, but in the small security room and lab through which Tap had taken her.

She got up quickly, dressed, and made her way to the doorway through which Tap had first escorted her. As she stood in front of it, the door slid open immediately. Entering, she looked about the small room with interest. The equipment looked different from any computer system she had ever seen. She moved closer and looked at a screen of data. It made no sense to her. Cautiously, she started to open data files, looking for something she could use to help her escape.

We were concerned, yet we could not interfere. Our role is to advise, not to change the course of events.

The computer screen contained mostly a jumble of symbols that she could not decipher but eventually, by sheer luck and perseverance, she stumbled on a file of correspondence to Tap. Courtney's hands were sweating and she wiped them on her jeans. There were emails from some of the most significant figures in the world about issues with which Tap had clearly helped them by opening dialogue and/or providing data that would lead to better understanding. Tap seemed to be exactly what she had told Courtney she was — an objective observer most of the time and a facilitator on request.

Courtney could feel the heat rising in her face. Tap and the work she did was top secret, and Courtney had blundered in and demanded information as if she had a right. Courtney Hunter felt she could now see why information was being withheld from her. She could even see why she was a security risk. We hoped this would satisfy her curiosity. It did not. What she could not see was why that necessitated the cancelling of all her accounts, her life.

Then a brief memo popped up that made her heart pound. It was a request for the termination of Courtney Hunter. Tap had casually emailed back that termination was not appropriate at that time.

"What are you doing in here?"

Courtney turned to see Tap standing in the doorway. We were relieved.

Courtney's heart skipped a beat but she held her ground bravely. She had nothing to lose now. Whether now or later, they meant to kill her. "Looking for answers. You've lied to me over and over. I know I'm a prisoner. I know my life has been erased and you plan to kill me. I want to know who you are and what you are up to, and why I'm being held as a prisoner until you feel like killing me."

"I do not wish to kill you. It is not possible, at this time, to answer your questions. I have asked you to trust me," Tap said with some annoyance, moving to stand in front of Courtney.

"Back off," Courtney snapped.

Anger flashed across Tap's face and for a second Courtney thought she might be struck, then Tap took one step back.

"You are not having a period. Why did you make an excuse not to meet with me?" Tap heard herself asking in a voice edged with angry frustration.

"Look, Tap, I admit I was fascinated by you, but I'm not some sixteen year old with no common sense. I have some intelligence and a hell of a lot of pride, and I'm not getting involved with a liar and God knows what else. Shit! You mean to kill me."

Tap's face was hard with tense muscles. Her eyes were dark with anger. "Ian." Courtney turned to see Ian standing in the doorway of the lab behind her. "Take Court away. She is to be detained until I decide how I wish to proceed."

Courtney dived for the door behind Tap, but strong arms grabbed her and held her in a gentle but tight embrace. "Do not be afraid. You are safe; you will not be harmed. I ask again that you trust me. There is so much that you do not know."

Courtney felt her arms being pulled back behind her back and secured by Ian with plastic strip handcuffs as Tap held her. "Then tell me, damn it!" Courtney yelled.

"No," was the curt reply as Courtney was dragged away.

Tap, things are out of control.

She behaves badly.

This is not acceptable.

Tap stood looking moodily at the screen Courtney had been reading. Courtney Hunter had proven herself to be intelligent, creative, and determined. She had the qualities Tap felt she needed, but they were also the very qualities that made her a difficult individual to handle. She nodded slowly and, having calmed herself, followed in Ian and Courtney's wake.

Courtney lay on a narrow bunk in a small cell. Tap indicated the door should be opened and she stepped in. Ian hesitated. "Yes, lock it." Ian quickly did so and then left them alone.

"Am I to be interrogated?" Courtney asked, looking up at Tap from where she now sat on her bed, trying not to show her fear.

Tap looked confused. "Of course not. You do not know anything worthwhile."

"Thanks!" Courtney snarled, standing up and pacing away from the taller woman.

"Would it make you feel better if I question you?"

Courtney sighed in annoyed frustration and brushed the hair from her forehead. "Tap, what's going on? I want to know why you're holding me."

"You have qualities that I want...in my organization. I do not mean to stress you by withholding information. I do not want you stressed. But there are things going on that are of far greater import than you realize. You have gone through some of my files. If those people choose to trust me, then why can you not?"

"Maybe they don't know that you terminate people," Courtney growled.

Honour is everything, but there are times when honour must be tempered by practicality. Tap chose to lie. "You have misunderstood, Court," she said calmly. "The message is referring to me firing you, not to my ordering the taking of your life. I think you have been watching too many gangster shows. Whatever you have convinced yourself happens here, it is far from the truth. There are some who rightfully feel that you have been a very troublesome employee of late and you should be dismissed."

Courtney went a deep red as she realized her fear had made her put an unduly dramatic interpretation on the message. No, she must not doubt herself. "What about the fact that my apartment has been emptied and my accounts closed? Even my library card is no good. Damn it, Tap, my library card," she repeated, her voice breaking.

Tap took a step closer but Courtney stepped away, crying more from frustration than from fear now. Tap thought quickly. Lying is not as easy as it seems. "I should have explained. It did not occur to me that you would make enquiries outside this establishment. You know you are in the process of being retrained. Part of that process, in order to protect you, is to create a new identity for you. You must trust me, as so many others do."

"Am I stuck being someone else forever then?" Courtney asked, wiping away tears with her sleeve.

"Our agreement is only until the end of your training period," Tap evaded. Tap moved forward slowly and, steeling herself, gave Courtney a brief touch. Physical contact, she knew, was comforting. Then she indicated that Courtney Hunter should sit on the bed. Tap sat down beside her.

For a long time there was silence while Courtney considered what Tap had said. Gradually, we felt her small body relaxing. Finally, Courtney straightened and wiped her eyes. "Is that all there is, Tap?" she asked.

"No. There is much more, but it is as much as I can say at this time." This was an honest answer, yet misleading all the same.

"I feel like a fool."

"You acted with great daring and intelligence, but you are very pigheaded, my Courtney Hunter."

The words had been said softly and with pride. The word "my" had not been one of ownership but of affection and respect, we noted with surprise. Courtney felt herself weakening. She had only Tap's word for all of this and yet it seemed so plausible an explanation. She had to admit she wanted to believe.

"One month, right?"

Tap nodded but said nothing.

The pain Percy Dingwall felt was excruciating. His skin blistered and his internal organs fried slowly. He had always fantasized if he was ever captured by the enemy, he would tell them nothing. He would die alone, with his secrets — a hero and martyr. Instead, after the first lance of pain he'd babbled like a baby, telling them anything they wanted to know.

All his life he had wanted to have people listen to him, to take his ideas and insights seriously. Now they were. The pain was worth the price of knowing he had been right. What he thought and knew was very important to others. Enough so they were prepared to torture him to death to get every bit of information out of him. The pain became part of him. It was dreadful and yet exciting, knowing it was because he was so important. It made him hard. When they finally stopped and he slowly sank into oblivion, his body was barely recognizable as his. Yet there was a smile on his lips.

Chapter Thirteen

"I want to go ahead of Father Time with a scythe of my own."

~ H. G. Wells

From Our Report

Courtney Hunter tried not to laugh. This was a sign that she was extremely stressed. After the strain of the previous day, she was feeling highly strung. Once again she had decided to set aside her better judgement and believe in Tap. This was a relief to us. It was important that Courtney Hunter stay calm. Believing Tap, we knew, was not a comfortable decision this time. The bottom line, as Courtney Hunter expressed it, was that all sorts of bells and whistles were going off in her head, warning her she was in big trouble, but her heart wanted to believe in Tap.

Courtney Hunter's mother would have said that pounding hearts drown out common sense. Her eyes would have sparkled when she said it and she would have looked at her husband, Courtney's father, with love and devotion. Her parents had dared to love and to live a Bohemian lifestyle, regardless of what others thought. We found this concept both appealing and illogical.

Tap was no Bohemian. We knew she was not soft and gentle like Courtney Hunter's parents. Not that she wasn't always polite and considerate, but there was an animal strength about Tap, an air of authority and danger that made others find her fascinating, sexy, and scary, all at once.

Courtney Hunter knew Tap was not her friend. She was her boss, her instructor, her jailer, and a woman with many secrets. Yet, we were surprised to sense Courtney Hunter cared for Tap.

We knew Tap would set aside any personal feelings for the good of her people. Illogically, we had come to realize Tap was also encouraging her own personal feelings, and those of others, for the good of her people. These were difficult and confusing times.

We noted the attributes of grim authority were not in evidence the next night.

Tap had been busy all day but called on Courtney that evening. She had led her, while they engaged in civil if stilted conversation, through the house to the courtyard. There, Tap had ordered set up a small table, complete with candlelight, and had soft music piped in. She'd ordered a meal for them. Tap was wining and dining

Courtney, as they say, and the whole situation, after the revelations of the day before, seemed to us absurd.

With formal dignity, Tap invited Courtney to sit and then poured two glasses of juice before taking her own seat. "I wish to make amends," Tap stated seriously.

From Courtney Hunter's Logs

I bit my lip so as not to laugh. Tap was attempting, rather obviously, to smooth the troubled waters between us in her intense, formal way. "I might have overreacted," I conceded. My heart felt this was so, although I admit my mind was still thinking defensively and considering escape. The human mind is quite capable of easily maintaining contradictory beliefs.

We ate and discussed some of the research I'd been doing. One thing led to another and I found myself telling Tap stories of my early childhood travelling with my parents. Tap listened with rapt attention to stories of sun-baked mesas, soaring mountains, and art colonies on rugged ocean shores. I'm sure for Tap it was a real and personal excursion into a world that she understood only through data. I had no doubt she would file away everything I told her in that amazing memory of hers.

We played racquet ball later, each keeping our competitive nature in check. I really enjoyed the camaraderie, and yet was suspicious of it. Tap must be up to something for which she needed my cooperation. I was amazed when Tap's stiff, formal manner seemed to melt away as she wholeheartedly entered into the spirit of the game. She was a good racquet ball player. I suspected Tap was holding back to make the game more evenly matched.

"You have enjoyed the evening?" Tap asked as we walked back to our quarters.

"Yes. Thank you."

I took my leave of Tap and showered in the privacy of my own bathroom. Once in my pyjamas, I laid on my bed in deep thought. When I was near Tap, the force of Tap's quiet confidence removed many of the doubts from my mind. Tap was charismatic. That made her a natural leader and dangerous foe. For me, the evening had brought the realization I wanted to be loyal to Tap. I wanted my boss's respect and confidence, and that was why I allowed myself to believe everything was all right when the worms of doubt told me otherwise. An ability to sway those that would doubt is the mark of a great leader. Tap was born to lead.

From Our Report

For Tap, the experience of the evening was first about trust, letting someone close, giving up the power, if only for a little while. Gene Lamount had advised her it was important that she and Courtney Hunter become friends. Friendship was not an experience Tap had been able to enjoy in her life. With power comes isolation. Friendship was about feelings so new, so strong, and so personal, Tap was left quite shaken and exhausted by the evening.

We are unsure.

Friendship means trust.

Trust can be betrayed.

For a long time Tap lay awake thinking over the evening. It had been carefully planned with input from Lamount and Haichen. The evening had gone well and hopefully had bridged some of the mistrust between Courtney Hunter and herself. Lamount was convinced that this was important to the success of the endeavour. Tap was not as sure. Friendship could be used against her as well as for her. However, time was short, and there was only one chance for success. Any machinations that might increase the chances of success were worth taking. To her surprise, she had found as the evening wore on she was actually enjoying herself.

The next day, Tap and Courtney Hunter sat side by side in the first class section of a commercial airliner. Each felt a little awkward as the parameters of their relationship had now shifted slightly.

"Tap?"

"Hmmm."

"About last night..."

Tap looked over with deep green eyes filled with gentle anxiety. "You did not enjoy yourself?"

"Of course I did, Tap, but...well...I was surprised. I mean...I didn't realize that you'd want me as a friend, and I'm still not sure what role I'm to play in your organization.

Tap looked at Courtney with an amused but perplexed look. "I have few friends. Friendship is important. I need to take time now and again for recreation. It took some time to come to this decision. I felt it was an unusual but necessary step for me. I enjoyed my evening and hope we can have others. But you must remember, Courtney Hunter, that I am your employer and the leader of many. Do not forget to show respect and defer to my authority when we are not alone."

"Yes, Tap," Courtney responded obediently, though with a mischievous grin, and was rewarded with one of Tap's rare but beautiful smiles.

Courtney tried to concentrate on her research. The author was trying to make a comparison between the plight of the worker in the late Industrial Revolution and the trends for the future for the echo generation, the children of the baby boomers. In the Victorian Age, many workers had part-time rather than full time jobs. Today, part-time employment was up twenty-four percent and growing at a rate three times faster than full time employment. In the late 1880s, more people were self-employed in small "cottage industries" than worked in the new factory settings. At the turn of the millennium, self-employment was up forty-three percent and, like a hundred years earlier, these jobs were primarily located in homes. Today, more people had more than one job in order to subsist, just like in the old days, and companies again were demanding longer hours and more work output for lower wages. Late in the flight, Courtney sighed, slipped her data pilot into her briefcase, and settled down with her head on her pillow. She wasn't really asleep, just drifting, enjoying the chance to relax. This we did not realize and we did not immediately monitor her thoughts.

She sleeps.

We will speak.

Our voice must be heard.

"Go ahead," Tap instructed us.

Later we realized Courtney Hunter had heard us. She also wondered whether anyone else heard the voices. She peeked out from under the blanket Tap had wrapped around her. All she could see was the back of the seat. Who were the three people who ran this mysterious security system of Tap's?

Events are changing too rapidly.

Your friendship is not acceptable.

Trust can be dangerous.

"Perhaps. But there is no other way. Time has run out," Tap replied.

She is not one of us.

She lacks intelligence.

She has no culture and little awareness.

"I am committed to the use of Courtney Hunter. There is no other way. Establishing a friendship means obtaining her cooperation. Go."

Courtney must have forced herself to keep her eyes shut and her breathing regular. Her report indicated she felt as if she was just another one of Tap's studies. She wondered how many lies had she been told by people she thought condescending.

These thoughts we did not access until later. It would not matter. We advised. We did not interfere with the course of events.

They touched down in Geneva and Courtney busied herself with getting her few things together. She followed Tap out, a look of studied calm on her face.

"You are okay, Court?" Tap asked, looking at her with worried eyes as they passed through Customs on their diplomatic passports.

"Fine, thanks. Just a little tired," she lied. She knew that Tap's security personnel, Franz and Rugia, were already ahead of them. She would not have much of a window to make her escape, yet it was imperative she do so.

She handed her phony passport to the Customs officer and watched calmly as he checked her information on the computer screen in front of him. She wondered what lies about her past he was being told. How much English did he know? Could she ask him for help, tell him that she was being held a prisoner? No, that would not get her anywhere but into more trouble. Tap had power and credibility; she had none. Her story would not be believed and she was sure Tap would have a reasonable explanation for Court's strange behaviour.

She took back her passport with a weak smile and joined Tap. Together, they walked through the maze of corridors until they entered the crowded main concourse of the airport. Courtney thought about making a break for it, but before she could, Tap took her arm and steered her through the crowds to the Arrivals door.

The glass doors slid open and, stepping out, Courtney saw the limousine pull out and move towards them. She acted before the thought had even completely registered, throwing her briefcase into Tap's face and darting out into the heavy airport traffic. Cars honked and slammed on brakes as she dodged across four busy lanes. Ahead of her, a cement wall separated her from a lower level road.

There was no time to consider caution. This was her only chance. Blindly, she vaulted the metal railing and dropped right in front of an oncoming truck. It slammed into her at hip level and threw her back over the rail, where she bounced onto the pavement and was struck by the front wheel of a taxi as it swerved into the railing.

Tap saw it all as if in slow motion. Her heart contracted with fear and without a second thought, she charged out into the mess of screeching brakes, car horns, and curses. "Court! Court!" Tap pushed the shaken taxi driver aside and slid onto her belly to reach Courtney, who lay partly under the car. Courtney was covered in blood, her body ripped and distorted by shattered bones. A pool of red spread quickly beneath her. There was so much damage, it was almost impossible to know where to apply pressure. Tap didn't need to be told Courtney was dying. "Court," Tap groaned.

Courtney's eyes opened and looked into Tap's and her lips moved. Tap leaned close to hear, "You lied to me."

Tap's face hardened in determination. With hands now scarlet with blood, she held Courtney's face and looked into her eyes. "Trust me!" Tap insisted.

We were shaken by these sudden events. We felt Courtney's new world of pain tunneling toward death as she found herself floating, drifting through a tranquil current. The noise around her disappeared and the pain that lanced through her body vanished. The next second, she was walking out of the airport again. She saw the limousine pull out to meet them, then Tap's hand clamped painfully around the wrist that held her briefcase. Before Courtney could even process the contradictory information, she had been pushed across the back seat of the limousine and heard Tap yelling to the driver to get them out of there.

We monitored her thoughts. *Am I dead? Is this some sort of dream within a coma that I drifted into?* She fought against Tap for all she was worth. *This whole thing is wrong. All of it.* "Let me go, damn you! Let me go!" Tap held her in an iron grip with ease. Her face was expressionless, only her eyes — dark pools of worry — revealed her emotion.

"You will be quiet, Court, or I will have to knock you out," she commanded.

Courtney stopped fighting Tap and lay quietly, not out of obedience but because she needed to regroup and figure out what was happening to her. Try as she might, the pieces would just not go together. With grim determination, she fought down the panic welling inside her. She had been hit by a vehicle, she knew that. She had seen it at the last second, when it was too late to save herself. She had felt the pain of the impact and felt herself thrown through the air as lightly as a feather. Then came the second and the third impacts as she bounced on the pavement and was hit again, sending explosions of pain even through the blackness of her unconscious mind. It had been Tap's voice calling her name that had made her fight back through the agony.

She had seen the horror in Tap's face, heard the confusion around her, then... What then? It was all a mass of undefined sensations, like an abstract picture, until she found herself walking out of the airport again. *I must be in an ambulance, not a limo. I must be dreaming. Maybe they have given me something for the pain. I'm badly hurt, aren't I?*

Nothing was making sense. Tap was still lying on her, holding her down with Court's hands held firmly over her head.

"You are hurting me," Court said softly. Tap looked down at her with concern. Those amazing aqua eyes were the last image Courtney saw for a long time.

Chapter Fourteen

"Birth and death are so closely related that one could not destroy either without destroying the other at the same time. It is extinction that makes creation possible."

~ Samuel Butler

From Our Report

Courtney woke for a change in a conventional bed. She was aware of only two things. First, she was naked beneath the bed sheet, and second, she was not alone. Her eyes shifted to her right. Sitting stiffly on a chair beside her bed was Tap. Tap looked tired and deeply upset.

Courtney lay still for a minute, trying to piece things together. Had she had a nightmare? She could feel no pain. She looked down at what she could see of her body above the bed sheet. No cuts or bruises. But the memory of being very badly injured was terrifyingly clear in her mind. Her eyes shifted again towards Tap. Serious aqua eyes dulled by exhaustion looked back at her.

"How do you feel?" Tap asked.

"Well, but very confused," Courtney managed to answer calmly, although she was feeling anything but.

"I need to talk to you. Please do not try to escape. It would be a pointless effort. You will be under constant guard from now on."

"I've escaped before," Courtney needled.

"You only escaped from a room, not the compound. This time they might kill you. I do not wish that to happen." Tap stood up in one quick and graceful movement, like a cat springing. For a second, she paced at the end of the bed and then stopped and faced Courtney. "I do not recall ever being really scared in my life until today. I have been scared enough today for a lifetime."

"I was hit by several vehicles, wasn't I?" Courtney asked, a fear growing inside her as she realized that she was involved in something that had no rules and no common experiences to fall back on.

"Yes."

"I thought I was hurt badly."

Tap squared her shoulders and looked Courtney in the eyes. "You were hurt fatally. You were only moments from death. I chose to step back in time and change the course of events."

Courtney's eyes got round with shock and panic. We were concerned. She thought she was being held prisoner by a mad woman who thought she could play God. Carefully, she moved her arms and legs. No pain. Everything worked. She felt up and down her body, no casts or bandages.

"You are drugging me, confusing my mind with scenarios that never happened. I couldn't have been hit by a car; I haven't got a scratch on me. I don't know what you want, but I have no information that could be the least bit of use to you."

"I am not drugging you; I am telling you the truth," Tap stated, frustration edging her voice. It had been the worst day of her life, we knew, and Tap had seen many dark days. Today, Tap learned she cared for Courtney Hunter. That realization had come almost too late. Courtney Hunter's actions had, in just seconds, jeopardized the entire endeavour. But more than that, Tap had felt depths of emotion that she had never before experienced.

Courtney snorted. "You wouldn't know the truth if you stepped on it. Everything you've told me from day one has been a lie."

Tap turned away and tried very hard to keep her temper. "I want you to listen to me. You humans think you see flying saucers and little green men from Mars. We talked about this once. You know as well as I do that the vast distances between this planet and others would make such travel impossible. Even a message travelling near the speed of light could not cover such distances in hundreds of years — in this dimension."

"What are you talking about?" Courtney snapped. She wanted to get up and run. We held her in place, gently but firmly. "Damn your Security. They're holding me down."

Suddenly Courtney Hunter went quiet, remembering she had no clothes on and not knowing for sure if she'd find any in the closet. Fear was creeping into her heart. For the first time, we sensed, she realized we were beings and not a mechanical system. She turned and seemed to strain her eyes to see us.

Tap sighed and tried again. "There are many dimensions, more than humans can yet conceptualize. In other dimensions, space and time are easily traversed."

"This human is aware of Einstein's theory of General Relativity, despite your low opinion of my intelligence," Courtney said with some sarcasm, folding her arms and glowering at Tap. "I have also heard of string theory. I'm confused enough with what's happening here; I don't need this crap dumped on me."

Her thoughts showed more fear than her brave words.

The sarcasm seemingly lost on her, Tap nodded, looking somewhat relieved. "My natural environment is in another dimension."

Courtney's eyebrows knotted in an annoyed frown. "You are telling me...you are an alien?"

Tap cringed. "I am a species that has a different origin than you, yes."

Courtney snorted and rolled her eyes. "Let me guess — you're really some sort of space monster and I'm about to find out I've been working for some kinky space lizard."

"I am *not* a lizard!" Tap snarled in anger. "How dare you. Just the opposite is true. I have been employing an animal."

Courtney picked up the clock radio from the side table, tore out the plug, and heaved it at Tap's head. Tap ducked and spun. She reached out her hand and just before the radio could crash into the wall, it stopped. Then it slowly moved backwards through time. Courtney could feel her breaths returning to her body. Slowly, the clock moved back along its path. Courtney felt as if she was in the frames of a video on slow rewind. The clock entered Courtney's outstretched hand and she watched as she lowered the clock to its original position; Courtney's hand put the plug back in place and then came to rest at her side.

"I repeat, I am not a lizard. I have no idea why humans insist on making other species into such disgusting forms. You are an animal. Your kind lived on the savannah. Five million years ago, you were a scavenger who had no more intelligence than it takes to knock two rocks together to make a hand axe. Despite that, we saw promise and started a seeding process."

"What?" Courtney asked, trying to take things in. Her mind was on such overload as a result of these events that all she wanted to do was sit in a quiet corner somewhere and try to pretend none of it had ever happened. Denial is very much a coping trait of humans, but not a very effective one.

"Millions of years ago, Earth time, we started to change your genetic coding, making you more like us. We were facing... problems, even then. We thought by introducing our genetic code into other species, we could create life as we knew it. That policy was aborted many years ago, seen as a dismal failure. We had some most unfortunate incidents on other planets. The variables are just too great and our genetics can place unrealistic strains on lower creatures. We didn't know then that genetic programming was not just unique to a species but that planetary life is genetically programmed to suit the planet.

"It would seem, however, that having started the process on Earth, it has continued unassisted with some amazing results. Because of Earth's remoteness, it was only when I was sent here that I realized that Earth might be the exception, the one success among hundreds of failures."

"Tap, this sounds like a science fiction B movie. You don't expect me to buy into this, do you?"

As we noted, Courtney's mind had decided the best way to handle all the contradictory data of the day was simply to go into denial: she had never been hit by a truck; she had never travelled through time; the clock had not flown backwards; and she was not the product of a laboratory experiment in genetics by some lizard race. Denial helped stop her head from spinning. We found this most interesting, but not productive.

"If you're so superior, like some Dr. Who, Time Lord, what are you doing bothering with me, or this planet?" Courtney challenged. From Courtney's perspective, there were so many holes in Tap's story it looked like Swiss cheese. Such similes are commonly used in expressing difficult concepts on Earth.

Tap felt the heat rise in her face and for a long time she stood staring at a wall, trying to find answers. When she spoke, it was with an effort to keep her emotions in check. "Just before you...I mean, at the airport, I was holding you, trying to hear your voice. Y...You said I had lied to you. Yes, I have Court. You were not ready to hear the truth. You still are not, but there is no other choice."

Courtney's heart skipped a beat. She had said that. She remembered now, lying in Tap's arms and needing Tap to know she knew she'd been lied to before she died. It was her turn to blush. "Of all your lies, this is the most unbelievable."

Tap seemed to slump in defeat. "You do not accept what I am saying, then, even though I have shown you time moving backwards?"

"A parlour trick, I suspect, or a drug-induced hallucination."

"What can I do to convince you?"

"Nothing. Your story has only complicated things. I don't see much future in working with someone who thinks she's an alien and thinks of me as an animal to be studied," Courtney stated, anger and hurt lacing her voice. The confusion within Courtney Hunter, we realized, was fuelling her anger.

We sensed Tap was near her breaking point. It should be noted Tap had experienced just as much data overload that day as Courtney. Courtney, though, was used to dealing with emotional surges; for Tap, these were uncharted waters. It is difficult even still for Tap to completely understand why she chose to take the course of action she did. "I need you to accept what I am telling you because my fate, and the fate of my people, rests with you."

For a second, a silence fell on the room as the two women absorbed the enormity of this simple statement. Then Tap sat beside Courtney's bed again. She reached out and took one of Courtney Hunter's hands. We were shocked.

"I was never so scared in my life. There was blood everywhere. I knew I was going to lose you and I could not risk that. You are our last hope. And...and I care about you. So I chose instead to change the course of events. I need you healthy. There are reasons...but that is not all. I did it because I think you and your planet hold the answer to the problems of my people. I did it because I am amazed by the qualities that this planet is developing in us. And I did it because I have come to like and respect you, and I did not want you to die as a result of my actions."

Courtney was pale with stress. With a shaky hand she reached out and touched Tap's warm skin. "Is this the way you really look?" she asked.

Tap took hold of both her hands and the next instant they were part of an endless sea. Their life forces intertwined, flowed through each other, a part of each other and a part of us, then they were back in the room.

Courtney bit her lip, trying to chart the wild emotional ride she was on. "You're part of an energy force, like a sea of hot tides? Like the pictures in your room?"

Tap smiled encouragingly. "Sometimes. Yes. We have a planet like yours, too."

"So, can you morph into anything?"

Tap tried not to smile. "No, not really. As infinite as the possible combinations are, there are limits to the abilities of carbon-based life forms. Courtney nodded, her façade of bravado starting to crumble.

Tap sighed and leaned back in her chair. "If I promise you that there is no lizard blood in my family and that I have never been a worm-like alien, would you feel more comfortable? I need you to believe me."

Courtney's answer was to burst into tears. We did not know how to advise Tap.

"This is ludicrous," Courtney sobbed, near to hysteria. "You are threatening to kill me if I leave this room. I've come back from the dead, and I'm talking to someone who thinks she's an alien and that I'm a stupid, mouth-breathing primate. And I haven't even had lunch yet."

Tap awkwardly patted Courtney's shoulder. Gentle physical contact seemed to provide comfort to humans, Tap knew. She could not yet admit she needed to touch Courtney Hunter to reassure herself, as well. "We have not dealt with humans in a very long time. I admit we had biases. I know that I have learned much from you, Courtney Hunter. I no longer believe that humans lack intelligence or cultural awareness. You have very different world views and thought processes, that is all."

"And I'm not an animal either," Courtney Hunter stated firmly. She was acting irrationally, she knew, but she had reached her capacity. Everything she believed in, her whole concept of reality, had just changed. We had cautioned Tap this would be the case. She would not listen. Now there were few options left to us.

"Actually, you are an animal, but a highly evolved one," Tap corrected in all seriousness.

"Yeah, well what are you if you aren't a lizard?" Courtney demanded through her tears. "Listen to me. I'm talking as if you *are* an alien now. I'm losing it."

Tap stiffened with indignation. "Unlike humans, we have been a highly developed, intelligent life form for millions of years," she said formally. "Our origins are obscure."

"Ah! You and your voices talk about me like I'm a lab rat. You think nothing about ordering my termination. There is no doubt in my mind, you lot are cold blooded and slithered off a rock somewhere. Oh, shit, how did I ever get caught up in all this?"

We sensed Tap was a bundle of contradictory emotions herself by this point. She was angry at Courtney's insults directed at her species, concerned Courtney would become sick because she was so upset, and frustrated by her inability to make Courtney believe her. Tap attempted to comfort her.

"Court, I know this is very difficult for you to take in all at once, but I do need you to try to calm down. This is not good for you in your condition."

"What do you mean, my condition? I was hurt, after all?" Courtney asked as she blinked back tears and looked at Tap with real fear.

"You have been honoured. You are carrying my child," Tap stated calmly.

The shock wave that shot through Courtney Hunter's body impacted against us. It took us a split second to react. By then, Courtney Hunter had attacked Tap, punching and clawing at her.

For the good of all three of them, we were forced to render Courtney unconscious once again.

Chapter Fifteen

"Insurrection is an art, and like all arts has its own laws."
~ Leon Trotsky

From Our Report

We observed. We listened. Torgga Appala Punra stood perfectly still. Around him he could feel the pure life force of his people. It helped to calm him. Calm was essential for clear thinking. He should have killed his sister Tay long ago. The people loved her, but she could have had an unfortunate accident. Instead, he had sent his rebellious sister as far away as possible, on a mission that had no significance, until now.

Now everything had changed. He should have known Tay would use the few resources at her disposal to achieve her goals. But what were those goals? His spies knew little — only that Tay had taken a human into her organization. A woman. There was only shame in this. Even if Tay were to launch an insurrection, who would follow her if her allies were these primitive life forms? The thought of his sister associating with one of those animals turned his stomach. He had been told the humans' distant cousins, the chimpanzees, were all hairy, had huge incisors, and swung from trees.

The seeding program begun millions of years ago was to help other promising life forms advance to a level where they could be useful neighbours. The idea was built on the erroneous hypothesis that other life forms were capable of developing culture and values. This had not proved to be so. His people had had to prove their superiority in numerous wars over thousands of years. Now another seeded area was threatening to be a nuisance, but this time Tay Appala Punra was there.

We feel your stress.

Can we help?

We are here to guide.

"Tell me what my sister is up to," Torgga demanded.

This is not our role.

We do not report.

We only offer wisdom.

Torgga's anger shattered the peace he had been labouring to bring to his soul. "I am a Tap! I *am* wise. What I need is information. Go!"

As you wish.
We are not far,
If we are needed.

"Kaysolna." Torgga felt the brush of another current of life close to him.

"Yes."

"I want to know everything my sister knows about these ape-people of planet Earth. Have your security personnel contact Rugia Malwala rather than Gene Lamount. Lamount has been a disappointment to me. Rugia heads Tap's communications division under the security department. Have her devise a way to access Tap's personal data banks."

"This could result in Rugia Malwala being exposed as your agent. Franz Scheidt is head of your sister's security. He is a seasoned warrior and fiercely loyal to Tay Appala Punra."

Torgga shrugged. "If Rugia is exposed, then she will have given her life for her leader. Go there and learn what you can as well."

"Yes, my Tap."

For a long while, Torgga stood staring out into space. The Earth solar system was so small, so far away, it could not be seen. It was located on the far edge of the outer spiral of the galaxy. A remote, cold wilderness. What was Tay Appala Punra up to out there?

Tay Appala Punra turned as Gene Lamount entered the room. "Well?"

"Her blood pressure is low — shock, I suspect — but it is not dangerously so," Lamount stated cautiously. "The trip back has not done her harm." He would have liked to remind Tap that the first three months are unusually risky in human pregnancies. To have told Courtney at such a time she was expecting a child by an inhabitant of another dimension was rash, but one did not correct someone of Tap's position.

"Nothing must happen to Courtney Hunter or our child."

"I understand."

Tap looked at her feet, a worried frown on her face, then she looked up at her medical officer with eyes as piercing as diamond. "I will see her now."

Lamount licked his lips nervously. "She does not wish to see you. To force the issue might lead to unnecessary stress." Lamount jumped as the data pilot Tap held in her hand was whipped across the room and smashed into pieces that bounced and rolled along the floor. Doors flew open and Ian and several other security personnel charged into the room. "Get out!" Tap hissed, and they hastily retreated.

"I want to see her."

We felt Lamount's fear and shock at the uncontrolled emotion Tap showed, yet he spoke. "You must understand, Tap, Courtney Hunter was never prepared emotionally for this, nor had she given her consent. In her mind, she is little more than a captive who has been raped."

We were shocked by Lamount's words. We felt the rage course through Tap. Lamount, too, realized he had gone too far. He quaked with fear.

Tap strode over to Lamount. Her movement was like a panther's, fascinatingly beautiful and inescapably deadly. She stopped so close to him he could feel her warm breath brush his skin "You will talk to her. You will make her understand," she hissed, barely louder than a whisper.

The power of the words, however, sent a chill down his back. Tap was always polite. When she was not, it was wise to be afraid.

"Yes, Tap."

We felt Tap forcing herself to calm and focus on other issues as she moved away. "What have you reported to my brother?"

"Only what we discussed — that you are doing a massive amount of research but that I can not find a focus to it. He grows impatient."

Tap nodded. "I need more time."

"Rugia worries me. I feel she has tested my loyalty to your brother a few times by setting traps for me to be more open with her. She is ambitious. She is capable of going directly to your brother rather than going through me, if she feels it holds an advantage for her."

"I will talk to Franz Scheidt. He is loyal to me and an old friend. As head of Security, he has every excuse to be close to Rugia; he can keep an eye on her."

"One other thing, Tap. I am sure Rugia has a partner. I was sent by your brother to spy on you. Rugia was sent to spy on me. Is it not logical that someone watches Rugia?"

"Yes."

"Be careful, my leader."

"I will. Go now and talk to Courtney Hunter."

"Immediately, Tap," he stated, and left as quickly as he could without appearing to run.

Tap paced about the room, barely controlling the frustration and anger that arose from the insult of Courtney's rejection of both her and their child. She did not understand. Courtney should be honoured. Who would not want to bear her child?

"Tap, may I enter?" Tap looked up to see Haichen standing in the doorway. That had never happened before. A Tap is always aware. She could see the uncertainty and concern in Haichen's face. Emotions, Tap was to realize, can cloud reason and dull perception and awareness.

"I have much to think about and do not wish to be disturbed. That should have been obvious," Tap responded coldly, trying to give the impression she had been aware of Haichen's presence. "You have done so, I am assuming, because the situation warrants it."

Relief, then fear showed on Haichen's face. It was not wise to displease a Tap. "I apologize for disturbing your contemplation, Tap. Torgga Appala Punra has attempted to access your data banks."

"How?"

"Franz Scheidt is following the breach to its source. He feels it might be Rugia Malwala."

A smile, cold and challenging, slowly raised the corner of Tap's mouth. One eyebrow arched up and she looked at Haichen with eyes sparkling with excitement. "Have you ever been in a war, Haichen?"

"Not direct combat, Tap."

"War is a horrible, abusive lover, who always leaves deep scars on your soul. Yet a lover war is, because it can draw and hold your heart like no other." We understood. We knew and felt what Tap had endured on the battlefield.

Haichen frowned. She had not ever seen Tap like this. Her commander was known for her clear, logical thought and calm assessments. She was speaking like a Guardian not a Tap. We knew this thought of Haichen's to be insightful, even if she did not. Tap was a good leader because her skills combined our talents and natural leadership ability.

"Your orders, Tap?"

Tap's smile widened into a grin. "Let my brother retrieve all the data he wants about planet Earth. He has neither the skill nor the flexibility to use that information to his advantage."

Haichen's eyes widened in shock. Tap had just openly criticized her brother. Most had thought her sitting in the presence of Torgga Appala Punra had been a signal that Tap meant to claim

Earth as her right, but maybe it was far more than that. Did Tap mean to rebel against her brother?

"Are you afraid, Haichen?" Tap asked with quiet confidence.

"Yes."

Tap nodded. "That is wise."

Lamount entered Courtney Hunter's room quietly and sat down on a chair beside the bed. Courtney did not acknowledge his presence but continued to stare at the ceiling. She had awakened to find herself back at Tap's home, in the room where she had originally been held captive. The only difference was the iron grate now welded over the hole through which she had escaped. How she had gotten here from Geneva, how long she had been kept unconscious, or what they had done to her, she had no idea. *We worry about her* and *the child.*

"Tap has requested that I talk with you," he started. Haichen had told him that the human greatly admired honesty.

"About what?" The tone of the question did not indicate interest. Courtney had not moved, not even shifted her eyes.

"Tap is not happy that you do not wish to see her." Lamount could feel the sweat running down his back. He must be careful not to undermine Tap's dignity.

"That's too bad."

Lamount tried not to show his fear. "She is most concerned, and has ordered me to make sure that you and the child are well."

Courtney's head turned and she looked at Lamount with eyes rimmed red from crying. "I'm just the incubator for Tap's little alien. She cares for no one."

Lamount frowned at his hands, trying to think of how to deal with this. "Tap is second in standing only to her brother. They are like a royal house. They have absolute power. With power comes terrible responsibilities and danger. Taps must always think of the well being of their people first. That does not mean that their personal loyalties are not as strong as anyone else's."

"I'm lying here wondering, why me? Why not one of her own kind?" Courtney asked, the hardness in her voice reflecting her suspicion.

"We can not breed anymore."

"What? None of you?"

Lamount shook his head and sighed. "Few. Our population is dwindling. For a long time, the Taps were still able to...but not now."

Courtney's hand went to her stomach. "Then what is in me?"

"You were fertilized by a synthetically produced sperm carrying Tap's genetic code. I have been working on the process for years." Lamount heard the pride creeping into his voice despite his fear.

Courtney's head shifted again and she went back to looking at the ceiling. "So that's it, then?" Her voice was flat and emotionless. "Tap needed a human incubator and I walked in."

"No. You do not understand. That is not the case. Our research was continuing and we had planned to create an egg using the embedded genetic code of one of the women of noble blood. Instead, Tap ordered that it was to be you. She sees in you qualities that are needed."

Courtney snorted. "I am aware of her thoughts. They tend to run towards my termination. What...I mean, the child...what will it look like? I mean, is it a puddle like that life force ocean?"

Lamount almost gasped in surprise. Then the rumours were true. Some of the humans, including Courtney Hunter, were developing an awareness of dimensions beyond the plane on which they existed. "Humans have evolved, over millions of years, to life forms very similar to ours. We, as of yet, have no idea why that would be so. It does not seem possible. We anticipate that the child will look much like Tap, but we are hoping that from you she will inherit some of the qualities that we have lost."

"Like the ability to be impregnated by someone without knowledge or consent?" came the angry response. "I've been treated as if I am no more than a convenient test tube. I do not want this child. It disgusts me." Courtney turned away and buried her face in her pillow.

Her words were strong and shocked Lamount, but we knew better. Courtney Hunter was very confused about what she believed. On one level, she did not want to be pregnant. On another, much against her will, she knew she was already feeling protective of the seed inside her. What really revolted her was not the child, it was the violation of her being. It was a form of rape.

There were other issues there, as well, ones far greater than just her. She had many questions. Why were aliens studying planet Earth? Was there to be an invasion? What part were she and the child to play in that? Again, Courtney found herself divided in her feelings. This was partly her child that she carried, and yet this child could be the key to the fall of the human race. Her name and that of her child could be forever associated with betrayal and the enslaving of the Earth's people. We are often surprised by the acuity of Courtney Hunter's reasoning.

Chapter Sixteen

"There are no rewards or punishments — only consequences."
~ Dean W. R. Inge

From Our Report

"When?" The question exploded from Tap. We felt its impact on Ian Phillips as he stood before her.

"Twenty-three minutes ago."

"Dead?"

"Nearly. Franz Scheidt and Gene Lamount are now trying to access any data we can from Percy Dingwall."

"Preliminary assessment?"

"He was tortured. The wounds are in keeping with our own culture, not that of Earth."

We felt Tap's dismay. This could only mean her brother had acted in an uncharacteristically bold manner. Tap's feelings did not show.

"Give me the circumstances."

"As you know, Tap, Percy Dingwall has been observing the compound from the hillside. Our initial investigation showed that he was not a stable character. He had little social interaction and lived in a fantasy world based around information he gleaned from delivering mail on his route. He was particularly obsessed with Courtney Hunter, who lived across the hall from him for a number of years.

"When Courtney Hunter disappeared, he reported to the police that she had been abducted. At your request, we appeared to cooperate with the police, providing the information that she had gone to South Africa on a training program. We also informed the police about Percy Dingwall's files on people. They checked to see that Courtney Hunter had indeed left the country and then did not pursue the investigation. The police records indicate that they interviewed Percy Dingwall and did not find him a credible source. We did not consider Percy Dingwall a threat."

Tap paced the room. We found this action disturbing. It indicated the depth of her stress.

"Go on."

Ian swallowed. We felt his fear. He knew it should have been Rugia Malwala making this report, but she said she was too busy. Ian felt victimized. He was right to feel so.

"Security personnel doing a routine patrol found Dingwall's body inside the compound. He was taken to Gene Lamount and I was sent by Rugia Malwala to report to you."

Tap nodded, approving of Rugia Malwala's political suavity. She had ordered Ian Phillips to be the bearer of bad news. No doubt she was busy making sure that Torgga got all the information about Earth that he needed. Rugia Malwala's loyalties lay with her brother.

"Report to me again when the security report is complete. And Ian?"

"Yes, Tap?"

"Make sure that Percy Dingwall's body and life disappear. I suggest that he might have become so obsessed by Courtney Hunter that he followed her to Africa."

"Understood, Tap."

With much relief, Ian Phillips left Tap's presence.

This is surprising.

What could he gain?

What could he learn?

"That is the question. What did he learn? I have been preoccupied and therefore careless. Percy Dingwall was tortured for information, therefore we must assume that he had somehow gathered some significant piece of data on us."

We fear.

Your brother is dangerous.

War is imminent.

"Yes. I need you to start instructing Courtney Hunter immediately in The Way."

This is necessary.

She will be a Tap.

We sense this.

"Yes, she will be. She carries my child. Go now."

As you wish.

We will obey.

It is fated.

We knew Gene Lamount's thoughts. He worried for the health of the mother and child. Events had happened quickly and she was only human. Courtney Hunter was in deep shock and depressed. He wished to keep her quiet and isolated. He did not wish Tap to go to her, yet he feared to refuse Tap this right. Nor could he.

He knew failure could mean his own disgrace. This he did not care about. He cared only that his disgrace might bring pain, and

even disgrace, to Haichen Lai. This we did not understand. These
feelings are beyond our understanding, even though they grow
stronger among our people. Gene Lamount and Haichen Lai had
not yet been together, but felt this need. They think their feelings
were secret, but Tap has known for sometime. Others were quick to
tell her. She waits. Information left to simmer becomes a strong
brew.

We must be careful then. We visit Courtney Hunter in her
dreams.

We have come to guide you.

To bring you to The Way.

We are the Guardians.

There are only two of you yet three voices. Why?

All things are paired.

Yet not the same.

United they are one.

I'm dreaming. This is not real.

Yes, you do dream.

But you also experience what is real.

We are here to help.

How can you help? Can you change what has happened to
me? Can you give me back my freedom? You are just dream
figures. Yet you are not the nightmare my life has become.

We see all.

Know all.

But we do not change Fate.

Then you are no good to me. Go.

We felt this command. This was a shock so deep we are left
confused. This could not be and yet it was. It was at this point only
that we realized the true importance of Courtney Hunter. Had Tap
realized so long ago when she hired this human? No. Yet, she
always said she felt there was something about Courtney Hunter.
Now we knew. And although we wanted to follow her command, we
had to resist. Training Courtney Hunter was now our single and
most important goal.

We can not go.

Although we wish to obey.

You are one with us.

What do you mean, one with you?

Like us, you will see.

Like us, you will hear.

Like us, you will travel free.

You speak in silly riddles. I'm an incubator nothing more.

No, you are far more.
You must learn.
The power is yours.
What power?
The power to see,
To hear,
To travel free.
You said this. I know this is a dream and I'll wake feeling stupid. Yet, tell me more.
All things are paired:
Dark and Light,
Earth and Space.

They are paired and yet are different.
Spirals and rings that look the same,
And yet are not.
This idea is nothing new.
Harmony comes when pairs are joined and balanced.
Neither must dominate or leave the other,
But work in unity as one.
What is the power? How do I travel free?
You must let go of form,
Join the oneness.
Return to your source.
Return to my source? I don't understand.
You will.
You are star stuff,
Like us. Come home.

Later, we reported to Tap. She had also received the news Percy Dingwall had died. We knew in his imaginary world, he had touched on truth. He had told the agent of Torgga Appala Punra Courtney Hunter was the Chosen One of the aliens and was picked to be their Queen. He told Tap's brother that it was his, Percy's, duty to save her. So he had died, with lies on his lips but truth in their meaning.
Will Torgga Appala Punra realize?
Will he see truth in this madness?
Will he now fear you?
"He has always feared me. Weak leaders always fear the strong. And because he fears, he will see patterns in Percy Dingwall's ravings. And those patterns, however delusional, might bring him to the truth."

We have news.
Courtney Hunter is one with us.
She has the power.

She now feels
The interconnectedness of all things.
She has reached the fifth level of awareness.

We felt Tap reel at this news and then calm herself, knowing in her heart it must be true. She had always known and yet was not able to give that feeling form. That is the gut feeling that humans prize so much and of which we understand little.

"I am shocked. Yet this news supports my decision. Courtney Hunter's life has been in danger since she chose to enter our world. That was of no real importance at first, and yet I felt drawn to her. Now she has conceived our child, and we must protect her at all costs. She is in grave danger. The news you bring increases that danger. Courtney Hunter will be doomed if we are not prepared to die for her. It would be a noble death. Some day, Courtney Hunter will save us all."

We must stay with her.
She must see no one else.
She has much to learn.

"She must see Gene Lamount. She must see me."

No.
It can not be.
It will not be.

And so we left Tap. We did not allow anyone near Courtney Hunter. This angered Tap and Gene Lamount. Still we insisted. Only the Guardians could perform this task. There was little time. Courtney Hunter must be strong and skilled to survive. We trained her. We cared for her. She grew strong and wise under our guidance until she saw us and walked with us. In the meantime, we left Tap to protect us. She knew her duty.

Her duty. We learned later that the cost would be high.

Torgga Appala Punra once again visited his sister.

He was wiser this time. She found him sitting at her desk when she entered her office. This left her standing in obedience. Such acts of social etiquette are not for the sake of manners alone. They establish social order and the pecking order that goes with it.

"Tay Appala Punra."
"My brother."

Two Taps together. Leaders, when brought together, either form uncomfortable bonds for mutual benefit, or politely tear each other apart. That day would be the latter. Tay was not about to submit in any way to her brother's authority. She smiled confidently, sauntered across the floor, and dropped into the visitors' seat Courtney Hunter had used at the beginning of her training. It took no effort for Tay to look relaxed. Thanks to her brother, she was used to war.

Torgga bristled with anger.

"You have forgotten your place, Tay. Isolated on this pathetic little planet, you seem to have come to feel you are master of these apes."

"I am master of no one; I lead. There is a difference. One, I am afraid my brother, you never fully understood."

We felt Torgga's anger, yet we could not respond. Courtney Hunter had to come first.

"I understand power. I was born to it, unlike you. I also understand the need for discipline and punishment for those that do not know their place."

Tay smiled.

"You wanted to be rid of me. You sent me to war when I was barely old enough to survive. When I did not die in battle making your empire great, you exiled me to the outer arm of the universe. Was this not enough?"

"I would have thought so, but now I know what you are up to. At first, I found it hard to believe that you would associate with this low species. Then I was shocked and sickened to know that you have actually bred with them."

His lip curled in revulsion, so we saw later in Tay's mind.

"You disgust me."

Tay shrugged.

"I do not wish to see our noble line die out, and it will under your leadership."

Torgga surged to his feet.

"Then it is war. I command a huge force. The Guardians are mine to command. You and those loyal to you will die a terrible death. I promise you this."

Tay stood slowly, careful to not take her eye from her brother. He was capable of great trickery. All cowards are.

"You might want to reconsider."

"I am not afraid of the likes of you."

He left, leaving Tay alone.

We do not know if she was scared, nor do we know if she had already planned her next bold move. We only know she rounded the desk and sat where once her brother had.

"You should be afraid," Tap warned her absent brother.

Chapter Seventeen

"Let them hate, so long as they fear."

~ Accius

From Our Report

Courtney Hunter had learned well. We believe she will someday fulfil the prophecy that the one from far away with the grey eyes will reunite those who have moved apart. We had no doubt now as to her importance to our people, and yet we were concerned. Her training was far from complete. Yet time, we felt, had run out. It was important that Tap see Courtney Hunter.

"Court?"

Courtney turned to see Tap standing there. "You lied to me. Then you forced your child onto me. I have no respect for you, nor do I trust you. Please leave."

Tap continued to stand there looking miserable and unsure of herself. This was not something we had seen before. "There is going to be war," she finally said, although it was not what she wished to speak to Courtney about. Emotions often make a person approach issues through a back door.

The statement did get Courtney's attention. She was across the room in a second, ready to face Tap down. "You are going to invade Earth, aren't you? That's what this is all about. Then you'd better terminate me right now, because I will do everything I can to stop you."

"An invasion of Earth would be foolhardy and unnecessary. The war will be with my brother. Tap against Tap. His forces greatly outnumber mine and are immensely powerful. I might not survive. I wished to...to say...I needed..." Tap stopped and turned away.

Before she could get to the door, Courtney was there in front of her. "Sit. You are going to answer all my questions and you are going to do it now."

Anger flashed across Tap's features. "Do not dare to speak to me like that."

"I do dare. It is my right. I am carrying our child. I'll not be treated like a concubine. I am Tap."

We felt the shock of these words on Tap, even though it was her actions that had brought this about. For the first time, she noted the earrings that hung from Courtney Hunter's right ear — one, a spiral of gold; the other, rings of gold.

"The Guardians have chosen you."

"Yes. And you are way out of line. You came here, so sit and explain. I will hear you out but I am warning you right now, at the moment, I am your worst enemy."

Tap's eyes were dark with emotion. They focused on Courtney like a weapon seeks its target. "I still have the power to do whatever I want with you."

Tap was a warrior. Courtney Hunter could feel the heat and strength radiating from her, yet she stood strong. We felt Courtney Hunter's strength and were pleased.

"You already have. But you won't go any further because of the child."

Tap looked up into the intelligent face of the spirited human she had come to respect. The anger of her frustration with Courtney's attitude disappeared. "The child means the world to me and to my people, but that is not why I am here. I wished to see you, in case I die."

"Don't go all melodramatic on me, Tap. You are here to try to pacify me with more of your lies. I have trusted you at least a half dozen times more than I should have. And now look at me — impregnated against my will with your child. Go on, I want to hear you explain this one away."

Tap paled and went strangely still. A muscle in her jaw worked. "I can take you back so that it never happened, like I did with your accident. It would be hard after this time span, but I could do this so that my child never existed, if that is what you want, Courtney." Tap's voice was heavy and toneless.

"No!" Courtney snapped and pushed Tap away. "No, no. Don't you dare take this child! I make the decisions about my body, not you." Courtney sat down and sobbed, finally undone by the stress of the events of the last few months.

Tap looked away from Courtney's shaking body, her anger spent by the enormity of the events that were unfolding. "I do not want to lose our child. Not now, not ever. I would die for our child, but for you, Courtney, if you asked me, I would give up even this. You are Courtney Appala Punra. You are Tap, a Chosen One. It is, in the end, your choice."

"No." The answer came whispered from the depths of Courtney's soul. Tap sighed with relief. All her hopes, and those of her people, rested with this one human woman.

"The events with my brother forced my hand and I needed to see that my seed would carry on my line if I were to die. But that is not why I chose you. Many would have been honoured to carry my child. I chose you because I saw in you something that we had lost and something that was also us. The Guardians saw it, too. You are one of them, a Chosen One. I feel that you and I, and our races, are meant to live together. I meant to honour you, not to violate your sense of self."

Tap spoke beautifully and sincerely, but Courtney was sceptical of ever again believing in this strange, alien woman. She felt as if her whole world had been turned upside down and given a shake. We had tried to overcome this limited perspective, but we had not yet finished her training. "How many of you are on planet Earth? Tell me the truth," Courtney asked.

"A few thousand. My personal household, that is all," Tap stated. She did not dare hold back the truth now.

Courtney Hunter was now Courtney Appala Punra. She was a Chosen One. Like we, the Guardians, she would move on to a higher existence some day. She would become one of the Three Voices of the Paired Entity, replacing one of us who had trained her so they could move on.

"Your household has a few thousand people? Who the hell are you?" Courtney asked, looking up far enough to meet Tap's eyes.

"I am Tap, one of those who carry the blood of our ancestors. I am of the ruling family and only my brother has more power. My brother and I have never seen things the same way. At first, I led my brother's forces into battle, winning victory after victory for him. When I returned a hero, I was sent to this out-planet to do research. It was essentially exile. From here, I have watched our race suffering and slowly dying under my brother's leadership. Action was needed and so I have used my isolation to my advantage. I have found that this planet has strengths for which we never gave them credit.

"More than that, this planet has changed us. We feel things, emotions we have not felt in a very long time. It is not just me that has been affected by humans. Nearly three quarters of my staff have confessed to such emotions and some, I know, have started to feel attractions. Several have become involved. I have encouraged others to do so. I feel we are regaining what we had lost."

Courtney stood and paced the floor. After a while she stopped and looked at Tap with grave, serious eyes. "So, it is not an invasion, it is to be an assimilation. Either way, you do mean to take over this planet."

"My people have become so insular and refined that we have lost significant traits which would allow us to grow and flourish as a people. We are a culture that has risen, dominated, and now dies of inner rot. I do not wish that to happen. I see humans as a way to regain the passion we have lost," Tap admitted.

"And what if we do not want your blood? What if we see that as a violation of who and what we are? How do I live with the fact that I, and my child, will betray this planet?" Courtney asked, tears rolling down her face as she stood, her arms at her sides and her hands in tight fists.

Tap frowned. "That is the same racism that I must battle with my own people. Court, your planet is dying, not of old age but by murder. It is a rose alluringly beautiful to off-planet people in its abundance of life and stable climate, but it is a bleeding rose. Without us, you are as doomed as we are. I am not asking you to commit treason against this world in accepting my child; I am asking you to help save this world, and my people."

Courtney snorted and shook her head. "No, Tap, that is not what this is all about. It is about the assimilation of Earth. You have been kicked off your planet and you want mine. You forget this is an *iron* rose bleeding. Humans might be rather stupid, short sighted animals, but we're survivors. We will find a way to solve our problems; we don't need a pack of aliens to show us how."

Tap sighed loudly in frustration and worked to keep her temper under control. She was not used to being questioned. She knew in her heart that this communication was a better way. It allowed for the exchange of ideas and the creative growth of thought, but it was very difficult to learn to listen and to deal with those who did not see things as a Tap would.

"Courtney, you have read the reports. You will be facing many major crises in the next twenty years. Rising sea levels will displace billions just as the world populations double; climate and growing seasons will change just when food is needed the most. The air is nearly toxic; the ozone layer is deteriorating, exposing your people to cancers. Deserts are growing and fresh water supplies dwindling. The world economy is failing as the gap grows between those who have and those who have not. Poverty and disease are rising at an alarming rate, and natural resources — fish, copper, oil, to name only a few — are running out. You are well past the point of no return. You need us. You are not bleeding, you are haemorrhaging to death."

"It would be better to die free than to live on as slaves of some alien race," Courtney stated quietly.

Temper won out. Tap was on her feet in a second. "You are a racist, who would die rather than see our bloods mix, even though the genetic structure of both of us is now nearly the same. You are incapable of accepting. I will always be seen by you as some alien lizard instead of a representative of the noble race from which I come. Perhaps invasion and the eradication of your kind would be a blessing to this universe rather than an atrocity."

Tap stood tall and rigid, pale with strain. "I ask again, do you wish never to have carried my child? I will not have my seed hated and looked down on." Tap waited, knowing if she had to reverse time, she would do so at great risk. Worse, the loss would rip at her heart and tear at the fabric of her being.

The silence dragged on. "I need to be alone, Tap. Please go," Courtney whispered.

Tap turned and left, relieved that, at least for the time being, their child lived on, yet hurt and angered Courtney did not hold the same feelings for the child they shared.

You must accept.

You carry the future.

So much is at stake.

"I appreciate the wisdom you have shared, Guardians. Understand, I am a human first. I will not betray my people."

History can not be reversed.

Tay Appala Punra is vulnerable without you.

Courtney Appala Punra is vulnerable without her.

"I know this. My life is tied to Tay's."

It is so.

And Tap's to those she serves,

And the world, to you.

"The world will be better off dead than assimilated."

All things are paired.

Spirals and circles.

The same and yet different.

"Are they? I do not see Tay's plans as an equal partnership."

Partners, yes.

They need you;

You need them.

"The peoples of my planet can't even manage to get along amongst themselves, do you really think they would accept an alien species as one of their own? No. Nor are there the resources to support us all. No."

You would accept Tap's offer to reverse time?

It comes with a heavy price.

Can you accept this?
"There is another way. There is death."
This would mean an end.
All would be lost.
Torgga will triumph.
"What?"
If Tay fails,
Torgga will not.
He will take this planet.

Torgga turned slowly and looked at the nervous official, Covel, who had brought the message. "What did you say?" he asked slowly in disbelief.

Covel swallowed and tried not to show his fear. "The Council has received word from Tay Appala Punra that she will return and address them. They are now forming in the Grand Circle of the Taporian Council. The Grand Council has requested that you honour them with your presence, Torgga Appala Punra."

"I will be there. Go," Torgga ordered, and watched with satisfaction as the official scurried from his presence like a scared beetle.

The time is near.
We see a cusp in time.
All is on a knife edge.

"I do not need such warning. I am not so stupid as to underestimate my sister. What is she up to? That is what I need to know? Tell me!"

We observe and advise.
We do not inform.
That is not our role.

"Then leave me. I have no time for riddles," Torgga sneered. "Send me Kaysolna. There are plans to be made."

The Council must approve.
They grow weary and cautious.
Opposing views lead to division.

Torgga smiled coldly. "The Council will support me. I am the supreme Tap. My sister is smart and daring, but she has lived with animals for too long. The Council will not support someone who lacks pride and judgement. Go."

Torgga walked over and knelt by the water that flowed through the room. It calmed him and he felt again the great flow of energy that was the soul of his people. They were *his* people and he would decide what was best for them. They were his to command. The people were the sea and he the tidal force.

"All is ready, Torgga Appala Punra," said Kaysolna. The officer stood by the door, waiting to be acknowledged before entering. The kneeling figure did not respond or move. Kaysolna waited, growing more uneasy by the minute.

Finally, Torgga stood and turned. "My sister must die. She is giving us the opportunity to achieve this goal quite easily. She has sent word that she will address the Council. On her way back to her little world so very far away, a shift in the inter-dimensional tides will result in her untimely death. It is regrettable."

Kaysolna smiled. He had waited a long time to prove himself to Torgga Appala Punra. Now was his chance. "I would be honoured to oversee such an unfortunate...accident."

"See that it is done," Torgga responded, and saw the smug smile of satisfaction cross Kaysolna's face as he left.

We saw it too. We knew that Torgga Appala Punra felt Kaysolna had the soul of a maggot. He would be used and then discarded. That was Torgga Appala Punra's way when dealing with those who lacked cultural awareness. Still, however primitive Kaysolna was, Torgga Appala Punra reasoned, he was so much better than the pathetic animals with whom his sister associated. This is what we sensed of Torgga's thoughts.

Tap lay alone on her bed. When she had first come to Earth, she had thought to live and work within the limits of a three dimensional existence would be easy. She now knew that this dimension was amazingly complex. Emotions were so much more intense and communication far more difficult a process.

You are determined?
You will not reconsider?
We fear the enemy within.

Tap nodded. "Yes, I do, too. Yet, I think that this way is better than another. I believe that if my brother destroys me, he will not have a second thought about destroying this planet. War is seductive. It is life on the edge rather than the humbling existence of daily life. How much more exciting to say you are a warrior than a scribe."

War can not always be avoided.
Some causes are great.
Some, honourable and noble.

"I have lived through war. I am not afraid of it. Yet, I know the emptiness that comes with victory and I have seen the horror of defeat. If I can take steps to avoid placing my people in battle, I will. If I can protect Courtney Hunter's planet, I will."

Are you so confident?

Are you so bold?

Are many not better than one?

"I am neither confident nor bold. I feel that this is the right way and I no longer have anything to lose."

Chapter Eighteen

"A good leader avoids bloodshed but is not afraid of it."

~ Taz Appala Punra

From Our Report

Haichen looked at Tap with worried eyes. "Tap, the Malasha has not been requested since ancient times. It is something belonging to our history. The Council—"

"The Council will have no choice. Whether it has been used or not, it is there in our laws and can be invoked," Tap mumbled as she clicked through documentation, deleting as she went. She was wise, we knew. No record must fall into the enemy's hands.

Haichen stood her ground. "Certainly Torgga Appala Punra will object, and he has supreme control over the Council."

"My brother's arrogance is his weakness. Remember that, Haichen, if I should not be around. He will agree to the Malasha because to decline would be to show weakness. He thinks he is all powerful and can easily defeat me."

Haichen did not choose her words carefully as she normally would. In her mind, this was no time for subtlety. "Torgga Appala Punra is powerful. Our forces are few, but you are an experienced and brilliant military leader. Would we not have a better chance force against force?"

Tap stopped sorting through material and straightened to look Haichen in the eye. "War, Haichen, is a fickle, diseased lover. Whatever the risks, and I do acknowledge that they are high, all out war must be a last resort. We can not win such a war. All we could hope for is to die honourably."

Haichen dropped her eyes and stared at the floor moodily. The truth was slowly being accepted by her consciousness; they would all most likely die. "Yes, Tap."

Tap nodded her approval then turned as Franz Scheidt walked in. "Franz, my old friend, I go to battle again. If I do not return, you will take charge. First, watch Rugia Malwala closely. It is likely that she is loyal to my brother, not me. It is better to observe the enemy within than to destroy her and not know the enemy's interests. However, if she grows too dangerous, neutralize her. Hand pick a small force to hold on while as many of our people as possible go into hiding. Tell them to spread out as far and wide as they can. Survival will depend on each individual's own cunning and strength. If I die, we cease to exist as a people and each of you must look out for yourselves."

"It will be done, Tap," Franz responded, not showing his surprise. He watched her put things neatly away with sad, knowing eyes. "I have always fought at your side before."

Tap stopped what she was doing and walked over to the older man. They looked at each other and then, to our surprise, and Haichen's shock, they embraced as comrades and equals.

"You have been my faithful protector, guide, and teacher. Now it is time for me to stand alone. I need you here. You are the only one with the experience and skills to carry on. More than that, no matter that your birth was common, you are Tap. You have acted as my family when there were no others. Now I recognize you as such. From now on you will be known as Franz Appala Punra. My brother."

We recognize Franz Appala Punra.

We are learning to change.

It will strengthen us.

Tap turned and looked at Haichen, who stood dumb with shock. "I know your heart. You must not follow it. At least not until we have victory."

We saw Haichen pale.

"Yes, Tap."

"Courtney Hunter must be protected at all costs. It will fall on you and Gene Lamount to keep her safe. But always, Courtney Hunter must come first, no matter what your heart tells you."

"Yes, Tap."

"Franz, assign guards to Gene Lamount. Pick your best. They are to protect him with their lives, but he must not be taken. He knows too much about Courtney Hunter and our research. If all is lost, Gene Lamount is to be neutralized."

Haichen gasped and Tap looked at her sharply. Haichen straightened. She knew her duty.

"Go."

The two officers retreated from Tap's quarters. We felt their shock.

Once gone from Tap's presence, Franz stopped and looked at Haichen with curious, intense eyes. "What does she plan?"

"She means to petition the Council for the right to a Malasha."

We felt Franz Scheidt's pride. "It is a daring and brave manoeuvre, worthy of a great warrior like Tay. But surely, Torgga would not agree."

Haichen's surprise at Franz Appala Punra using Tap and her brother's given names rather than title did not show. He had a right now, as Tap's adopted brother, and he should show no respect to her brother. Torgga was the enemy. Everything was changing. The old ways would soon be gone.

"She feels he will agree. Nothing is left on balance. We must be prepared. If the worst happens and Tap's gambit fails, Torgga will declare war on us all. Our only chance of survival will be to run," Haichen responded, using the familiar form of Tap's brother's name as Franz Appala Punra had done. She saw he was pleased by her bravery in slighting Torgga. We approved too. There was no point in showing respect to the enemy. We have learned to change.

"Yes, we must prepare, but I am confident that Tay will succeed. And Gene Lamount?"

"What of him?"

Franz sighed. "I am not blind, Haichen. I know, just as Tay does."

Haichen blushed and stood ridged with tension. "We have our orders. We must obey."

"Yes."

"What is this nonsense?" roared Torgga, turning to glare at Covel as if his minion was personally responsible for the turn of events.

Covel cringed in fear and responded to the question carefully. "Our spy tells us she means to ask for the right of Malasha when she meets with the Council."

"I will destroy her and send her parts scattering through the universe! My sister has gotten arrogant and ignorant, living among those animals." Torgga fumed.

Covel licked his lips nervously and thought carefully before he answered. "Torgga Tap, your sister is well liked by the people. She is also well seasoned in combat and a hero of the Pleaidenian Wars. She is, of course, not of your ability, but a dangerous foe nevertheless."

Torgga looked at Covel with disdain. "I am not without combat experience. I trained under the great Taz Appala Punra, not my sister. Her training was only such as her rank deserved. She learned her skill from common field marshals and honed them in combat against lesser species. She might fight well for a soldier, but I am well aware that it is the art and skill of a weapons master that will triumph."

"Yes, of course, Torgga Tap. But as you noted yourself, she has lost her sense of culture in living in a lesser dimension and mixing with these animals. Can you trust her to fight strictly by the rules of the Malasha? I fear not. Perhaps if you would allow me to put in place some...safeguards." Covel smiled at this, knowing he had handled Torgga Tap's arrogant attitude well.

Torgga returned the smile, his lips thin and cruel. "Yes, this would be wise. Tay Appala Punra is not to be trusted. I can easily defeat her if the Council supports her in this nonsense, but it would be wise to have a secret force on hand if my sister uses treachery. Go."

Covel bowed and left the room.

Torgga felt a presence disturb the fiber of the dimension and Kaysolna appeared. Torgga turned to face him. "You have analyzed the data?"

"Yes, Torgga Appala Punra."

"Any weakness in these primates that my sister studies?"

Kaysolna snorted. "So many as to make them unworthy of our attention. This is not a planet of any importance to us and not worth fighting for. Why Tay Appala Punra would rebel for such a useless rock makes no sense."

Torgga frowned and looked out the window. "My sister never does anything without good reason. That planet is important. Somehow it holds the key to solving our problems. We must learn what Tay Appala Punra has discovered among these primates."

Torgga's eyes shifted and focused on his commanding officer. "Our spy has sent word that my sister will request the right of a Malasha."

Shock followed closely by worry showed on Kaysolna's face. "This is not good news. Will the Council support such a mad request? Should we...talk to a few members to make sure that they see things our way?"

"Not to agree would be to show weakness. I will not only agree to this madness, but encourage the Council to support the request. I will do so with the confidence of knowing that my sister has sealed her fate."

Kaysolna frowned. "Tay Appala Punra is an outstanding warrior."

Torgga stepped forward and grabbed the sleeve of Kaysolna's jacket, pulling him close and hissing in his ear, "You underestimate my abilities. I am not so stupid as to let my sister put herself in a position where she can win. Forewarned is to be prepared. I do not mean to let my sister pick the time or place for battle. I will. And you, Kaysolna, will be waiting to ensure a victory."

Kaysolna smiled cruelly and considered the implication of what Torgga Tap had said. "The people might suspect a trap if the Malasha time and location suddenly switches."

Torgga chuckled and let go of Kaysolna's jacket; he went to pour himself a drink from the ornate nectar jar that sat on the table. "Of course there will be a trap. Covel is working right now to set one up. He will be exposed, of course, as Tay Appala Punra's spy and accomplice, and be eliminated." Torgga turned to look at Kaysolna and took a sip of the bitter nectar before going on. "I will triumph despite Tay's treachery. You will see to that."

It was Kaysolna's turn to laugh. What Torgga Appala Punra lacked in military leadership, he made up for in cunning. We observed, but did nothing.

From Courtney Hunter's Logs

In Southern Norway, eighty percent of all the rivers and lakes are dying or are already dead. The smog layer over Beijing can be so dense that the city itself can not be seen from satellites. The longest recorded drought was in Arica, Chile. They had no rain for fourteen years. In one year, Cherrapunji, India received 2646 cm of rain. 7098 different varieties of apples existed in the Americas in the early 1800s. Today, the genetic pool has shrunk to 977 varieties. The World Health Organization predicts by 2075 there will be more than 153 million cases of skin cancer worldwide. Scientists believe the world passed the point of no return on global warming in 2005.

I woke with a start, heart pounding, and fought to push the stream of depressing facts from my mind. The future wasn't just mine now, but the inheritance of my child. Given the state of the world, that thought was very depressing.

I lay very still on the bed, staring at the ceiling. My activity was internal as I tried to make sense of all that had happened to me in such a very short time. The Guardians were observing my thoughts. I sensed them but did not care. I was coming to realize that I was Tap.

To me, the recent events seemed like madness, and perhaps they were. But I could only deal with my perceptions and my perceptions told me I was carrying the child of an alien being in a world rushing headlong into crisis. What new world would I bring my child into? I had been told that the foetus was a girl. Tap, being a female, could not pass on the chromosome for a male. Could my daughter be happy caught between two realities foreign to one another? Would I be betraying the human race by having this child?

Humans had not been responsible caretakers of planet Earth. Now the planet teetered on the brink of an environmental crisis that would plunge the planet into years of economic and social chaos. It could be a slow, depressing descent into the new Dark Ages. Could an alliance with Tap's people prevent the inevitable? Or would we be selling out our humanity for a quick fix to our problems?

Was Tap right, that my initial reaction had been rooted in racial intolerance? I didn't think so. Even after all the unforgivable deceptions and being controlled by Tap, I had to admit a part of me still respected and was attracted to Tap. No, my anger stemmed from the same resentment so many non-European peoples felt in the years of exploration. Now I could understand, both emotionally and intellectually, why it was better to be poor than under foreign rule. I hated the thought the yoke of colonialism might fall on the human race if they tried to make an alliance with these alien beings. Look what Tap had already done to me. I could sense the Guardians understood my pain.

Tears dripped slowly from the corners of my eyes. I felt them trailing down my cheeks. I had lain here for hours, going over and over things. The bottom line was the daughter I now carried bound my future to that of Tap and my race. My own life continued, I feared, only because I carried Tap's child. Whether right or wrong, Tap had to triumph, because the alternative, it would seem, was an unbeatable invasion force led by Tap's brother.

Finally, I came to the only decision left to me: I would not support any alliance with Earth, nor would I actively undermine it unless it became clear Tap was planning a takeover. I would try to make a life somehow in Tap's world and remain a neutral observer in order to protect my child's humanity. I smiled bitterly at this decision. A neutral observer, the very thing that I had lectured Tap it was wrong to be.

From Our Report

We observed. A bell rang far off in the distance. Its echo brought with it a wall of emotion from Tap's people. Courtney Hunter sensed it, but did not understand.

Haichen walked in. "Courtney Hunter, please, I must ask you to come with me. Tap has instructed that you be kept safe at all costs."

Courtney smiled with sad cynicism. She had no doubt Tap's concern was for their unborn child, not her. "What is that bell?" Courtney asked as she got up to dress and follow Haichen.

Haichen strove to look calm and unconcerned, and failed miserably. "It is the tolling of war."

May the Ancient Ones give you wisdom.
May your heart strike fear in your enemies.
May your soul lead you to honour and mercy.

"I thank you, Guardians," Tap murmured. We left, knowing she would feel suddenly alone as the life force of her people swayed to accept the return of we who watch. We can not be a part of such action. War is for those who have not achieved the seventh level of enlightenment.

We sensed Tap striving again to find an inner peace. In only a short time, she would go before the Council. She needed to focus. The future of her people, those who had willingly followed her into exile, depended on her skills, yet she could not find the calm she sought. Her mind came always back to Courtney Hunter and the child she carried. This, we did not feel was wise.

She had objectively observed the institution of marriage as it was practised in different cultures on planet Earth. She had been both moved and appalled by the forms it could take. Good marriages, loving marriages, had a magical depth of happiness, the golden ring all reached for on the merry-go-round of life. It was a rare reward, though, and to fall short of the goal could lead, at the very least, to boredom and, at the worst, to violence and fear.

Tap had always known the happiness of a good marriage was not possible for her. At best, she would have been joined for a good political alliance for her people. Now she found herself bonded by a child to a human woman. Courtney Appala Punra would be her partner, of sorts, in life, and that meant any sort of traditional marriage was not feasible. She needed for Courtney to be with the child to nurture the human qualities she lacked. On the other hand, the child would be Tap and would need daily training by her to be the leader she was meant to be. The events of the universe were strange. She had come to respect and like Courtney Tap, yes Tap, for Courtney would now have to be part of Tay's house. To her surprise, she had to admit she more than respected Courtney, she was attracted to her. If the Guardians were right, she and her people would come to honour Courtney.

We were right. We now had no doubt of Courtney Appala Punra's destiny.

The day when Courtney Appala Punra could accept such a partnership seemed remote to Tap. Courtney Tap was revolted to be carrying her child and contemptuous of her leadership. To Tap's surprise, she felt tears prick her eyes and a hard lump of emotion wedge in her throat. Now was not the time to feel emotion. She fought to pull herself together. She would need all her focus to face her brother in combat. Failure would condemn her people to death.

We sensed Courtney Appala Punra's presence before Tap did. Courtney Tap had, in a short time, become very powerful. She had come to sense the oneness and was moving in her understanding to the sixth level of awareness. We knew unlike Tay Tap, Courtney was aware we still observed.

"Tay?"

Tap turned in surprise at the sound of her name spoken. Only her brother and Franz would dare to use the familiar form of her name without House name or title. Courtney stood across the room, looking pale but determined. "That is your real name is it not, Tap?" she asked softly.

Tap swallowed hard and blinked back the tears. She did not wish to appear weak before Courtney Tap. "Tap is a title. Tay is my given name. It is used only by my family. Tay Appala Punra is my titled name. It is the formal way to address me. Tap is an abbreviation of my family's House. It is acceptable to call my brother or myself by this title as some of your royalty are addressed as Your Highness. Now you and Franz Scheidt also have the right to use these titles. Taylor Alexandria Punga is an Earth name I took that matched my title and name."

Courtney's hands were balled at her sides as she listened to the response. She stood rigidly. "So I should address you as Tay Appala Punra?"

There was a time for pride, and a time to recognize that being humble also reflects a personal strength. We knew this was a valuable lesson Tap had finally learned from her time on Earth. She walked over to Courtney and looked down into the remarkable woman's eyes. "I would wish for you to call me Tay. I hope some day that you will feel that we are allies and partners in the raising of our child. I...I feel close to you."

Hesitantly, Courtney reached out to Tap and drew her into her arms.

Tay allowed this for several heartbeats before reluctantly pulling away. She was not sure when she had come to enjoy Courtney Tap's touch.

"Courtney Hunter, I respect you. I wish that we could be... friends...partners. I wish that you would help me raise Tamma Appala Punra as our daughter. But I will honour your wishes if you do not want contact with me after the birth of our child. I was wrong to assume that you would be honoured to carry my child. I was wrong not to talk to you about my wishes and needs. I...I am sorry."

Courtney stepped back and looked at Tap with a raised eyebrow. "Tamma Appala Punra?" she questioned, trying to capture the same lyrical quality to the name as Tap had used.

Tap blushed deeply. "If the name is suitable to you. It is a family name," she added by way of explanation.

Courtney got a combative twinkle in her eye. "And in English, Terry Alice Punga, after my parents."

Tap smiled in relief. Courtney was going to give her, and their child, a chance. "Agreed."

Courtney chanced hugging Tap once more. We knew Courtney's decision to raise the child with Tap was also a decision to try to humanize Tap, to form a life with her. Human contact seemed a necessary part of this process. Quickly letting go before Tap could pull away again, Courtney Appala Punra crossed to sit by Tap's desk. "Tell me about this war."

Chapter Nineteen

"If I could define enlightenment briefly I would say it is 'the quiet acceptance of what is'."

~ Wayne Dyer

From Our Report

We listened.

"There are so many things that I don't understand," Courtney Tap stated, running her hand through her hair in frustration. "Like: is that really you? I mean, *are* you that body or are you just in it?"

Tap raised an eyebrow. "Do you think I got it from Rent-A-Body? Yes, this is me. I told you, we are genetically very similar. The origin of my people is in the third dimension. We have simply developed the ability to live in other dimensions, as well. Lamount and I have come to hypothesize that seeding does not explain our likeness. We feel that my people might have originated from your Earth, but one in another dimension. Our genetic structures are amazingly similar."

Courtney nodded, a worried frown forming between her brows. "Then Torgga could kill you."

Tap met Courtney's eyes with a steady gaze. "Yes. He is a ruthless man. I'm sorry to tell you that he has already killed Dingwall."

We feel Courtney Tap's shock.

"The mailman who lived in the apartment across from me?"

"Yes."

"But why?"

"Dingwall was obsessed with you. He went so far as to quit his job and spy on this compound. I thought him harmless. That was my mistake. I have lived with humans for so long that I have come to accept their illogical ways without question. Dingwall thought you had been captured by aliens. He thought they were going to make you their Queen."

Courtney Tap snorted. "That's ironic."

"Yes, it is. Sadly, his madness touched very close to the truth. That cost him his life. My brother had him tortured and killed for information. With it, Torgga might piece together your importance to me."

"I feel so sorry for Dingwall. He was just a sad, disturbed man who, like me, walked into the middle of a civil war."

"I am sorry too. It was careless of me and it cost Dingwall his life. My brother is a dangerous man."

"Would he go so far as to kill his own sister?"

"Yes. If he can get away with it. I am a threat to his authority, as you will be, if he finds out that you carry my child. If anything happens to me, trust Franz and Haichen. They will look after you," Tap explained. It was her duty to make sure these matters were settled. She owed it to her people. Yet it hurt to think of never seeing her child or helping her to reach her full potential. Had she allowed herself to admit it, it also hurt not knowing whether she would see Courtney Tap again.

"Why do you have to fight this Mal..."

"Malasha," Tap stated. "Because the alternative is war. I know war, Court. I know it well. It is something I will avoid for my people if I can. Nor do I want to bring such devastation so close to this planet. I was born to lead, and good leadership means being prepared to defend your people. This is something our child needs to know. If I fail, Tamma will carry on the struggle for us when she is of age."

"What if I do not want that for her? What if I raise her to think she is human, call her Terry, and raise her on Earth?" Courtney questioned.

"She will be no safer on Earth. You know that. Your world is on the brink of chaos. She is born to rule. You can't stop that, Court. Nor do I think you would want to."

Courtney's eyes sparked. "Oh, I would want to, all right. But if she's anything like you— Well, she has a right to be what she needs to be. I will not deny Tamma her birthright."

Tap sighed and relaxed. "I do not have long."

Courtney turned away while she considered Tap's words. "I'm not the person I once was. The Guardians have opened a world to me that I thought the stuff of science fiction. I see and feel things now that none of my species have ever felt before. I don't just hear and feel their presence now, I see the Guardians. I feel our oneness."

"They are not here. That is surprising."

Courtney turned and smiled. "They're here through me. I am here and I am one with them."

Tap felt the jolt of this realization. Courtney Appala Punra had indeed become powerful in a very short time. "Oh."

Courtney Tap sensed her surprise. She walked over to Tay and faced her again. "I have much to learn yet, but I'm coming to accept that I might indeed be the Chosen One of your people, the one who was prophesied. But understand this, Tay, I am and always will be human first. I will be your greatest supporter, but also your staunchest foe. I'll not stand by and allow you and your people to in any way assimilate this planet or its people."

Tap felt the thrill of the challenge. Courtney Tap had become a rival who commanded respect. "My people and I are Earth's only hope. Your planet is bleeding to death from wounds inflicted by humans. Only I and my people can bind these wounds."

Courtney Tap smiled. She, too, enjoyed the challenge. "Ah yes, your bleeding rose. But I once told you not to underestimate this planet or its people. We have iron wills."

Tap laughed. "The Arctic sea ice hasn't reformed in the last few years. That means global warming is now irreversible. The rising ocean temperatures are creating stronger and more deadly hurricanes in areas already threatened by rising sea levels. Pesticide levels in the soil and foods are so high that they are a likely cause of cancers in young children, and fertilizer run-off is causing algae blooms in the ocean that form massive dead zones. The pollution of the oceans is killing shelled creatures and the coral. In Africa and the Indian subcontinent, a hundred million people are now in danger from massive flooding, drought, famine, and disease directly related to the world's industrial pollution. There is a significant escalation in war and terrorism as you humans fight over control of the depleting natural resources brought on by sky-rocketing overpopulation. In your world, every minute ten children die of malnutrition and another twenty-six thousand species of plant, animal, marine, and bird life are now in danger of becoming extinct. Should I go on? Do you really think your precious rose can be saved from the very species that is killing it?"

"No, I don't. Nor do I believe your species can go on without the help of my people. You need us and we need you. Most of all, this world needs us. Planet Earth will not die. It is a beautiful rose that is forged in iron. This little planet, on the outer arm of the universe, developed an amazing abundance of life and clung to that life despite many near extinctions in Earth's history. In the vastness of cold, lifeless space, this one planet bloomed and thrived against impossible odds. It is a very special place. You know it and I know it, and as equal partners, we will both fight with everything we have to make sure it survives."

Daring, Courtney Hunter reached out and took Tap's hand. We are no longer surprised that she would be so bold, nor that Tap would enjoy such a gesture. Things are changing. We do not always understand, but we are learning.

Courtney Hunter held on tightly, knowing when she had to let go, it might be forever. We sensed everything in her being cried out for her to stop Tap from going, but she remained quiet. Her future was at the side of a hereditary leader. She now understood she shared that burden with Tap and with this alien race. She would not send Tap off to battle burdened down with her fears.

"Win this battle for our people, Tap, and come home to us. Tamma and I need you," she whispered instead, and was rewarded with a nod of understanding and a small smile of thanks.

Neither would we have expected from Tap.

"I have everything to live for now — a child and a chance to save my people from extinction. I have the Chosen One to protect and as a worthy partner in this endeavour. I mean to win."

Courtney Tap nodded and moved away a few steps. "Although it was forced on me, I am Tap. As strange as it seems, we're now partners in the raising of a child and in the quest to save this Earth. Do not betray my trust. My safety, and that of our child, lies with your success."

Tap nodded. We felt Tap's determination and strength. It pleased us.

Later, Courtney Hunter watched as Haichen assisted Tap into her armour. The black material was lightweight, flexible yet strong. A material that would spread and reflect energy blasts, Haichen had explained. Tap pulled on thick gloves that rose almost to her elbows and flexed her legs to bounce on the heavy soled boots. She nodded her satisfaction.

Tap turned and walked over to stand before Courtney. Her face was lined with concern. A smile slowly softened her features and, in front of Haichen, she leaned forward with a ripple of muscle to kiss Courtney on the cheek. "We are family."

"Haichen, Courtney Hunter is now Courtney Appala Punra. She will rule at my side. If I should not return, you and Franz Appala Punra are tasked with the protection of her and our child, and you will counsel her in raising our child and in ruling until Tamma Tap is old enough to accept that responsibility. Do you understand?"

Haichen tried her best not to show her shock at Tap's actions. She was both intrigued and excited by the tension and energy in the air around her leader and Courtney Appala Punra.

These new feelings and emotions they had found on Earth were both wonderful and scary. In one bold move, Tap had not only established an alliance with the human but had handed to her incredible power.

All is well.

It is as we have foreseen.

Courtney Hunter is Tap.

We felt Haichen relax at our words.

"Yes, Tap."

We heard Haichen's thoughts. She considered the mild attraction and comfort she and Lamount had experienced in their hesitant courting and realized they had a long way to go to achieve love. Could they find this passion and so be able to produce an offspring? If Courtney Tap and Tay Tap could find the mutual respect and trust to reach such a partnership and, yes, affection, then maybe anything was possible.

Courtney Hunter turned and looked at Haichen. "Tay Tap has placed a terrible burden of responsibility on you and Lamount, yet I know it is necessary. I believe that this adversity will bring you and Lamount closer together. I'm happy for you. We're happy for you."

Tap nodded in agreement but we felt her surprise. Giving power to Courtney Hunter was necessary and strategically wise under the circumstances. Accepting she would be sharing power with the human was a harder step, yet one she was determined to take. Tap came to stand by Courtney and spoke to Haichen.

"There are spies in our midst. Make sure that no word of Courtney's condition spreads. I suspect that my brother will use treachery to win this battle if he feels the fight is not going well. Monitor the situation carefully. You have my permission to interfere only if you feel that treachery has put me in a dangerous situation. Do you understand, Haichen Tay Tap?"

Haichen looked up, her eyes wide with shock. Tap had just called her by the title of commander, second only to those of the ruling House. She swallowed, squared her shoulders, and managed to respond with dignity, using an ancient title. "I understand, my Sovereign Ladies."

Tap smiled. "It is time for me to talk to the Council. Go, Haichen Tay Tap. I wish time alone with Courtney Tap." Haichen stepped back and faded away before a startled Courtney.

"Can you all do that? Where did she go?"

"Yes, we can all do that. She has released the energy that binds her molecules together to drift back into space/time. You have become aware of that flow of life but as yet your body remains behind."

Courtney shook her head and looked at Tap. "There is so much for me to learn, so much responsibility that I will have to assume. Don't die, please, Tay. Come back to us. I need you," she choked out.

There was no answer. Tap was embarrassed by Courtney Hunter's sudden display of emotion and yet pleased by it. Tap hesitantly reached out and touched Courtney Hunter's belly, then she slowly vanished from Courtney's world.

We observed the dark eyes desperately scanning the screens in the lab. All other resources had revealed nothing of why Tap was willing to revolt against her brother in order to keep control of this small and insignificant planet. A number of times, the human Courtney Hunter had been brought to the labs. At first, it had seemed as if this was because she had been ill, her mind overtasked by the workload she had been assigned. Now, the spy was not sure that was the case.

Tap's sudden decision to rebel after all this time in exile had to be connected to the arrival of Courtney Hunter and whatever Lamount had been up to in this lab all this time. Gene Lamount must be a double agent working for Tap and not a spy for Torgga Tap, as they had thought. They had been fooled, but not anymore. There was more going on here than the study of Earth diseases. The spy meant to find out what.

The screen flashed to another file and the dark eyes blinked, at first unable to accept what they were reading. Surely not! The spy slowly sat in the swivel chair and started to read. It was all there, kept safely in a computer not attached to any system. That was why Torgga Tap had been unable to access the data. Tay had mated artificially with the human animal and the insemination had been successful. There was to be an heir to the Tap line, after all, but the cost was to be their purity.

The spy moved to another computer, stepping over the unconscious body of Lamount. It was not possible to worry about security now. Torgga Tap must know this information before Tay went before the Council. Then the next step would be to kill Courtney Hunter before being captured or killed.

From Courtney Hunter's Logs

I worried and chafed at the inactivity. I paced restlessly around the dark computer room, watching as stern faces anxiously scanned screens of rolling data. Haichen stood to one side, eyes closed, focused on the faint trace of energy that was her leader, now light years away. I bit my lip and frowned. Haichen had said that even with Tay Tap's remarkable abilities, it would take time to cross through dimensions to their world. Haichen had told her it was called Tappor, the Peaceful One. The little I knew about Tapporian history suggested the planet had been anything but peaceful.

"She has arrived and is before the Council," Haichen stated, and moved to stand in front of a monitor. I moved with her, although the strange markings meant nothing to me. Haichen had explained these were not like the computers of Earth but ones that used the low microwave energy of the dark matter of space to send untraceable impulses through the universe along the strings of space/time. To me it was pure science fiction. The terms, I was aware of; the concepts behind them eluded me.

I took to pacing again. The wait seemed endless. Fear gnawed at my gut. I found myself second-guessing all my decisions in the last few days and finding no better answers. I was now the alien, one human woman relying on the loyalty of a group of Tapporians who were virtual strangers. Their world view, their thought patterns, their concepts of right and wrong were so different from mine. I needed Tay here. Without her, I had to admit, I was scared and lonely.

Haichen straightened from the screen and looked across the room at me. "The Council has agreed to the Malasha. Torgga has supported this decision. It will start when—"

"Haichen Tay Tap, look at this!" interrupted an excited voice. Officers manning modules took off earphones and hurried to stand behind the excited officer and Haichen as they watched the computer screen.

"What is it?" I demanded.

"Shit!" exploded Haichen, turning on the officer and using an English word that she had found to be particularly expressive. "Sapata, scan for her. Lucentern, I need details."

"What is going on?" I repeated louder as I watched Haichen's people manning their centres again and working feverishly. Fear spread like fire through my gut.

"We don't know where Tay Tap is. Something has happened. Give me a minute to sort through all this mess and I will be able to tell you more," Haichen finally answered me, not taking her eyes off the screen of data that rolled past.

I felt my heart contract. This was my worst nightmare coming true.

Haichen scanned the screen madly, trying to make sense of the reports of the observing recorders in the Hall of the Council. It made no sense. A plot against Torgga Tap had been exposed at the last minute and Torgga had managed to escape, pulling Tay Tap with him into another place/time. The Council was in an uproar.

From Our Report

Not far away, the spy walked calmly into the main rotunda and looked around. They were in the computer room, monitoring Tap's progress. It was likely that Courtney Hunter was with them. The human had courage and daring. It was likely that she would insist on an active role in all this. That meant getting to Courtney Hunter would be easy. It also meant that death was inevitable in the shoot-out that would follow. To die for one's leader was honourable.

We saw. We cared. We could do nothing.

Give me strength, Guardians, to face what I must, Ian thought as he flipped the safety off the gun and opened the door.

Courtney looked up with worried eyes that widened into shock as the gun in Ian's hand raised.

"Ian, no!" cried Haichen.

Courtney went down in the crossfire that followed.

Chapter Twenty

"Our doubts are traitors and make us lose the good we might win, by fearing to attempt."

~ William Shakespeare

From Our Report

Tay remembered relaxing at Courtney's touch and letting the energy of her being draw in. Gradually, the bonds that held her molecules together weakened and she could feel herself drifting off into a dimension without form. The sense of oneness stole over her, of tranquil belonging within a sea of like souls. The current in which she flowed travelled at near light speed and yet, relative to her own awareness, time stood still.

She had ached for this tranquil belonging when she first arrived on Earth. She had found it very difficult to confine her being to a limited form. Her movements had seemed heavy and clumsy, and she was revolted by the feeling of touch and the germs and dirt associated with it.

Now, to her surprise, she found her old dimension sadly lacking in stimulation. Here there could never be the heady scent of flowers warmed by the sun, or the shiver of excitement when thunderclouds mounted on the horizon and the wind got up. The texture of soft hair and warm flesh could never be felt, nor could one taste the salt of a tear shed at separation. There was only tranquil sameness. Here a sliver could not sting, a bump could never give soreness, and a word said in anger could not hurt. Yet it was feeling that gave colour to life, gave it passion and drive. What they had lost in throwing off the shackles of the third dimension was their sense of being.

Slowly, she felt herself crystallize into solid form. She stood on a hilltop surrounded by a rugged, arid land. The purple Nareenians were in bloom and their sweet peppery scent filled the air. She had never been aware of their fragrance before. Her time on Earth had changed her. Forty individuals stood as she materialized. They were the hereditary members of the Council. Forty leaders from the great tribes of the plains now ruled by the house of Tap and guided by the Guardians, Keepers of the Way. They had been sitting in a circle on rough cut blocks of stone, waiting. One stone for each clan and three left empty in symbolic respect to the Guardians. We watched. Each wore the costume and colours of their tribe with pride. When she had fully arrived, they bowed in respect, not in servitude. Tay wondered how they felt when they bowed before her much more powerful brother.

"Welcome home, Tay Appala Punra. You have been too long gone from our lives."

Tay acknowledged the Speaker of the Council with a slight nod of her head. "Necessity has brought me back once again. I invoke the right to a Malasha."

There were gasps of surprise and murmurs of disbelief, but Tay was totally focused on the tremor in the atmosphere around her. Torgga was arriving. She turned to face him as he appeared on the other side of the circle. The members of the Council again rose, but this time their bow was deeper and fear made them hesitate to straighten again. Tay did not bow. She looked her brother in the eye defiantly. Her message was clear. She would no longer honour or follow him.

"So, my younger sister, you are here to request the Malasha. You have never known your place. You were wild as a child and disobedient as a youth. Now I am shocked to be told that you even mate with animals."

The Council looked fearful, at a loss as to what to do. Some gasped at this revelation, others protested, some still stood, others sat. Tay walked nonchalantly over to her brother. "I have sired a child by a human. That might offend you, but at least, dear brother, I am capable of passing on my seed."

Torgga's face went red with anger. He turned his back on his sister and moved closer to the Council seats. When he spoke, his voice was etched with ice. "Honourable Council and most noble of Guardians, you see the rudeness with which my sister addresses me. By right, I could have her terminated, but unlike my sister, I was raised to rule. I will not insult my lineage by having Tay Appala Punra executed like a commoner. I, too, request the right of Malasha. I will defeat and kill my sister in fair battle, as befits the rank she now mocks."

Tay laughed as she walked to stand beside her brother. "Pretty words, my brother, and as meaningless as the wind echoing through an empty canyon. The Ancient Ones introduced the Malasha into our laws so that if a Tap was found not capable of leadership they could be removed by combat." She looked at her brother with disdain.

The Speaker looked at the anger in Torgga's eyes. He was well aware that Torgga's leadership had been harsh and tight. He was feared not loved by the people of the endless plains and space, yet it was his right to lead. One would be mad to cross this man. Slowly, the Speaker walked from councillor to councillor, stopping each time to see how each folded their hands. Then he went to stand again in his own position. "The Council recognizes the sovereign right of Torgga Appala Punra. At his request, we grant the Malasha. Torgga Appala Punra, Tay Appala Punra, you will go now to the fields of Ternsal where the battle of Tarmalasha ended the civil wars and brought peace and balance to the forty tribes so very long ago. There you will battle one another for the right to lead. Go now."

Tay allowed her energy to draw within. She was ready to dematerialize when she felt Torgga grab her by the wrist. "It's a trap, look over there! She and that official are trying to pull me to a new arena," she heard her brother cry, and then she was gone, her energy redirected at the speed of light.

The angry Councillor turned to where Torgga was pointing and released a bolt of energy that broke the connection that the official had placed on the brother and sister. The Councillor's second bolt hit the unlucky man in the chest and he dropped to the grass, unconscious. The Council was in an uproar. Never had anything like this happened.

Tay did not fall to the ground, she floated, hitting and bouncing high again in a mist of dust particles. She twisted like a dancer in the thin atmosphere so that she would land this time on her feet. It was incredibly hot. Torgga had chosen well. After her time on Earth, fighting in low gravity in a dry, hot environment would be very difficult for Tay. She was in trouble, big trouble, and she very much feared that her people would have lost contact with her.

From Courtney Hunter's Logs

I got up slowly with Haichen's support. I could feel Haichen trembling with emotion, but her face appeared serious and calm. "You are okay, Courtney Appala Punra?"

I nodded. "Believe me, I got out of the way as soon as I saw that gun. I'm fine, Haichen." I saw Haichen's worried eyes shift to the door and back again, and knew immediately the source of Haichen's tension. "I think you'd better go check on Gene Lamount while I get some of the others here to find out what's going on and where Tay is."

Haichen eyes widened in surprise and then softened into gratitude. I gave the arm that supported me a squeeze of understanding.

Haichen shook her head. "Sapana, go see if Gene Lamount is all right. If he is alive, we need to know if any files were accessed by the spy. Have him report here."

Sapana, a young man crouched beside Ian's body, rose and made his way to the door. Haichen stooped to make sure Ian was dead as she passed to the computer terminals. I steadfastly refused to look. Ian might have been a traitor who had tried to kill me, but I could not imagine him as anything but a friend. I felt sick inside and despite what I had said to Haichen, I was anything but okay. I was terrified. "I can't believe that Ian... Well, I just can't," I muttered through tight lips as I watched chairs being righted and screens brought back on line.

"I am surprised. I am sure Tay Appala Punra will be also." For a minute, Haichen watched the screen as data flowed rapidly across it. "The Malasha was granted and Tap and Torgga were on their way to the fields of Ternsal to battle. A spy appeared and tried to force the two of them into another realm. At the last instant, Torgga cried out and pulled Tap somewhere else. The Council has the man, Covel, who is a low official of Torgga's court. He is refusing to talk. But just before Torgga and Tap disappeared, Torgga yelled out a warning that it was a trap, pointed to the official, and then grabbed Tap and pulled her with him.

"Convenient, that it was Torgga who saw this Covel. It was a pre-planned deflection and they have Tay."

"Where is she?" I snapped, barely controlling my anger at the turn of events.

"Courtney, I am sorry; we do not know. It could take us hours to sift through data to try and find a trail of ionized particles that might lead us to them. I only sensed their destination for a split second. It was very, very hot there."

"Then start looking," I commanded, turning on my heel and heading for the door. "I'm going to try another method."

"Courtney, Tay commanded that I stay with you," Haichen argued, quickly following.

"Haichen, I'm in command now. Our first priority is to save Tay Appala Punra. Emergencies call for drastic and creative action. Besides," my voice filled with sadness, "the spy is dead. Stay at your station. This is a job I must do alone."

Haichen took a step back in respect. "Yes, Courtney Appala Punra."

I walked purposefully down the hall, only stopping for a second to question Gene as he came limping down the hall, supported by a worried looking Sapana. "Did Ian find what he was looking for?" I asked cautiously.

Gene nodded sadly. "Yes, that file was open."

"Then he would have transmitted the information before he came looking for me. Meet Haichen in the communications room. Wait there for further instructions," I ordered, and saw the shocked look on Lamount's face as I opened the door that led into Tay's private quarters.

I stood in the room with the beautiful abstract paintings that I now knew were painted by Tay of other dimensions. I tried to calm and focus my mind. *Guardians, I need to speak with you. Guardians, Tay is in trouble. I need your help. Guardians, please.*

Help is not ours to give.

We offer only wisdom.

And our opinion.

"Forget neutrality!" I roared in anger, turning to face them. "What did objectivity get you? You are a dying people. And I'm not about to let Tay die. You know where she is and you are going to tell me. Today your people start on a new path. It is not an easy path, being involved and having emotion. The third dimension is dirty, raw, and in your face, but let me tell you, Guardians, here you are really alive. Don't you want a future for your people under Tay? Come on. Forget tradition, just this once, and tell me where she is."

This is not who we are.

Dare we do so?

Can we not?

"Tell me! For God's sakes, he'll kill Tay."

You are only human.

So weak and frail.

You would have no chance.

"Believe me, I have a weapon that will bring him to his knees," I sneered, with more confidence than I felt.

You can not travel.

You are confined to this dimension.

It is not possible.

"I have felt your world, sensed the ocean of currents, the tranquil life force. I know its beauty. I also know that with your help, I can do this. I might have only started my training, but I am Tap. I am the Chosen One. Guardians, there is no time to waste. Isn't this what you wanted me to understand — that I am the ring to Tay's spiral, that our child is the link between us? Because of this, the Earth will not be conquered or assimilated; rather Tay's people and my people will be as one, opposites balanced."

A shocked silence hung in the room for a few minutes while they tried to cope with the enormity of what I was visualizing. I was just about to argue again when their response came.

Change we must.

It is the only way.

Yes, we will take you there.

"Good. Give me a minute to get organized and then you can zap me wherever I need to be," I stated, as I headed for my quarters.

From Our Report

We felt the relief flow through Haichen as she saw Gene Lamount come through the door. He was pale and shaky but otherwise seemed okay. In past days, she would have smiled softly then waited for an opportunity to talk to him. But she had now realized the path that Tay and Court had chosen meant accepting human emotions and learning to deal with them. She knew she wanted that passion, so instead she walked over to Lamount and wrapped her arms around him, reaching up to kiss his lips softly.

The room went totally still. Lamount looked down at Haichen in wonder and then wrapped her closely in his arms. Slowly, Haichen heard the others recover from their shock and return to work. The soft click of keyboards did not drown out the beating of her heart.

Haichen Tay Punra.

We will speak with you.

There is news.

Haichen jumped back as if she had been given a jolt of electricity. Experimenting with physical contact was one thing, doing so in front of the Guardians was quite another. "Yes, Honourable Ones."

Times must change.

We have sent Courtney Tap.

She has gone to protect Tay Tap.

"What?" Haichen gasped in fear imagining what Tay Tap was going to do to her for not protecting Courtney Appala Punra. Then she remembered to whom she spoke. "I mean, Honourable Guardians, she is only human and Torgga is so powerful."

Her humanity is strange to us.

It is her weakness and her strength.

She is our only hope.

"But you do not understand, Guardians. Courtney Tap, she... ahhh they..." Haichen struggled to explain why Courtney had to be protected without revealing what she knew.

Do you think we do not know?

We are the Guardians.

We say again, there was no other way.

As we spoke, we saw the spy Rugia Malwala accessing her computer terminal.

Haichen, stop her.

She is a spy.

She will betray us.

We saw Rugia spin around in her chair in surprise, then she leapt up and ran for the door. Haichen's shot brought her to the ground beside Ian.

To survive, there must be change.

This we have learnt from the Chosen One.

We have involved ourselves.

Chapter Twenty-One

"Victory at all costs, victory in spite of all terror, victory however long or hard the road may be, for without victory there is no survival."

~ Winston Churchill

From Our Report
We observe and record.
We have interfered and hope.
Fate balances on a knife edge.

Landing on her feet although she was still off balance as a result of her momentum, Tay blocked the blast of energy that instantly came her way. Even so, it was much more powerful than anything she had experienced before. Allowing her body to use the energy rather than resist it, she spun back, twisting sideways as she reached out and sent a charge directly into her brother's chest. She might not be as powerful as Torgga, but years of combat had made her reflexes sharp. She aimed not to neutralize, but to kill.

In his overconfidence, Torgga was not prepared and staggered under the blow. This gave Tay the time to bounce closer and send an attack from the side. Again she caught Torgga in the chest, but not before he had sent a glancing blow of ionized particles off her shoulder. Her exposed neck and face burned with the impact, but she now believed she could win this battle. Her confidence was shattered a split second later by an incredible energy blow to the back. Tay crumpled, unable to straighten for the pain, even as she absorbed the realization this was a trap.

Gritting her teeth against the pain, she rolled over and aimed at the shadowy figure making its way towards her through the dust clouds. She knew she was now totally vulnerable to Torgga's attack, but she could not fight on two fronts. Gathering her strength, she focused everything she had into a single deadly shot. The shadowy figure glowed bright at the impact, turning the grey dust particles around him to bright yellow. Then the light faded and the assassin folded to the ground with a thud. A second later, Tay was hit full on and sent spinning across the ground. Then another blow left her protective armour smouldering and hot. The pain was almost blinding and Tay struggled to breathe through her own blood. She lay still. Her only hope would be if she could raise enough energy for one last shot before her brother killed her.

Her thoughts drifted to her people, then Courtney and their unborn child. There was still hope. Courtney Appala Punra would survive. She must. The prophesies could not be wrong. She could hear her brother's heavy boots crunching the gravel under his soles as he walked over to her. She reached inside herself, but there was no energy left. There would be no last chance.

A heavy boot caught her in her raw and bleeding side and sent her rolling over and over. Her own scream echoed painfully in her ears. Tay bit down on her lip. She would die with honour. Through blood caked lashes and eyes stinging with sweat, Tay saw the black form of her brother looming.

"This is the end, Tay. You, first, and later, your pregnant human. But have no fear for your child, Tay, I will raise her as my own," he laughed.

Anger and fear helped Tay find the energy from somewhere within. Her hand shot out and delivered a blow to Torgga's chest. He blocked it easily, laughing still, and kicked once again, sending her body sledding painfully across the rocky surface. When the dust settled, Tay's body lay still in the sand. Her wounds were barely visible through the thick layer of dust matted into her blood.

We feel her pain.
We feel the pain of the people.
Our hope is the Chosen One.

We hear her thoughts. Courtney wondered whether something had gone wrong or whether we, the Guardians, had tricked her. We had told her she would be travelling great distances, light years away through strings of energy present in the dark matter of space. Yet she felt like she floated quietly in a warm ocean, gentle currents nudging her around. There was no sensation of form or speed, only a timeless band of energy flowing through an endless sea. Nevertheless, she had to force herself not to panic. The lack of physical sensation was terrifying. Then her world rushed in on her and she suddenly felt heavy and confined. Sensations hit her like arrows: incredible heat, a bruised shoulder from her dive behind the computer console when she saw Ian raise his gun, and the dust that filled her mouth and gagged at the back of her throat.

She materialized beside Tay's body and looked down in stunned shock, not realizing at first that the still, dust covered, bloody mass was Tay. Slowly, as realization struck, she sank to her knees. She rolled the dead weight into her arms and held her close. "Tay, I'm here; please don't give up on us. Please Tay, we need your leadership and our daughter needs to know you. You need to teach her all the things that she must know to lead. I want her to know your smile and I want to see the two of you play together. Tay, fight, hold on. You owe it to Tamma, to me, and to your people."

Eyes opened with difficultly, blinking dust and blood clear. "Court? No...leave. Get out. D...Do not want y...you hurt."

A shadow fell across them. Courtney looked up into a face so similar to Tay's, only lacking the warmth and kindness. "He knows. He w...wants our...ch...child," Tay warned, trying without success to shield Courtney with her own body.

Courtney lowered Tay's body to the ground, trying not to show her pain at hearing Tay's moan of agony. She got up slowly, a smile on her face, ignoring the woman who now lay at her feet, helpless. "So, we're to be allies then."

Torgga's shrewd face showed surprise for a split second. "I am Torgga Tap. I need no allies, especially not a human animal."

Courtney resisted the urge to kick him. With that protective suit on, it probably would do no good. "Sure you do. It is going to take nine Earth months for me to have this child and then there is the whole raising process. You have no idea how fragile and breakable the little sucker is going to be. You can't just zap this kid into your celestial genetic pool, you know. She's half human. Her better half, I might add. I mean, look at Tay. Not much to write home about."

Torgga blinked in surprise as Courtney stepped over Tay, wobbling because she was having trouble keeping her balance in the low gravity. It seemed to him Tay was no more important to her than an annoying bump in a path. The human looked around at the flat, dusty plain. "Please tell me this isn't home. Hell, even an alien couldn't love this dust bowl. I've seen kitty litter pans with more relief."

We are proud of Courtney's bravery and cunning.

Torgga looked down at the small creature beside him. He did not understand all she referenced. What was a kitty litter pan? Still, he had to admit, he found her interesting. Humans were not as revolting as he had imagined. "How did you get here?" he demanded.

"The Guardians sent me," Courtney responded honestly as she measured distance and calculated her chances.

Torgga's face distorted in anger. He grabbed Courtney by the shirt and lifted her off the ground. "I do not believe you. They will help no one. Not even me."

It was now or never. Courtney steeled her courage, knowing that whether this worked or not, she could get hurt badly. "Wrong again," she stated quietly, lifting her hand and pulling the trigger.

Torgga cried in pain and dropped her as he covered his eyes. Courtney tried to maintain her balance as she bounced. She kept firing at Torrga's exposed flesh, avoiding Torgga's blind swipes at her. She was getting tired. The intense heat and lack of gravity were taking their toll. Her plan now seemed stupid and it clearly had not worked. A big mitt of a hand, covered in a steel-like material, caught her chin and sent her reeling away. She hit the ground on her back and skidded painfully. Looking back, she could see Torgga looming, hand raised in her direction. Then his knees buckled and he dropped to the ground.

Courtney leapt to her feet and bounded awkwardly over to wrap Tay in her arms. "Get us out of here, Guardians. Please!" Courtney sobbed.

We sent Franz Appala Punra. We had other more important matters with which to deal. He arrived at the Council feeling the weight of responsibility heavy on his shoulders. Tay Appala Punra had carried such a weight since she was a young child with great wisdom and dignity. It was only now, as Franz Tap stood in the circle of forty-three, that he realized just how great a burden that must have been.

"Honourable Councillors, I am Franz Appala Punra, and I have been instructed by the Guardians to present myself to you." A murmur of disbelief rippled around the ring of distinguished Councillors.

The Speaker stood with indignation. "Quiet please." His eyes fastened on Franz Tap. "Tay Tap has taken you as a brother?"

"Yes."

"You are Tay Appala Punra's second in command?"

"Third, Honourable Speaker; I also serve Courtney Appala Punra." Now the ripple became a rising tide of voices.

"Silence, please," the Speaker commanded again. "Tay Tap has given such a noble rank to a human?"

"Yes."

The Speaker seemed at a loss for words. He held up a hand to Franz Appala Punra to signal him to wait and then hurried to join the buzz of conversation around the circle. Councillors got up and formed groups, talking and arguing. Franz Tap waited, not knowing what to do.

The Speaker returned to stand by his chair and with a wave of his hand signalled the other Councillors to do likewise.

"Franz Appala Punra, we need to know more. You will explain the events that have led to this day when sister turns against her brother, who rules us all." He sat solemnly, folded his hands and waited. So did the other Councillors. This was to be a sort of trial, and the fate of Franz Tap's leader depended on his convincing the Council that Tay Tap had done no wrong. He took a few minutes to settle his thoughts. He was a soldier not a politician, but we had sent him because it was his right. Tay Tap trusted him.

Only a few weeks ago, the idea of him standing there supporting Courtney Hunter and Tay's decisions would have seemed impossible, ludicrous. Now everything had changed with Tay Tap's bold actions. Only time would tell if those decisions had been wise.

Eventually, he began. "Torgga Tap and Tay Tap have never seen eye to eye. That is well known. Tay Tap objected to the conquests into which his leadership has led the People of the Plain and Space. She objected to his oppression of ideas and control of lives. As a result, after she led his forces to victory, she and her Household were sent into exile to a remote and unimportant planet in the far reaches of our universe."

Franz Appala Punra stopped and slowly turned in a circle, making eye contact with each of the individuals who sat there before continuing. "Tay commanded that we observe everything about this planet and understand it completely. She also ordered that research be done to fabricate a synthetically produced sperm that would carry her genetic code. She did this because there was no male of rank suitable with whom she could mate who was capable of producing offspring."

A murmur passed around the circle. The Speaker glared. "Tay Tap's actions are startling. Go on."

Franz Tap steeled himself, unconsciously straightening his shoulders and standing tall. Here was where it was going to get interesting. He hoped Tay was alive, because if not, he and all Tay's Household would probably be dead or in hiding from Torgga's anger by tomorrow. "We discovered that the humans, who are the dominant animal on planet Earth, were nearly genetically identical to us. At first, we thought that it was a remarkably successful result from the earlier seeding attempts. Then Tap started to study the human Courtney Hunter, and she questioned this hypothesis. She began to realize that humans held the key to our survival as a species."

At that, the Councillors broke out in loud protests and arguments. Franz Tap ordered them quiet. "Listen to me, please! You need to be objective and hear all of it. I, too, was shocked, but I have since realized that I was wrong. Tap called a meeting and told us frankly that we all needed to work to cultivate the emotion and passion of the human race. As much as she realized that humans were self destructive in their behaviours and erratic in their thinking, she also realized that it was their passion and creative thought that had allowed them to survive one crisis after another. She noted that merely living and working on the planet was changing us, whether or not we were prepared to admit it. She asked us to speak honestly about our own feelings. Some of us did; others of us could not bring ourselves to be so open. What Tap found was that over half of us had been attracted to the humans that we had been observing over the years. Some even admitted to having close relationships with them. I was sickened by that revelation at first because I had not experienced such feelings, even though I had felt friendship towards some of them."

Franz Tap stopped, checking eyes to see what reaction his words were having. He felt mostly disbelief and shock. He went on. "It was then that Tay Tap and Gene Lamount presented their research on genetics. We and the humans are very closely related, far more so than seeding could explain. Tay observed that our planet, our plains, have no evidence of dwellings on them. We know nothing of our distant past. Don't you see: we didn't evolve here; we evolved on Earth."

For a minute there was stunned silence, then chaos. "You do not dare. You are mad. You insult us. We are not animals."

Franz Appala Punra waited, maintaining his ground against the onslaught of abuse. The Speaker rose. "Silence! We will hear him out. It is our way."

Franz Tap felt himself relax in relief. There was a small chance that he just might fulfil his directive. "Our research indicates that we might have originated from an Earth, perhaps not in the same dimension or even in the same universe, but from an Earth. Tay Tap believes that we are, at the very least, a parallel people."

There was no stopping now; he plunged on with his revelations. "We are both species in crisis, for different reasons. We need to help each other. We have perfected the process of coding genes into synthetically produced sperm. Tay realized that this was not enough, that we had to deal with the problem that has caused us to lose our ability to reproduce. She believes the root cause is our neutrality, our lack of contact with the emotions and feelings that exist only in the third dimension. Tay Appala Punra and Courtney Tay Tap are expecting a female child, an heir to the House of Tap. Tay means to overthrow the tyrannical rule of her brother if she can."

This time there was no outburst. The Councillors sat in stunned silence. The wind rustled through the endless plains of grass and flowers, moaning down valleys and around the figures that sat in a circle. A sleeve flapped, a dry leaf bounced across the circle. All else was still.

Again Courtney found herself drifting in a dimension of energy without form or boundaries. She was aware of Tay's presence but there was no response, only a feeling of closeness. Then again she felt her awareness funnel and her being condensed within. As she lost consciousness, she was aware Haichen reached for them.

She woke to darkness, her body sore and exhausted, weighted down even by the sheets that covered her. "Tay?" she called. There was no response.

Chapter Twenty-Two

"Blessed are the peace makers, for they shall be called children of God."

~ Matthew 5:9

From Courtney Appala Punra's Logs

It was some time before the sickness and dizziness passed and I was able to crawl from my bed, shower, and dress. With effort, I staggered through Tay's private quarters and opened the door to her room. Gene Lamount sat by Tay's bed. The shock of seeing Tay again so badly burnt, along with the stench of her cooked flesh, sent my stomach heaving. I ran to Tap's bathroom and threw up.

Gene Lamount came and helped me up. He offered me a wet towel. "You shouldn't be here. I fear for the baby. You have done enough."

"Will she live?"

"I do not know. She is very badly injured."

"I'll sit with her."

"I do not think that is wise."

I looked at him coldly and, I hoped, with the command I had seen in Tap's bearing.

"You forget I am Courtney Appala Punra. I am Tap. While Tay is unable to rule, that power falls to me. I will sit with Tay. Call Franz Appala Punra and Haichen Tay Tap to me."

Lamount paled and bowed as he took a step backwards. "Yes, Courtney Tap."

Once he had left, my façade of confidence crumbled and I sank into the chair beside Tay's bed. She was a charred form. Inert and vulnerable. For the first time, she needed my protection far more than I needed hers. Yet, I was acutely aware that my safety and power was founded on Tay's name. Opposites balanced. One could not survive without the other.

"Courtney Tap. We are here."

I turned to see Franz and Haichen standing across the room. "I've not yet developed the ability to materialize or to be fully aware of those that do. In the future, when you or anyone else arrives, please do so outside my door and knock. It is our way on Planet Earth."

"Yes, Courtney Tap."

"Franz Appala Punra, you are Tay's closet friend and, I hope, now mine. I need to know honestly what has happened while I've been ill."

"Little. I have talked to the Council and explained all. Nothing like this has ever happened. Things are in a state of confusion. The Council is demanding to know where Torgga is and is insisting on an enquiry. I have been stalling them."

"Where does their support lie? Can I trust them?"

"Yes and no. Most would be greatly relieved to see Torgga ousted by Tay, but they will not show support until they know for certain that Torgga is no longer a threat. They fear him."

"Tell them then that Torgga no longer rules, that Tay Tap and Courtney Tap defeated him and his assassin in battle. Tell them the enquiry will occur only when Tay has recovered from her wounds. They're not to know how serious Tay's condition is. Understood?"

Franz smiled. He was pleased and relieved that Tay had triumphed. "Yes, Courtney Tap."

"You are also to take command of our enquiry. We had two of Torgga's spies in our midst, there might be more. I want anyone who is not loyal to Tay removed and held."

"Understood."

"Haichen, you will take complete command of the household until such time as Tay recovers. Make sure no one is in a position to doubt the leadership of the House of Tap."

"Yes, Courtney Tap."

"I hope I can look on you both as officers who serve, but also friends. Please call me Court in private. Thank you for your loyalty, bravery, and help. Tay and I need both of you."

It was Franz who hesitated. "Court, how is Tay?"

I signalled for them to come closer and felt their dismay. "Tay fights for her life, but she will win. She is Tap. Do not worry."

They left and I returned to sitting by Tay, not sure at all whether she would live or what would happen to any of us. Tay and I were opposites needing balance. If one was lost, both were lost.

From Our Report

Courtney nursed Tay for days. Tay's flesh was badly burnt and the regeneration of her skin was a slow, painful process. Worse, her nervous system had been severely damaged. She remained barely conscious, and Lamount could give no reassurance as to whether Tay would regain mobility or even live. Through it all, Courtney Tap was there, providing comfort and aid in any way she could.

She also continued her studies with us, growing stronger and more aware with each day. She has achieved the sixth level of awareness and some day she will reach enlightenment and become a true Guardian. As the Chosen One, she will bring in a new age of understanding and reinforce our beliefs. As Tap, she will help Tay Tap find a way to balance two worlds, thereby saving both.

Most surprising of all to us was that she had taken command of Tap's people with the guidance and advice of Franz and Haichen. For so long, Courtney Tap denied her destiny. Now she had reached within herself and found the strength and wisdom of a true leader.

It was eight days before Tay tried to communicate. Her eyes fluttered open to see Courtney leaning over her, gently applying ointment to her new skin.

"It is never good news to wake broken and looking into the face of one who has declared herself my worst enemy."

Courtney smiled, realizing that Tay was teasing. "There have been some changes in my world views since you were last with us."

"You and our child are well, Courtney Tap?"

"Yes."

We felt some of the tension leaving Tay. "How long have I been unaware?"

"Eight days now."

"Where is my brother? What has he done in my absence?"

"I'm not sure where he is, only that the Guardians hold him. You are now the head of the House of Tap. With the help of Franz and Haichen, I have been ruling in your name. That hasn't been very hard, as everything has virtually come to a standstill. The Grand Council plans an enquiry, but they are awaiting your recovery."

"Will I recover?"

Courtney reached out and took Tay's hand. "You are badly hurt. We feared you would die. Lamount will be greatly relieved to know you are conscious and communicating. Can you move your limbs?"

Slowly, painfully, Tay managed to move her feet and wiggle her fingers. The effort exhausted her. Worry flashed across her face. The fear of dying in battle she had long ago conquered; the fear of living in a broken body was a different matter. Courtney Tap understood this.

"It will take time. Don't worry. Lamount will be delighted that you have movement and are aware again."

Tay forced her pain and fear behind her and focussed on the future of her people. "And you, Courtney Tap? Now that you rule my house, what do you plan to do?"

Courtney laughed. "Somehow I think Franz and Haichen would not let me stray too far from your wishes or from your house, not yet anyway. Tay, I have come to realize that all things in this universe are balanced. For each extreme there is a counterpart, and for the universe, for this planet, to survive, these elements must be of one accord. I no longer fear that Earth will be conquered or assimilated by your people. If you try, you will fail. Your people and my people can only survive if we are joined in harmony. We're meant to be equal partners in a great enterprise, and our child will be the joining of two people who have been too long apart."

Tay's eyes closed but Courtney felt the weak hand gently tighten around her own as Tay slipped back into sleep.

A few days later, Courtney Tap entered to find Tay alert but still in considerable pain as she struggled to sit up in bed.

"I need to get up."

"Is that wise? What does Gene Lamount think?"

"Gene Lamount hovers over me, fearing he will be responsible if I die. I need to get up and I can not do so without help. You are the only one available that I would let see me so weak. Help me, please."

We knew Courtney had reservations also, but she did not hesitate. She knew that weakness was vulnerability. She wrapped an arm around Tay and helped her to a sitting position and, after a minute, to her feet. Courtney was shocked by how thin and frail Tay felt. Her skin no longer had that inner warmth she had so often noticed. Tay clung to her. Courtney allowed it, wondering when she had stopped seeing Tay as a danger and started to feel a partnership with her.

"I will need to sit at my desk."

"OK." They moved slowly, Tay suffering with each step until they made their way to the outer room and Tay sank into her chair with a groan.

"Give me a few minutes and then I will see some of my staff."

"Let me straighten your hair." Courtney disappeared into Tay's quarters and returned with a comb and a lab jacket. With care, she parted and combed Tay's hair back into place and then helped her slip into the jacket so that most of her healing flesh was not showing.

"Thank you."

"You are welcome."

Tay looked at Courtney with those beautiful but alien aqua eyes. "Why?" A small question that always demands a good deal of information.

"Why, what?" A stalemate.

"Why did you risk your life and that of our child to save me?"

Courtney frowned. "I can tell you my justifications in hindsight, but at the time I simply reacted. I knew you were in danger and I knew I had to go to you. I've come to care very much about you. That is totally irrational. You have lied to me, endangered my life, planned to terminate me, changed my identity, and even forced your child on me. You are a threat still to my planet, yet I care about you. I didn't want you to die. I think your actions, however misguided, were for noble reasons. I could tell you that I realized that my safety was very much tied to your own, but that is not why I went. I went for you, just like you went for your people, our baby, and me."

Tay felt uncomfortable, yet she did not hide her feelings as she might have done, not so long ago. "This is difficult for me. Not long ago, the only real passion I had ever felt was in the heat of battle. Slowly I, and the others here, have become aware of new emotions, new feelings. It has changed us. These feelings are all foreign to me. I, too, could justify my actions. The truth is my first concern was you and our child."

Courtney knew Tay well enough to know that if she was pushed too far, an emotional wall of defence would slam into place. Tay might care for Courtney and be grateful for her help, but as yet, Courtney knew, Tay still saw herself as the sole ruler and the superior being. A balance had not yet been achieved, but Courtney was now enlightened enough to know it would be.

"I have supported you in your escape from under Lamount's watchful eye, but I will not be responsible for you having a relapse. You have one hour, Tay, then I will come to take you back to bed."

"Am I not Tap?"

"Am I not also?"

Tay laughed. "The Guardians have created a bully."

"Not a bully, an equal, who is not afraid to stand up to you."

Tay raised an eyebrow in surprise and then nodded. "One hour will be all I need."

Courtney stood to leave. She knew she could stay, but she also knew that Tay needed to show she was strong enough to stand alone. Courtney Appala Punra had learned much. As she left, we sensed Tay's respect and affection for Courtney Tap. Both ran deep.

"Guardians, Courtney Tap has changed."

She has learned and grown.

Through her, we, too,

Have learned and grown.

"How so?"

We have involved ourselves.

We feel.

We care.

"Where is Torgga?"

Where he can do no harm.

His reign is over.

Yours has just begun.

"She is the Chosen One?"

Yes.

It is so.

Of this, we are sure.

"Then it is time for a new beginning. Please call Haichen. I will see my senior staff."

Chapter Twenty-Three

These are the events as we know them.
We recorded them factually and objectively.
And now we report them to you.

The Speaker materialized before Tay's Household, who stood in respect, waiting. Franz Appala Punra stepped forward. "Welcome, Loedan."

The Speaker looked around with curious eyes. "How is Tay Appala Punra?" he asked.

Franz Tap tried not to show his concern. "She is recovering."

"Good. Let us proceed then."

Franz Tap led the way to their library where chairs had been set up for the questioning. "You will excuse me, Honourable Speaker. I will go and inform Courtney Appala Punra that we are ready to start. She is with Tay Tap." The Speaker inclined his head in assent and, with relief, Franz Tap made his exit. He was a soldier not a diplomat.

It had been nearly an Earth month since he had spoken before the Council of forty-three. Since then, nothing had been resolved. No one had seen the Guardians, no one had seen Torgga, and few had seen Tay Tap. All they knew was Courtney Tap had arrived back on Earth holding the bloody and near death body of their leader in her arms. Lamount had worked night and day to save her. Even now, nearly a month later, Tay Tap's complete recovery was not assured.

Franz Appala Punra knocked gently on the door. This was out of respect to Courtney Tap, who, although she now sensed all, preferred to maintain some traditions of her people. There had been many small changes like this one in the last month.

"Enter," came Tay Tap's voice.

Franz Tap found the two sitting in chairs, looking relaxed, as if the conversation they had been having was agreeable. "It is time. The Speaker has arrived."

"Very well. Inform the Speaker that we are coming and ask him to be patient, as it takes me some time to walk. I can not yet muster the energy to materialize."

Franz Tap looked at Courtney in surprise. Courtney shrugged, which is the human way of not dealing with an issue not being resolved to their satisfaction. "Tay Tap has decided." Actually, they had argued, but Tay had been determined; however, that was not a matter to be discussed, even in front of someone as trustworthy as Franz Tap. Franz Tap, loyal as ever, left to do as he was told.

"You won't reconsider?"

Slowly and with Courtney's help, Tay got up from her chair and stood. Pain shot across her face as she straightened.

"No," Tay stated firmly, then smiled when Courtney laughed and gently squeezed her arm.

They all stood when Tay and Courtney walked in. Courtney did not touch Tay, but walked close at her side in case she should need assistance. Tay moved to the two chairs quickly arranged at the end of the table and pulled one out for Courtney to show the respect she had for her. Then Tay seated herself and the others followed.

"Loedan, welcome to Earth, and to our home and research base. We appreciate the Council allowing Courtney Appala Punra to be questioned here."

"The Council does recognize the unusual nature of the situation and is anxious, as are all others, that this child be born healthy and safely."

"Proceed," Tay stated.

The Speaker hesitated in order to collect his thoughts. "Courtney Appala Punra..." Here he inclined his head in respect, so as not to sound too accusatory. Tay Tap could now very well be their supreme ruler, so discretion was essential. "You have been involved in events that are both politically and spiritually catastrophic. Never in our known history has a Tap been defeated by a member of an alien race. The implications of this are staggering enough, but we are also filled with foreboding. Torgga Appala Punra has simply disappeared, and our spiritual leaders, the Guardians, have not been heard from. We need answers so that judgements may be made. Out of respect to the seriousness of your injuries, Tay Tap, we have delayed our investigation of the alien that you have taken into your Household."

"Excuse me!" interrupted Courtney Tap, and everyone turned to look at her in shock. "Let's just get a few things straight here. First, I am very proud to say that I'm a part of Tay Appala Punra's Household, but don't ever think for a minute that she 'owns' me."

We sensed that Tay was trying not to smile. Courtney was as feisty as ever.

"Second, I am not going to be judged by anyone. If your Guardians aren't speaking to you and Torgga has disappeared, that's too damn bad, but it's not my problem and I will not take the responsibility for it. I'm here to explain what happened, that's all."

The Speaker turned red, spluttered a bit, and then pulled himself together. "Tay Appala Punra, you must realize—"

"I realize," came Tay's cold voice, "that I rebelled against my brother's oppressive and violent rule. If you choose to judge Courtney Tap, you also judge me. Remember that," she finished softly.

The Speaker paled and around the table the others squirmed uncomfortably, caught between the warring forces of their loyalty to Tay, their sense of tradition, and their fear of an uncertain future. The Speaker wisely decided to go ahead with the questions outlined by the Council. It was unwise to proceed with any further discussion of any ramifications the Council might consider having once weighed the information the Speaker was transmitting to them as the meeting went on.

"Courtney Tap, we wish to know how many of you humans have developed the ability to travel through time and space."

"None of us," Courtney replied, not realizing the significance of her response. The look of shock on faces turned towards her made her realize for the first time that this had been a loaded question.

"Courtney Tap, how else would it have been possible for you to transport to where Torgga and Tay Tap battled?" the Speaker grumbled in frustration.

"I called on the Guardians and demanded that they find Tay Tap and send me there." The gasps of surprise and hurried remarks confirmed to Courtney she might have stepped over some significant line in the sand. "Hey! Tay Tap was in trouble," she justified.

Tay Tap, who was herself in shock as a result of this revelation, reached over to touch Courtney's hand. "Courtney Tap's loyalty and courage know no bounds," she stated calmly.

The Speaker was not so easily convinced. "Courtney Tap, the Guardians do not become involved in the events of the people. They are the keepers of wisdom and provide us with guidance only."

"Yes, I know that has been their way in the past. It is not now. I am one with them. I am their Chosen One. We chose to be involved."

This time the Speaker sat slack jawed as a thousand questions and ramifications exploded on his thoughts. Courtney Tap sensed this and went on.

"The Guardians and I argued about it. I suggested to them that it was your people's very neutrality that was the problem.

Respectfully, I suggested that they get off their backsides and get involved because if they didn't, the wrong Tap was going to rule and you could probably kiss your future good-bye. They thought about it for a bit and then sent me to Tay."

Still there was not a sound. Everyone sat in stunned silence. Courtney decided to fill in the silence with the rest of the story.

"When I got there, Tay was unconscious. She had been attacked not only by her brother, but also by a second assailant from behind. This assassin she had killed, but Torgga was still very much alive and ready to finish Tay Tap. Tay was able to tell me that he planned to kill us both and raise our child as his own. I wasn't about to let that happen."

Tay smiled, despite her shock at the events being revealed. She had known Courtney had defeated Torgga and come to her aid, but like the others, she had assumed that somehow Courtney had gotten there through her own devices. That it had been the Guardians who had aided her had far reaching implications. She focused on what Courtney had to say.

"So, I pretended that I was prepared to double cross Tay Tap and work with Torgga so that I could get close to him. When I did, I let him have it right in the face and anywhere else where his skin was exposed. I didn't think my plan was going to work at first, but then, just before he zapped me, he dropped."

Tay felt her insides turn to jelly. Courtney had no idea what a horrible death she had faced so bravely.

Courtney was winding up her explanation. "Before Torgga could get up again, I ran to Tay Tap and yelled at the Guardians to get us out of there. I sort of have memories of floating about in that cosmic ocean of yours, but my next real clear memory is waking up back here last month."

It took a few seconds for the Speaker to respond to these startling revelations. "You are saying that some primitive Earth weapon defeated the mighty Torgga Appala Punra and that you left him there alive and returned with Tay Tap to this time and place with the help of the Guardians again?"

"Yes."

Silence filled the room, while people looked around the table in wonder, trying to gauge each other's reaction.

"What is this deadly weapon?" the Speaker demanded.

"I have no intention of answering that question. To do so might put Tay's life in danger."

Loedan blinked then gathered his thoughts together again, hearing the thoughts of the other Council members in his mind and weighing their opinions fairly. "Courtney Tay, have you talked to the Guardians recently?"

"Not since yesterday afternoon. They usually pop in each day to ask me how Tay Tap is doing. They have been quite concerned, naturally."

Once the Speaker was capable of getting to his feet, he rose. "Tay Appala Punra, the Council feels that, under the circumstances, it is not suitable that this human be addressed by the royal title of Courtney Appala Punra." Courtney felt the anger ripple through her partner. "From this time forward, she will be addressed as Guardian Courtney Tap, as befits one recognized by the Council as a royal member of the House of Tap *and* a Chosen One." He bowed and Courtney sat in surprise as in turn each in the room stood and bowed, including Tay Tap herself.

It is we who hold the deposed Torgga.

Our path now lies in a new direction.

Courtney and Tay Tap will show us the way.

So spoke the voices of we Guardians, and all present knew that a new era had begun.

Tay and Courtney remained seated as first the Speaker and then the House officials bowed again and took their leave. "Can you make it back to our rooms?" Courtney asked softly.

Tay nodded, lost in deep thought. "Courtney, what is this Earth weapon that I must watch out for?"

"Alcohol."

"Alcohol!" exclaimed Tay in surprise.

"Rubbing alcohol. I knew from my experience with you that cold bothered you terribly. Haichen told me that the only thing she knew about where you were was that it was terribly hot and dry. I dosed him down good and the heat evaporated the alcohol almost instantly, dropping his skin temperature drastically. He went into shock and passed out." Courtney smiled.

Tay laughed explosively. "Humans!"

From Guardian Courtney Tap's Logs

The events of the last few months have been strange, fearful, and yet wondrous. I have come to a much greater understanding of my planet and a greater love for its people. I have also come to understand, to some extent, the philosophy of an alien people. My people now, too, for I am Tap and the Chosen One. How impossible this would have all seemed on the day I decided to break into Tap's private quarters. The Guardians would tell me that it was meant to be, that my decision was just the Universe unfolding as it should, no matter how surprising and shocking that might seem to us. I have come to accept that we are star stuff, as is the entire universe. Whether for good or bad, we are part of the same web, the same universal conscience. We have only to listen quietly to understand each other, our planet, and its place in the universe. I hope we can do so before it is too late.

Tamma is the first to be born into a new era. Ahead of her are turbulent and hard times for both her peoples. They must learn that the future, however uncertain, lies in the hands of those who can leave behind the hatreds and biases of the past and move on courageously with open hearts and minds. They must learn to respect this planet and our universe.

Planet Earth struggles for survival. It is a rose lying on the black velvet of space. Its future lies in our understanding of the balance of nature, its resources, and the universe.

From the dark depths of time, turtle watches the rose Earth she created and is sad.

Anne Azel is an award winning author. Her novel *Gold Mountain* won the Golden Crown Literary Society Award for dramatic general fiction. She was awarded the CLFA Readers' Choice Award and the LFRCA Readers Choice Award. Her work has also been recognized for its cultural diversity and its informed and sympathetic portrayal of world cultures.

Anne's writing covers a wide spectrum of genres including murder mysteries, contemporary issues, romance, and futuristic novels. As one reader wrote, "This is writing for readers who demand more."

Even the covers of Anne's books are unique. The cover illustrations are copies of original works of art by the artist B.L. Magill.

Anne is retired and lives in northern Ontario when she is not travelling the world. She enjoys kayaking, canoeing, and skiing. Anne has degrees in art history, archaeology, and forensic anthropology. Her hobbies include writing, painting, and travel.

Other works by Anne Azel:

Gold Mountain

ISBN: 978 - 1 - 933720 - 04 - 3
(Winner of a 2007 Golden Crown Literary Society's Award for Lesbian Dramatic General Fiction)

Seasons

ISBN: 978 - 1 - 933720 - 23 - 4

Murder in Triplicate: The Aliki Pateas Mystery Series, Book 1

ISBN: 978 - 1 - 933720 - 37 - 1

Three Doses of Murder: The Aliki Pateas Mystery Series, Book 2

ISBN: 978 - 1 - 933720 - 38 - 8

The Little Book of Big Christmas Tales

ISBN: 978 - 1 - 933720 - 50 - 0

Available at your favorite bookstore.

Printed in the United States
154327LV00003B/10/P

9 781933 720630